Murder at the
New York World's Fair

PHOEBE ATWOOD TAYLOR
Writing as Freeman Dana

MURDER AT THE
NEW YORK WORLD'S FAIR

Introduction by Dilys Winn

Afterword by Ellen Nehr

A Foul Play Press Book

THE COUNTRYMAN PRESS
Woodstock, Vermont

*The publisher would like to thank Ellen Nehr for the energy
and enthusiasm she has brought to this project.*

This volume is a reproduction
of the 1938 Random House, Inc. edition.

Introduction copyright © 1987 by Dilys Winn
Afterword copyright © 1987 by Ellen Nehr

This edition is published in 1987 by Foul Play Press, a division
of The Countryman Press, Woodstock, Vermont 05091.

ISBN 0-88150-095-X

Printed in the United States of America
By Capital City Press, Inc., Montpelier, Vt.

Introduction

by Dilys Winn

I THINK I now know how a devoted Rex Stout fan must feel when he comes across a title he hasn't read, gets it home, settles in, and after several pages discovers he is slogging through a Tecumseh Fox tale: 'Rex, how could you do this to me?'

My vice is Phoebe Atwood Taylor. Well, actually, I'm an addict of her alter (writing) ego, Alice Tilton, but let's not quibble—I devour them all. So can you imagine with what glee, with what utter relentlessness I unfettered an afternoon to feast on one of her books that had somehow slipped by me? I soon dropped the book from my hands, the better to wring them, and pitifully mewled, "How could you do this to me, Phoebe, how could you?"

I understand that Bennet Cerf is to blame. And the Westinghouse corporation. And high noon of the autumnal equinox. And if this is starting to sound like a bad mystery in and of itself, let me explain: back in '38, New York decided to host a World's Fair, Westinghouse decided to inter a time capsule in its pavillon courtyard, and Mr. Cerf, the publisher of Random House, decided that among the 10,000,000 words going down in it on September 23, 1938, 60,000 or so would belong to one of his authors. Namely, Phoebe Atwood Taylor, writing for the first (and last) time as Freeman Dana.

The result, of course, is the book at hand, *Murder at the New York World's Fair*, and if I find it amiably frustrating fifty years after it was written, imagine what folks in 6939 might make of it—that's when the capsule's due to be opened (assuming anyone's still around for the task). Clearly, however, the work is at least as interesting as the other items snuggling alongside it on microfilm, which include a mail order catalogue, a dictionary of slang, and snippets about a New York fashion show, Howard Hughes at the conclusion of his round-the-world flight, and Fiorello La Guardia pressing flesh, a maneuver politicians will still, no doubt, be doing in 6939.

I have no idea why Mrs. Taylor chose the name Freeman Dana for her excursion into 5000-year immortality, but I have two suspicions why she used a female protagonist and they're spelled Marple and Christie. Mrs. Christie had recently pulled off a coup: successfully introducing a series character to rival the popularity of Hercule Poirot. Once Miss Marple strode on the mystery scene, Mrs. Taylor's own little grey cells sprang into action with the creation of Mrs. Boylston Tower of Boston's Louisburg Square. I don't know, maybe snuggling next to politicians, even if only on microfilm, is not such a good way to make it on your own. Mrs. Boylston Tower disappeared, almost as soon as the time capsule was lowered.

Is there any earthly reason to resurrect her? As any Rex Stout fan can tell you, any Stout is better than no Stout at all. Same here. This may not be Phoebe Atwood Taylor at her best, or even Alice Tilton at her medium-best, but there is one saving grace: Slapstick.

Surely, under whichever pseudonym, Mrs. Taylor is the mystery equivalent to Buster Keaton. And never more so than here, where she surrounds her patrician Boston grande dame with fan dancers, licentious potentates from countries with unpronounceable names and unspeakable practices, officious dignitaries, demented relatives, spurious artwork, window-shades in private train compartments, tour guide disguises, marching bands, traveling salesmen, a suitcase stuffed with a snake, fairground jitneys, fairground VIP limos, private eyes tailing the wrong people, wallpaper samples, and a newspaperman sidekick who hero worships our heroine's nephew. Whew.

With all this going on, is it any wonder the plot dangles a bit, the murders are less mesmerizing than the snake in the suitcase, or that Mrs. Tower herself is not as beguiling as Alice Tilton's sleuth, Leonidas Witherall, or Asey Mayo, Phoebe Atwood Taylor's "Codfish Sherlock"? Indeed the parts are greater than their sum. Though in fairness to the author, I must note that the Westinghouse people did not accept just any old book that came their way; they ran a contest, and this was one of the winners. Westinghouse undoubtably hoped the people 5000 years hence would like to laugh, too.

Some backtracking at this point may be in order. Phoebe Atwood Taylor wrote 33 books. The first one in 1931 featured Asey Mayo, and is listed as a mystery milestone by Howard Haycraft and Ellery Queen in their "Cornerstones of Detective Fiction." This and the 23 Aseys that followed it are, technically, Mrs. Taylor at her best. They offer less in the way of drifting plotlines, outrageous characters and sheer wackiness. Their greatest following is among Holmes' disciples, readers from the northeast, and partisans of the exemplary American mystery novel (who also seem devoted to the works of Emma Latham and Tony Hillerman). As much as I like them, I am *truly* addicted to the 8 titles that appeared under the nom de nonsense Alice Tilton. Closer in feeling to *World's Fair*, these books don't make all that much sense, but they go a long way in proving that making sense is immaterial— a guffaw is more vital. Tilton books are so busy, so complicated, so Marx Brothers that it seems superfluous to tell you that Leonidas Witherall looks like Shakespeare, used to own a bookstore, and writes a detective series featuring Lt. Haseltine. That makes them sound as if they might have a plot, doesn't it? Bad assumption. They drift from incident to incident with the style of the crash'em cars at a carnival.

Where exactly does *World's Fair* fit in? Between *Annulet of Gilt, Banbury Bog* and *The Cut Direct*. About a third of the way along Mrs. Taylor's career, during a period of optimum creativity. So I think it only fair we forgive her a weaker moment. After all, it's not every time out an author can serve up such a tempting tidbit as a body embedded in the deep freeze (*Dead Earnest*).

Unlike the Christies, the Stouts, the Marshes, who wrote practically with their dying breath, Mrs. Taylor packed it all in by middle age. Born in 1909, she gave it up in 1951, then had 25 years left to repent all her bad puns. I like to think she spent the time cutting up at New England clambakes, wise-cracking at Boston teaparties.

Murder at the
New York World's Fair

1

No WOMAN ever missed a train more deliberately than Mrs. Boylston Tower missed the six-thirty-two.

There was nothing psychic about it. She missed the train because she wanted to. That was all. Mrs. Tower simply did not choose to go home, and extra-sensory perception played no part in her choice. If she had not missed the six-thirty-two, there would have been no World's Fair opening in New York the next day. There is even a remote possibility that there would have been no World's Fair at all.

But in missing the evening local, Mrs. Tower was moved by the increasingly distasteful thought of returning to her nephew Egleston and his statuesque wife Elfrida, and to their hideous imitation Early American house.

She had been rebelling inwardly against Eggy and Elfrida for nearly a year, but she had not really felt unkindly toward them until that very morning, when she had been moved to a point of surreptitiously slipping away in the laundry truck to catch the Boston train.

The thought of that truck ride brought a smile to Mrs. Boylston Tower's face. She would never forget that ride with the Home Beautiful wash. She would never forget the jouncings, or the affectionate overtures of the driver's dog, or having to duck back into the dirty linen at the stop light, to avoid being seen by Mrs. Lizzie Trimmingham. At the light, Lizzie Trimmingham drew alongside in her coupe, and leaned out to tell the driver all about her lost pillow-cases and the tea towel, and how she expected them back before she left for the World's Fair. Lizzie Trimmingham was a club woman, with chairmanship in her eye, and although it had been many months since Daisy Tower had been active in Lizzie's special sphere, Lizzie would have recognized her. Lizzie recognized everybody. And for Lizzie to find the wife of a former governor in a laundry truck! Mrs. Tower chuckled.

In two shakes, Lizzie would have cross-questioned her and found out everything, why she was in the truck, and how she'd got there. And in two shakes more, Lizzie would have whisked her home to Elfrida. No explanations would have mattered, Daisy Tower thought. She could have explained till doomsday, and Lizzie would not have understood the events which had led to her borrowing money from the cook and setting off to Boston and the station in that laundry truck.

4

It had all begun at five minutes to nine that morning, while Mrs. Tower, wearing a blue hand-embroidered nightgown and a Persian housecoat, was sitting in her room at Egleston's house, wishing for a ham omelette and a cup of black coffee.

She had heard Fannie, the housemaid, clicking up the stairs and down the hall in her silly heels, and suddenly they irritated Daisy Tower more than they ever had before. Those clicking heels meant that Fannie was bringing beef tea. The usual morning beef tea. The kind of innocuous, mild, steaming drink which Elfrida said was so good for Mrs. Tower, at her age. Probably beef tea was an excellent drink for the average woman of sixty-seven, but Daisy Tower felt only about fifty that morning, and quite well again.

Daisy got up from her chair by the window and briskly locked the door. She did not pause to look for her cane. As far as she was concerned, that gold-knobbed cane was sheer affectation. She did not need it. But it was easier to use it, when Elfrida was around, than to convince Elfrida of its uselessness.

Listening to Fannie's knock, Mrs. Tower smiled. If she had not been Mrs. Boylston Tower of Louisburg Square, it might be said that she grinned. She could imagine Fannie standing there at the door, her haughty nose tip-tilted, her cap becomingly set on her bronze curls, the unwanted drink held almost scornfully in her highly manicured hands. Fannie was almost like a maid in a play. Perhaps that was why Egleston smiled at her more often than he did at Elfrida. But no one could be blamed, not even Eggy, for failing to smile at Elfrida.

Fannie knocked again.

Daisy kept perfectly still, so still that she could hear the clock ticking in her radio. One of her son Boylston's idiotic presents. He always wanted her to share in all his fads. The house in Boston had been a welter of clocks while Boylston was writing those articles on Happy Mosello. She wished he were doing them now, instead of writing up the war in China. Then she wouldn't be sitting uncomfortably on the edge of Elfrida's guest room bed, holding her breath, while Fannie snorted outside the door with a cup of that damned beef tea.

Fannie did not knock a third time. She did something rather peculiar instead. Very gently, very softly, almost too cleverly, she tried the door. The knob turned, ever so little.

"Now what in the world!" Daisy frowned for a moment, as the clock on the radio chimed nine.

So now they were taking to trying her door handle, were they?

Daisy closed her eyes.

Life suddenly assumed an unbearable aspect. Here it was, nine o'clock on a perfect spring day, a day so perfect that most people with any gumption were getting ready to go somewhere. If they couldn't go to

6

the opening of the World's Fair—here Daisy sighed, and then, drawing in her breath in sheer relief because Fannie had tiptoed away, sighed again gustily. If they couldn't go to the World's Fair opening, where Daisy Tower longed to be, they could at least go to Boston to buy clothes, or to the White Mountains. Or to an auction, or something.

But Elfrida said that Daisy was to sleep late. Elfrida said she needed rest. She was not to have coffee. Elfrida said it keyed Daisy up too much. If only the statuesque Elfrida, Daisy thought, would get keyed up once in a while, maybe Eggy wouldn't be making passes at a housemaid with red hair. Then there was the Louisburg Square house. Elfrida said Daisy mustn't even consider occupying that until her hip was better and her lungs were better. She wasn't even to think of it.

"Bosh!" Daisy said aloud.

A broken hip and a bout with pneumonia were fun, approaching the frolic stage, when compared to living with Eggy and Elfrida during the convalescent period.

A silver-framed picture of her son Boylston stood among the papers on the desk beside her. Daisy looked at it and speculated about writing Boy and telling him that she was leaving for China on the next boat. Nothing would surprise Boy. He had enjoyed his mother's lust for living too long to be disturbed by a mere hop to China. If he knew Eggy and Elfrida better, Boy wouldn't wonder at her desire to go anywhere, anywhere at all, as long as it was away from them.

Looking at the picture on her desk and the papers surrounding it, Daisy suddenly stopped speculating about Boy, and merely looked. From seeing papers vaguely, surrounded, as it were, by a pink and green map of China, Daisy saw papers alone. Papers which had been disturbed by hands other than her own. Just as cautiously disturbed as the door knob had been cautiously turned a moment ago, But disturbed nevertheless.

Daisy was not orderly, but she had a keen and immediate perception for any disorder not her own. Her check book was upside down. That little monogram was wrong side to. And that letter about the insurance renewal had been in the other pigeonhole on the left.

Daisy closed her mouth tightly. She looked more like the wife of a former governor than she had a few minutes before. Leaning back, she allowed her head to droop a little, while she did some thinking which did not include a trip to China.

Only when a laundry truck chugged up the driveway and came to a halt beneath her window, and cook's vociferous command to come back in half an hour rose throatily to the upper story, only then did Daisy lift her head and gaze out at the white truck with the silly cupid in diapers on the side.

She had had an idea.

Clothes, of course, were a problem, owing to Elfrida's horrible habit of laying things away in dichloricide. But cook would help. For cook was Daisy's slave, and had even substituted fried clams for rice flakes the night before, when Eggy and Elfrida were dining out.

And cook had helped. Cook outdid herself. Cook had provided her new spring outfit, her last month's wages, and a mysterious arrangement with the laundry man to act as chauffeur to the station.

It was marvellous to have escaped from Elfrida's solicitous care. Daisy had got to Boston without discussion, argument, or plans. She'd intended to call her lawyer at once, and to telephone a few friends, with a freedom never enjoyed while her conversations had been carried on in the listening hush of Elfrida's suddenly stopped activity. She simply could not endure, now, to go back to a place where her food was censored, where they choked beef tea down her throat, tried her door knob when she refused to answer a knock, and tampered with the private papers on her desk. And with her check book, too.

In the light of this morning's developments, the affair of Cherry Chipman's leaving her took on a different aspect. How she did want Cherry back, to drive her around, to go to the theater with her, and to amuse her when she actually felt sixty-seven instead of late fortyish. She wished she knew where Cherry was.

If she telephoned to Jackson to open the Louisburg Square house, she could stay in the city long enough to see her lawyer. For Ben Bassett had not been in his office when she called, and she had had to choose between missing the advance newsreels of the World's Fair opening, and seeing Ben. And no Bassett was worth missing those pictures for, particularly since she had to miss the fair itself, the first important exposition she'd missed since the Philadelphia Centennial. Heavens, how much she'd missed since crawling into seclusion with Eggy and Elfrida!

Just this one day in Boston had waked her up to the fact that she had been almost imprisoned. And she felt exactly as well as ever. Queer that Eggy had kept fussing about her health, and about how little she was able to do. And here she had gone to two movies, lunched extensively at the Parker House, and she felt as fit as a fiddle.

Braced by these reflections, Daisy leaned on her cane—cook had insisted on her taking it—and watched the rear lights of the six-thirty-two as they disappeared into the dusky murk of the South Station yards.

Ignoring the gateman, who was staring at her curiously, and ignoring the bells and the engines and the trains and the crowds and all the rest of the station hurly-burly, Daisy stood by Track Four and continued to think things out. They had to be thought out, and this was the time, if not the ideal spot for meditation.

If she had gone home to Eggy's, she would have been whisked into bed with litters of hot-water bottles and a bowl of that stuff referred to by Elfrida as a nice hot drink. Mrs. Tower's hot drink, Fannie. But Daisy had had hot buttered rum with her lunch at the Parker House. Hot buttered rum, Daisy thought, was something you could honestly call a nice hot drink.

But not beef tea. Never. No!

With a firm step, Mrs. Tower turned and started for the telephone booths in the waiting room.

She would call Eggy and tell him her decision to open her Boston house and remain there. On second thought, she would write Eggy. He would be away fishing, during the week-end, and then there was a certain effective simplicity about a letter. She could state her decision without any interruptions, and any protests from Eggy would necessarily be defensive, and in the nature of an anticlimax. Elfrida, too, was more efficient at interruption than rebuttal.

A smile played around Daisy's lips as she walked over to the phone booths that were big enough to sit down in. She would phone Jackson and tell him to start opening and airing the house. His wife could cook until Marie was found. And perhaps Jackson would know where Cherry Chipman was. Of course, Eggy said that Cherry wanted a job with greater scope and opportunities, and that was why she had departed so abruptly after the accident and the broken hip incident. But there was always the chance that Cherry would be tired of being a department-store buyer, or a secretary, or whatever it was she'd gone in for. The bait of a trip to England would probably lure her back. Cherry loved to travel, and she adored England in the spring.

Daisy fumbled in her purse for a nickel and wondered why lights in phone booths so rarely worked. Phone booth lights and post office pens—

She jumped as someone wrenched open the door of the booth.

A man darted in, jerking the door shut behind him, and jamming her against the wall.

"Really!" Daisy gripped the gold knob of her cane and stared coldly at the intruder.

He was a tall young man, breathless, visibly perspiring, and there was a hunted look on his face. Somewhere, Daisy thought nervously, she had seen that aquiline nose before.

"Sorry," the young man said in apologetic haste. "Couldn't see you—thought it was empty."

He paused.

The woman had been a little frightened by him at first, he knew, but now her eyes were twinkling, and Sam Minot decided to take a chance on that twinkle. He practically had to take the chance, anyway. He wasn't going to back out into the waiting room and spoil everything at this point.

"Now I've dropped in, ma'am," he said, "could I stay till I find out if Comrade Glue's been shaken?"

12

"Glue?" Daisy said.

"Well," Sam said critically, "he's more persistent than glue. More dogged and rugged. Like granite. But there's an amorphous quality about his face. Gluey. His features run together, if you know what I mean."

"You mean," Daisy said, "you're being pursued by a policeman."

"Oh, no. He's no cop. I've walked and run him twenty miles this afternoon, and he's still going strong. He can't possibly be a Boston cop. And I'm sure he's not sent by the office. They don't care that much for me. They made that clear."

"I gather," Daisy said, "that you've recently been fired?"

"Booted is the word," Sam told her honestly. "Don't ask me why, because I don't know. Unless the city editor's stomach ulcers took a turn for the worse. Maybe you could guess why. You seem to be pretty perspicacious."

"I know the fired look," Daisy returned. "I have a son who was constantly being fired by newspapers and pursued by the police in his youth. Until Boylston finally grew up, and got to be a war correspondent in places like Manchuria and—"

"You're Boy Tower's mother!" Sam said. "That accounts for it. Your twinkle and all. No, I don't really know him," he added in response to her quick question. "But he used to come back to football games at school when I was there, and we all worshipped him from a distance. In fact, it was Boy's exploits that started me out on what I laughingly call a newspaper career. You've got another son who went to the school, haven't you?"

Unconsciously, Daisy sighed.

"You mean my nephew Egleston. He never played football, but he religiously tacks the team pictures on his study walls. That's where I saw your nose, in a picture of a team about six years ago, and you were holding the ball. And now," Daisy said briskly, "what about Comrade Glue? I'm beginning to suffocate in here—"

"I'm sorry," Sam said. "If you'll just slide past me—"

"Oh, I've no intention of going now," Daisy said. "This is like old times. Tell me what about Glue."

"I don't know what," Sam said. "He's just there. Whither I goest, there also he goest. I run, he runs. I dally, he dallies. I turn to ask him what the hell, and he's gone. I start along, and there he is behind me. It's the sort of thing that gets on the nerves."

"It also," Daisy said, "has a sinister sound. Why don't you talk with the police?"

"The cops," Sam said, "would like nothing better than to have me ask their help. I scooped 'em this week and they still don't like it. But Glue's no cop. I don't understand it. I don't understand anything. It's been a crazy day. Look, Mrs. Tower. You're hot and all jammed up. I'll flatten myself, and you just go—"

14

"I shan't go anywhere," Daisy said, "until I've heard about Glue and everything. You don't know it, but this is practically my first contact with life and the outside world in over a year, Mr.—Minot, isn't it?"

"Good for you! You even read the names under the team pictures, didn't you? I'm Samuel Minot. And you really don't mind if I tell you everything? Because maybe you can make sense of it. To begin with, I called Harris, my editor, and started to tell him that I didn't get an interview with Cassell—think of it! Harris is still naïve enough to send people out to interview Conrad Cassell. Isn't that quaint?"

"*The* Conrad Cassell? Why," Daisy said, "even Boy gave up trying to interview him!"

"Exactly. He popped up to Boston to take a look at Mrs. Bottome's new Gainsborough—"

"That tiresome woman!" Daisy said. "She sent me one pink lace bed jacket for my broken hip, and another for having pneumonia. So she has a new Gainsborough?"

"She thinks so, and Cassell came to see it. All very hush-hush and incognito, but of course Bottome's gutters oozed reporters. Anyway, I called Harris and started to tell him nothing doing, and he interrupted me and said it wouldn't matter if I'd got the interview, I was fired, and a messenger would leave my money in Tim's bar. And he hung up. Can you figure that one out?"

"Didn't you call back and ask—"

"Harris wouldn't talk with me, and none of the boys knew anything. And then, a while later, there was Glue. Look, you wouldn't—I mean—"

"Of course I'll go out and see if he's still around," Daisy said promptly. "What's he wearing? A grey suit and a black felt hat—"

She strolled along the line of phone booths to a news stand and requested change for a dollar.

"To phone with," she said, idly scanning the headlines, and ignoring the man next her, who was obviously Glue in person. "Oh! Oh, and a paper, please—"

She returned rather hurriedly to the phone booth.

"Glue's right there," she reported to Sam. "Doggedly watching by the arcade door. He probably trailed you this far, and is waiting for you to emerge. He can't possibly miss you if you step out. And my plan won't work—"

"What plan?"

"I was going to call a policeman and tell him that Glue was annoying me, and get him to lead Glue away for a few minutes. I did that once for Boy when he was being followed. But I seem to be hunted, myself. It's all Elfrida's work, I know. Eggy wouldn't have called the police."

"You mean," Sam said blankly, "the police are hunting you? *You?*"

"Yes. I'm more or less running away from Eggy and Elfrida, you know, but I didn't tell them, and they seem to be terribly upset. See, here on the front page. 'Prominent Elderly Woman Missing From South Shore Home. Wife of Former Governor and Mother of Famous Correspondent'—and so forth and so on. Ponds are being dragged—did you ever hear of anything so utterly ridiculous? When last seen, I was wearing a blue hand-embroidered nightgown—aha! Cook didn't give me away! Here, you read the rest."

Sam chuckled as he scanned the columns.

"They think," he said, "that you rushed out in a nightgown and a state of intense melancholy and hurled yourself into some convenient pond. They are at a professed loss to understand why."

Daisy began to laugh. It was an infectious laugh, and Sam caught it. They laughed until they cried.

"A nightgown!" Daisy said weakly, wiping her eyes. "What an idiot they must think I am! Sam, you don't want to go to the World's Fair, do you? To the opening tomorrow?"

"My God, no!" Sam said anxiously. "Why?"

Daisy pointed out that they could hardly spend the rest of their respective lives in the phone booth.

"Besides," she said, "I yearn to go. I love fairs. I always go. I've been to 'em all, since I was a mere child at the Philadelphia Centennial. That's why I ran away to the movies today, to see all the advance pictures. And I'm so annoyed with Eggy and Elfrida that for two cents I'd take one of those Fair specials, and not tell them, and let them keep on dragging

17

horse ponds. It would serve them right. You know, I *am* annoyed with those two!"

"If you're revolting against them," Sam said, "I feel sure they deserve it. But hadn't you better go easy on the revolt, at first?"

"How cautious you are, for a reporter," Daisy said. "Boylston, in your place, never would have hesitated an instant. But of course you're right. I can't go wandering off in a peeve. Only I've been hoping all day long that something would give me an excuse to go, and—well, maybe it will, yet. Now, I'll phone Jackson to expect us."

"Us, like me and you?"

"Yes, I've thought of a way to get you out. Past Glue, I mean. I'll buy some glasses and a top coat for you, and we'll get a wheel chair. I did it once with Boy."

"Now listen," Sam said. "You'll get pinched, yourself, Mrs. Tower, if you—"

"My dear boy, the police and the public think of me as a slightly cracked, elderly hag with a hand-embroidered nightgown on. I'm safe until cook breaks down and tells, and she won't. She likes me. Now, I'll phone Jackson."

After an impatient monologue, during the course of which half a dozen nickels were wasted, Daisy turned to Sam.

"I don't understand this," she said. "They say

there's no such number, and of course there is. It's my own house number. What would you do?"

"Perhaps they've changed it," Sam said. "Ask information for the number belonging to your street number—want me to do it?"

"What's the matter?" Daisy demanded, after Sam had carried on a long conversation with at least four people. "What's wrong?"

Sam looked at her.

"It seems," he said, "that your house is rented."

"What!"

"To some people named Lansing."

"But I never told—who rented it? Not Jackson?"

"They said, Mr. Tower. Maybe your nephew has a power of attorney?"

"I was not," Daisy said briefly, "that sick. Sam, hold these nickels while I call my washwoman. Katy always knows everything."

During her conversation with Katy, which cost twenty cents, Daisy's voice assumed a note of frightening calm.

"Jackson and his wife have been dismissed by Egleston," Daisy told Sam after she replaced the receiver. "My furniture is in storage, my house is rented, my cars sold—that will give you a brief idea. Ben Bassett's my lawyer; I don't see how he allowed—but then, he was ill this winter, and I suppose his office thought that it was perfectly all right for Egleston to act for me. To think that Egleston should—why, how dared he! No wonder I was kept from Boston! No wonder they told me not to think of the Louisburg Square house! Sam, do you want a job?"

"I'll beat Egleston up for nothing," Sam said.

"I'm not thinking of him," Daisy said. "I'm afraid to. I'm too shocked to think. Sam, I'll pay you what you've been getting to escort me to the World's Fair. With all expenses. Thank goodness, I've got my check book with me, and even though someone's been looking at it, I'm sure my bank balance hasn't been touched. I suppose it's the market that's made Eggy—well, after a trip to New York and the Fair, I may feel equal to coping coolly with the situation. Sam, are you going to the Fair with me?"

Sam hesitated, and then grinned at her.

"Get the glasses and the wheel chair," he said, "and we'll see if they work. Glue will take a lot of shunting, and I'm not sure that I shan't be pinched for kidnapping you. But let's go to the Fair. Why not?"

Privately, Sam could think of any number of reasons why not, but if Boy Tower's mother, in her present mood, was determined to go to the World's Fair opening, it was better that he rather than some stranger should escort her.

"Fine," Daisy said.

She started off briskly, but her footsteps were lagging a little as she returned to the station from her brief shopping expedition across the street.

She hadn't thought of the problems involved in

cashing her own checks, and her supply of cash on hand was very limited. When Elfrida's cook had lent her her month's wages, Daisy assumed that the wages were what she had paid her own cook. But apparently Elfrida paid starvation wages. The bills left in her pocketbook were ones, not tens. And there wasn't enough to start for the Fair.

Absent-mindedly, as she went in the station's side entrance, Daisy took the sample packet of Life Savers from the girl who held them out, and from a bearded man she accepted a handbill which announced that the world was coming to an end the following Wednesday at noon, sharp.

In the same preoccupied manner, Daisy held out her hand for the pink card that still another girl was thrusting under her nose.

"What kind of gasoline do you—" the girl broke off suddenly. "Daisy! Daisy Tower, darling, it's you, and you're well and whole and—oh, how swell to see you!"

"Cherry! Cherry Chipman, my dear child!" Daisy dropped her bundle and stooped to pick it up so that Cherry wouldn't see how full her eyes were. "Cherry, what are you doing here?"

"It's some sort of a survey. I ask people what kind of gas they use, and give 'em a card telling 'em to use another. I don't know why, but they pay me for it. Daisy, lamb, you're well! And have you forgiven me?"

21

"For what? For wanting to work in a department store with scope?"

Cherry stared at her.

"A what? Daisy, what do you mean?"

"I have this feeling," Daisy said, "this horrid feeling that—tell me, what did Eggy tell you after the accident?"

"Why, he said your broken hip was all my fault, because I was driving when the truck hit us. And that you were mad at me, and tired of me anyway, and I was fired. And he personally thought I was a bad influence, and better gone."

"I was told," Daisy drew a long breath, "that you wished a job with greater scope, and that you had no time to waste on an old lady with a broken hip. It was not your idea of fun, and fun was all you stayed with me as a companion for—"

"Egleston said that! He never! Oh, what you must have thought of me! Why, I begged to see you! I went to the house again and again, and they said you refused to see me! Daisy, whatever made Eggy do a thing like that!"

"Eggy has been doing a number of things," Daisy said, "which can only be described as strange and unaccountable. I thought the house renting was for the money, but why he should have told you lies—here, let's move out of the way of this mob. I wonder, Cherry, if Egleston wasn't afraid of my becoming too attached to you. He worries about the future of the

Tower money. That is, Elfrida does. It must be all Elfrida's work."

"How is that living statue?" Cherry asked.

"Momentarily," Daisy said, "she's dragging horse ponds for my body clothed in a hand-embroidered nightgown. Cherry, I've forgotten about Sam. I've got to get him out of that phone booth in disguise so Glue will get shaken. Sam's really very nice, he's a reporter and he knows Boy, and he's rather like Boy used to be."

"It all sounds haywire to me," Cherry said. "But I'm so glad to see you again, I don't care. By the way, am I re-hired?"

"Don't ask foolish questions, child! And remind me to look into my will. And do get rid of those silly pink cards!"

Cherry, Daisy noticed, was thin. And her clothes were shabby. And her shoes! The state of those shoes told Cherry's story. And to think that Egleston Tower was responsible for this, too!

"Hurry!" Daisy said.

"But I really ought to give these cards away, Daisy. I've been paid to. And these special envelope things."

"What are those?"

"Prizes, I think. I didn't quite understand. I had five, and I was to give them to certain sorts of people."

"How absurd!"

"I thought so, but this doddering old gent who hired me had a very fixed idea about them. Isn't it funny, that man reminded me of Egleston. He had those same silly eyebrows—"

"Don't talk about Egleston!" Daisy said. "And those envelopes—what's in 'em?"

"Oh, a stick of gum, or a coupon for free gas, or something. He didn't tell me, but he was very particular about my giving them out. I've done away with the middle-aged man and woman, and of these three left, one's got to go to an elderly lady—"

"Give it to me at once, then," Daisy said, reaching out her hand.

She frowned as she opened the envelope, then, making little sounds of incredulity, she smiled.

"Cherry! It's a railroad ticket to the World's Fair, a ticket to the Fair! With a sort of admittance card attached! How utterly amazing!"

"Probably the doddering old gent with the eyebrows like Eggy's is a philanthropist, incognito," Cherry said. "Like misers who give away circus tickets. Isn't it fantastic, the things people do. Probably someone who didn't want to be known put on that cloak—"

"Who're you supposed to give the others to?"

There was a gleam in Daisy's eyes.

"A nice-looking girl—you've no idea how surprisingly few nice-looking girls there are, Daisy! And a young man."

"My dear," Daisy said, "take one yourself, and we'll give the other to Sam Minot, and we three will go to the fair. I'd intended to go, but I was short of cash.

24

Elfrida pays her cook simply disgusting wages. This is providential, simply providential!"

"But—"

"Now you listen," Daisy said, "to me."

Briefly, she summed up the story of her day in Boston, the cook's wages and the cook's spring outfit, the laundry truck and the lost six-thirty-two, her meeting with Sam in the phone booth, and her series of discoveries about Egleston.

Cherry eyed her at the conclusion of her recital.

"But, Daisy, if they think you've hopped into a pond, should you go dashing off without telling them that you're all right—"

"My dear, I can't even think of Eggy now. I'm too mad. It's more charitable of me to go away and think him over before I see him or talk with him. And we'd planned to go to the Fair opening, you and I. And here is our opportunity."

"But the tickets," Cherry said. "Hadn't we better make sure they're all right before we wander off and embark on anything? They're awfully funny-looking tickets, if you ask me. 'De Luxe World's Fair Train, The Golden Dart,' " she read off the ticket heading. "They may be phoney. They have a phoney sound."

"Ask that train man, the one over there," Daisy stopped him with the point of her cane. "Can you tell me about a train named the Golden Dart, and if these tickets are good?"

The man paused, glanced at the tickets, and smiled.

"Track Fourteen," he said. "Seven-thirty."

"Now I think of it," Cherry said, "the old gent told me to give the five envelopes away by seven, but I forgot, with all that's being going on. Give me your bundle, Daisy. You've no idea what a madhouse this station has been, with the mob, and all the special trains going to the Fair. It's worse than a Harvard-Yale game crush. They've lost scores of children already, and twins got born in the waiting room—"

"Wait!" Daisy grabbed Cherry's arm as they started off. "Look at that man in the grey suit! It's Glue, and he's going! Yes, he really is, he's hailing that cab! Oh, that's fine. He was the man who's been following Sam. There, he's gone. Now, let's get Sam and get going— have you any money?"

"Two dollars," Cherry said.

"Well, there are always my rings," Daisy said. "They'll tide us over—"

"Daisy," Cherry said, "do you really think that we're wise in—I mean, shouldn't we sort of stop and think?"

"I can't hear a word you say," Daisy returned. "All this noisy crowd! What did you say?"

"I said, this is a sort of mad expedition, and I think we ought to stop and ponder!"

"There's the phone booth," Daisy said, "and there's Sam."

Sam's eyebrows went up when he saw the girl at Mrs. Tower's side.

"Glue's rushed away," Daisy told him, "but you'd better put on these glasses and this awful topcoat, anyway. And this is Cherry Chipman, who used to be my companion. And we've got less than ten minutes to make our special, so hurry. Track Fourteen."

"But—" Sam began.

"Hurry!" Daisy said. "Come on!"

At the sight of the sleek, streamlined train on Track Fourteen, Sam stopped short and gulped.

"What a lovely train," Daisy said. "Isn't that a beautiful thing? That must be the Golden Dart."

"It *is* the Golden Dart," Sam said in a choked voice. "But you haven't any bizarre—any whimsical notions that you are taking the Golden Dart, have you?"

"We've got tickets for it," Daisy said with quiet pride.

"Oh, Mrs. T.! Where'd you get 'em? Who's been pulling your leg like that!"

"They're perfectly good tickets," Cherry resented his tone. "A train man said so."

But she remembered, uncomfortably, that the train man had smiled a rather odd smile.

"It's certainly de luxe, isn't it?" Daisy said. "I don't think I ever saw a more de luxe affair—what are you making all those noises about, Sam?"

"Listen!" Sam said. "Do you know—of course you don't. You can't, or you wouldn't take all this so matter-of-factly. That train—my God, how can I tell you? That is the most famous private train in America!

That's more famous as a train than the *Nourmahal* is as a yacht. You can't get on that train with tickets, Mrs. Tower! You can't!"

He swallowed hard as Daisy passed the three tickets over to a guard, who scrutinized them, and waved to a gateman to let them through.

"Hurry, please," the gateman said. "Leaving at seven-thirty."

Sam looked at the gateman, then he surveyed Daisy and Cherry, calmly walking along beside him. Then he pinched himself.

"Whipple's statistics," he said aloud. "Whipple's statistics."

"What *is* the matter with you, Sam?" Daisy said. "What are you muttering about?"

"I know I'm awake," Sam said, "because it hurts when I pinch myself. I can say 'Whipple's statistics' with great clarity, so I must be sober. I—well, you're not *on* it, yet!"

Two minutes later, on the blue and silver observation car, Sam sat down limply.

"You're acting so strangely," Daisy observed. "Was it the heat in that phone booth, or are you tired from trying to shake Glue?"

"Mrs. T.," Sam said in a voice he hardly recognized as his own, "I have just gone through a very moving experience. I have achieved something that Boy Tower never achieved. I am limp. Shattered. Emotionally torn—"

"For goodness sakes, get to the point!" Daisy said.

"I'm not easily moved," Sam said, "but this day has been the maddest—"

"Daisy," Cherry interrupted, "we're going! We've started, see?"

"Maybe we've started," Sam said, "but I hope the cinders are soft when we get thrown off—"

"Sam," Daisy said, "what are you talking about!"

Sam smiled.

"This," he said, "is Conrad Cassell's private train."

2

Sᴀᴍ leaned back in the blue leather chair.

That, he thought proudly, was building up your story to the old sock line. That was a bit of news that would knock Mrs. Tower and her girl friend for the well-known loop.

He felt considerably deflated when Daisy merely nodded, and said simply to Cherry, "He's that multimillionaire, you know, dear. That one who came to see Mrs. Bottome's Gainsborough."

"Oh, is he?" Cherry said. "Aren't these chairs marvellous things!"

"They're heaven," Daisy said. "Particularly after Elfrida's fiddle-backs. Not a comfortable chair in that whole blessed house. Sam, those glasses certainly change you. You don't look the same. You look like Harold Lloyd."

"Maybe you didn't hear me," Sam said. "I told you, this was Cassell's private train. The private train of Conrad Cassell. Did you hear?"

"We heard," Cherry said. "I suppose the old gent who gave me the tickets has chartered it. I wonder if he kept Cassell's chef. I'm awfully hungry, aren't you, Daisy?"

"Starved," Daisy said.

Sam closed his eyes and groaned.

"They don't care," he said loudly to the curved Venetian blinds. "They're on the private train of the most eccentric tycoon in North America, and they don't give a damn! They're sunk in luxury, and they wonder if there's a chef! You've got transportation to the Fair, and admission when you've got there—and you think only of your stomachs! Did Cassell leave a chef! Say, did you know that Cassell almost *was* the Fair? One wave of an eyelash, and Cassell would have been the director!"

"Really?" Cherry said politely. "That's very interesting, but do you suppose we could get a sandwich or something, if—"

"And when he didn't get to be director," Sam continued, "he was so sore that everybody thought he'd never come near the place. But he had a change of heart, and stuck up a building that looks like Venus de Milo having nightmares—"

"It's simply wonderful, all you know about him," Cherry said. "But *is* there something to eat?"

"And Cassell's even going to be there for the opening pageant," Sam said, "to keep an eye on the Old Masters he's lent, and the ones he's wangled for the exhibition. They said in Boston that if Mrs. Bottome's Gainsborough was genuine, he was going to make her lend that, too."

"Anyone who could make that woman part with anything," Daisy said, "is a sheer genius. I seem to remember, now, reading about Cassell coaxing people to lend pictures for the Fair. Thousands of Madonnas, and the Mona Lisa—"

"Who," Cherry said reflectively, "was that lad who used to paint girls dancing under trees, and then swap his canvases for bowls of onion soup? I would love a bowl of onion soup."

"Corot," Daisy said. "Sam, you might do a Sunday supplement article on these murals here. 'Do His Pictures Show Cassell the Man?' I hope they don't. I think they're terrible!"

"I once—" Sam began, but he stopped short as the door at the end of the car opened, and two people rather hesitantly entered.

"They're the ones I gave the other two tickets to," Cherry whispered in Daisy's ear. "Middle-aged man, middle-aged woman. But they don't look so middle-aged in this light. Particularly the woman."

Daisy surveyed the pair with interest.

The man was short and plump and brilliantly bald, and Daisy guessed at some time his doctor had warned him about high blood pressure. He looked rather like the man Eggy knew who ran a lumber yard, and was always smashing golf clubs when he missed putts.

The woman was not so easy to sum up. She was, Daisy thought, between thirty-five and forty, and she might be almost anything from a professional contralto to a smart-shop saleslady. You couldn't tell from her clothes. They had about them an elusive quality that might mean the stage, or just slightly flamboyant taste. The small suitcase she carried was worn, but expensive. Daisy had learned from Boylston always to notice luggage.

"Good evening," Daisy said pleasantly. "Won't you join us? And you didn't see anyone broiling a steak or carving a chicken, did you?"

The woman's hesitant expression gave way to a grin, and she started to speak. The man, however, beat her to it.

"I want to know," he waggled a stubby, accusing finger at Cherry, "the meaning of this! What kind of a racket is this, huh? What was the idea, giving me that ticket?"

"You didn't have to use it," Cherry said. "You needn't waggle your finger at me. You didn't have to come."

He took her seriously.

"Of course I did. They wouldn't give me any rebate on the ticket, and I couldn't let it go to waste. I thought I'd see what was up. This country's chock full of free chances to get something for nothing. But there's always a catch to it!"

"Found any catches yet?" the woman with the suitcase asked. "If you ask me, it's a newspaper stunt. They get you to the Fair, and then ask your impressions with a lot of ballyhoo to boom trade. Say, what do you make of it?"

"You mean me?" Sam said. "I wouldn't know. It just seems we're getting a free ride."

"When do we get there?"

"Can't tell, with a train like this," Sam said. "We won't run on schedule, certainly not with all the other Fair specials and things. I suppose we do station-to-station stuff and get there tomorrow morning. Maybe we'll get there late tonight. I wouldn't know."

"Well, I wouldn't mind if it was a newspaper stunt," the woman said. "I might get a break out of it. My name's Duplain. Madame Duplain," she added, as she carefully set down her suitcase and took a seat beside Daisy. "Who owns the train?"

"Sam says it's Conrad Cassell's," Daisy told her. "That millionaire with all the pictures. And tell me, aren't you a singer? It seems to me I heard you at some club once."

"Sure, you might have," Madame Duplain said. "I warble around. Clubs aren't much in my line, but I get stuck once in a while and take a date. Say," she lowered her voice, "is there a ladies' room around? I want to wash my hands."

"Cherry," Daisy said, "do see if you can't find a button or a bell cord. And won't you sit down, Mr. —" she hesitated over the bald man's name.

"George Edward Whitty. Whitty and Glum, Meats and Vegetables."

"Do sit down and be comfortable, Mr. Whitty," Daisy continued hospitably.

Whitty glared about for a moment, and then sank into a chair.

"I sat down on two things in that smoking room where they put me," he said. "Two different things, and both of 'em turned out to be bars, and one played music. I'm glad this is meant to be sat on."

"Here's a button," Cherry said, jabbing at it with her thumb. "Let's see what happens."

The steward who appeared seemed a little startled at the sight of the group. He stared at them, and then instinctively turned and bowed to Mrs. Tower. Sam noticed that people had a habit of bowing deferentially to Daisy Tower.

"Yes, madam?"

"Dinner," Daisy said brightly. "What about dinner, steward?"

"Certainly, madam. Should you prefer to dine here, madam, or in the dining salon? Oh—"

"What's the difference where we eat," Whitty interrupted, "what's the difference?"

"Perhaps, sir," said the steward with infinite tact, "if you are dining informally, you would prefer to remain here, but—"

"I don't care how informal I eat," replied Mr.

Whitty hotly, "I just want to eat. What you got? Where's the bill o' fare?"

With an apologetic little bow to Mrs. Tower, the steward presented Mr. Whitty with a card.

"French, huh?" Whitty said disgustedly. "Here, take it back. What I want, waiter, is some tomato soup, and a rare steak—and mind it is rare, too! And French-fries, and ice cream and coffee. And bring me a good ten cent cigar."

The steward whisked a humidor from a table.

"Say!" Whitty stared at the band. "Corona, huh? Well, well!"

He retired with the cigar to the oval room at the end of the car, and the steward gave the menu to Daisy, who glanced over it, and nodded.

"Fine," she said, "perfectly splendid. And we'll dine here. And we should like to wash."

"Yes, madam," the steward said, "if you will follow me."

Mr. Whitty wandered back, after their departure, and sat beside Sam.

"What's the matter?" Sam inquired. "You look mad."

"This damn cigar." Whitty shifted it between his teeth and talked around it. "Can't taste the damn thing."

He removed it from his mouth, inspected it carefully, and then looked at Sam.

"Say, brother, what *is* the idea of all this? Of course,

business is bad, and I'm tickled to come if it's on the level. But what's the big idea? This fancy train, and the tickets—"

"Why worry?" Sam asked.

"Well," Whitty said, "if this is a newspaper stunt, I won't be exploited. No, sir! Nobody needs to think because they give me a free ride and a free meal, they can exploit me!"

He looked again at his cigar, and thoughtfully removed the band. Then he produced a stogie from his breast pocket.

"Three for ten," he said, slipping the Corona band on it, "and you know you're smoking something."

"We all know it," Madame Duplain said, returning to the car and wrinkling up her nose. "I thought someone's hair was burning."

Sam added his contribution. It was a temptation to tease the little man.

"Come clean, Whitty, you know you're itching to get to the Fair. You want to see the packers' exhibits, don't you? Wilson and Swift and all the rest?"

"Well," Whitty hooked his thumbs into his vest pockets and clamped his stogie at an angle in the corner of his mouth. "Well," he said self-consciously, "I don't care so much about them. But I would sort of like to see Sally Rand."

Sam and Madame Duplain hooted. But Daisy Tower, entering at that moment, got a fleeting impression, as she surveyed the naïve Mr. Whitty, that perhaps he was not as transparent as he seemed. No one who looked so much like a meat man could possibly be one.

"That was Chicago," Sam was saying. "You've got the wrong fair. But don't you worry. If Sally Rand isn't at the Fair in New York, you can depend on it there'll be someone just like her. She may not have bubbles, but there'll be a Sally Rand. Or a Little Egypt."

"Little Egypt," Daisy said. "You know, I enjoyed her thoroughly."

"You saw her?" Sam asked. "You really did?"

"Oh, my, yes. Boylston—I mean my husband, not Boy, of course. He said I simply couldn't—here, let's move out of the way of these waiters. Boylston put his foot down, but I went just the same. Carrie Phelps and I dressed up in his clothes and sneaked in. I don't know when I've had a better time. I had a marvellous time at the Columbian Exposition, anyway. Why, I led the grand march at the opening ball!"

"You never told me that!" Cherry said.

"Didn't I? I took the place of my hostess, who was sick—"

Her stories of the Columbian Exposition carried them gaily through dinner.

"Don't stop," Sam said, "just because you're pouring coffee, Daisy. What about your cousin Henry? Didn't he ever go on the ferris wheel, after trekking all the way to Chicago just to go on it?"

"The day he left," Daisy said, "Boylston and I marched him to the wheel and practically threw him on. He closed his eyes and stood like a statue. Wouldn't sit down, even. We had to lift him off. He was petrified. He never said a word all the way to Boston until he got to the station. Then he said Boston was good enough for him. And to the best of my knowledge, he never went any farther away than Dedham till the day he died."

Daisy did not think it was such a terribly funny story, but apparently it struck Mr. Whitty as one of the most comical things he had ever heard, and he laughed immoderately.

"Say," he said, "that's good. That's a good story. And do you know what? That was a good dinner. I never got any better food on a train except once in 1920, at a convention. The meat packers, the big fellers, they hired a whole train, and you couldn't hope to see such steaks as they had. But this was almost as good."

"Indeed!"

The five at the table swung around and stared at the man who spoke from the doorway.

Cherry, who did not recognize him, decided that he looked like the ex-dictator who'd had the next villa in Cannes one year. Sam, who did recognize Conrad Cassell, stiffened into silence and waited to be thrown off the train as he had been thrown out of Mrs. Bottome's house earlier in the day. But Cassell simply glared at him, and then turned his head to glare at Whitty. Sam couldn't understand, at first, and then he remembered the glasses. He'd forgotten to take off the glasses that Daisy had bought and given him, back in the station. Those glasses, Sam thought, were practically the only lucky break he'd had all day. For recognition by Cassell, in his present white, cold fury—Sam swallowed.

And Cassell was in a fury. His small blue pig eyes were glittering from between the rolls of flesh. His thin mouth seemed to go almost around his convex jaw. His nostrils were quivering, and the muscles in his throat were tense. Sam wouldn't have been surprised if the man had sprung at them.

"What," Cassell made a furious gesture with a fat, unnaturally small hand, "what is the meaning of this?"

Each word fell like an icicle on concrete pavement.

"I repeat, what is the meaning of this!"

Whitty's face was blank, but he continued to hold his stogie clamped between his teeth. Daisy noticed that the cigar did not even waver slightly. Madame Duplain reached for her suitcase, from which she had refused to be separated, and gripped the handle tightly. If there was going to be trouble, she was prepared. Cherry tried to display a poise which she did not feel, and leaned forward, cigarette in hand, her face alert as if she were just about to speak.

With all the courtesy of a hostess soothing an irritable guest, Daisy smiled.

"We'd like to know the meaning of it, too," she said. "We don't understand it all any better than you do. You see we—"

But Cassell did not listen. Waving that fat small hand, he launched on a violent and vociferous denunciation of people who had the brazen effrontery to enter and use his private, personal train.

After his opening barrage of insults, Daisy turned and traced the broadloom patterns with the tip of her cane. Mr. Conrad Cassell, she decided, was either a remarkably rude man, or a show-off, and she had long since given up listening to either type.

Strangely enough it was Mr. Whitty who decided that something constructive should be done. He was on a vacation, he felt, and he didn't have to listen to that sort of talk. And he didn't think anyone should talk that way before ladies.

Getting up from the table, he marched over to Conrad Cassell, thrust an angry forefinger into that gentleman's midriff, and told him as much.

"Brother," Whitty said, "I don't know who you are, but you hadn't ought to talk that way before ladies. Shut up."

Cassell glared at him speechlessly.

"And apologize," Whitty added, prodding again with his forefinger. "Quick!"

41

Sam waited for the explosion. But Cassell was almost too furious to explode.

"Take your hands off me, sir!" Cassell said. "And remove that offensive cigar!"

"Now you listen here, brother!" Whitty's face got very red. "No cracks about my cigar, see? They're a hell of a lot better than your damned Coronas, if those Coronas belong to you, see?"

He snapped his fingers under Cassell's nose.

The two waiters looked at each other and averted their eyes.

"Sam," Daisy said, "intervene, please, before we have bloodshed. Mr. Whitty, you come sit beside me, will you?"

"Aw, Mrs.—aw, Dais—"

"Yes, I really feel it would be best. Now, Sam, my son, stand beside Mr. Cassell."

"Yes, ma'am," Sam obediently went and stood beside him.

"There is no need," Cassell said, "for your son to—"

"Now, Mr. Cassell," Daisy said, "to sum it up, you wish to be told how we happen to be here?"

Cassell drew a long breath.

"Yes, Mrs. Days," he said. "I most certainly and assuredly do, Mrs. Days!"

Daisy started to correct his impression that her name was Days—he'd picked that up from Whitty's incoherent speech—and that she was Sam's mother.

42

Then it occurred to her that perhaps it was all for the best. There was no way of knowing to what extent her own name and her supposed disappearance in the horse pond might have been bandied about in the papers. Neither Mr. Whitty nor Madame Duplain knew her as anything but Daisy. Introductions had somehow never been formally accomplished.

And it was better for Sam, too. It was doubtful as to whether or not his name was sufficiently well-known to be recognized by Cassell, she thought, but if Cassell were to find out that he was practically nursing a reporter in his bosom, life might well be very grim for Sam. What Cassell thought of reporters was legend.

"I'm waiting, Mrs. Days!"

"Samuel, my son," Daisy said, hoping that Sam would catch on, "Samuel, my son, you—no, Cherry, perhaps you had best begin with your story of the doddering old man."

Cherry's story was simple enough. While waiting for a call in an employment office, the doddering old man had doddered in, looked over the assembled group, pointed to her and asked if she had had any advertising experience.

"Of course I said yes," Cherry said. "I'd have said yes if he'd asked me if I'd spent much time at the South Pole—"

"Why?" Cassell interrupted sharply.

Cherry looked at him. "I needed the job. So he gave

me those pink cards telling about that gasoline, and those five little envelopes for the different kinds of people."

For Cassell's benefit, she explained about the envelopes, just as she had explained to Daisy, at the station.

"How utterly absurd!" Cassell said.

"That's what Daisy said, too. She thought it was absurd. I suppose it was. I didn't really understand about it, and I told the old gent so, and he said there was no need for me to understand. All I had to do was to carry out his orders. He was a funny old dodderer, with that cloak and his hat brim pulled down—"

"Hah!" Cassell said. "A disguise!"

"That's what I thought later," Cherry said, "after we found out that the envelopes had tickets in them. I thought it was probably some philanthropist in disguise. But I didn't think about it at the time. All I thought about then was getting a job and being paid for it."

Daisy let her talk on for several minutes.

"Then," she said, "my son Sam and I came along, and we were given two of the envelopes, since we met the—er—the specifications." Daisy paused long enough to kick Cherry's ankle to keep her quiet. Cherry was clearly bursting to tell everything, but Daisy could not see any sense in presenting Cassell with all the extraneous detail, like the story of Glue,

44

or the story of Egleston and Elfrida. The simple truth of the ticket situation was not going over any too well with him. Details like Glue would probably only serve to convince Cassell that his uninvited guests were a pack of escaped maniacs. "We opened the envelopes there," Daisy continued, "asked about the tickets, and Cherry told us what she knew. Then, because it was getting late, we suggested that she take the remaining envelope herself, and come with us. She did. And, Mr. Cassell, before you say that it's the most incredible story you ever heard, perhaps you can explain to us why your personal guards and your train employees saw fit to let us board your train without question?"

"Orchids, mother," Sam said approvingly. "Orchids."

Daisy smiled. Cassell, looking into her face, smiled also, but it was not a very pleasant smile. Mr. Cassell seemed to be thinking very hard and very quickly.

"Mrs. Days," he said, "something has gone wrong. Very wrong indeed."

His pig eyes closed in a still more expansive smile. Daisy turned away from him. She didn't like men whose eyes closed when they smiled.

"The individuals who are to blame for this error," Cassell continued, "will pay, I assure you, Mrs. Days. They will pay."

"I hope," Daisy said, "that you won't be too harsh with them. After all, we did have tickets, you know.

And it seems too bad that people should be taken to task for our very pleasant journey and our excellent dinner."

"Five of you," Cassell said. "Five. Five people allowed on my train. It's remarkable. It's unbelievable."

"I don't see anything so queer about it," Whitty said. "We showed our tickets, and they let us on. That's all there was to it."

"You have your tickets?" Cassell asked. "Oh, you do. No one collected them. I see. Then if you will allow me to collect them and look at them, possibly I may be able to get to the root of this. Ah. All five. Thank you. If you will excuse me just a moment."

He disappeared so quickly and so quietly that Madame Duplain whistled under her breath.

"Light on their feet, these heavy boys," she commented. "Well, can anybody laugh this one off? What's going to happen to us?"

Sam shrugged his shoulders meditatively. "If he hasn't thrown us off yet," he said, "there's hope."

"What do you mean, throw us off?" Whitty demanded. "We had our tickets, and he can't—"

"My dear Whitty," Daisy said, "if Conrad Cassell wishes to throw us off his train, he will, tickets or no tickets. Hasn't he a peculiar mouth? It's awfully hard to connect a mouth and a face like that with all those Madonnas and the Mona Lisa."

"D'you see now," Sam asked her, "why he wasn't made Fair director? He's a marvellous organizer—"

"But," Daisy said, "he hardly has a winning manner, has he? He—"

"Hush!" Cherry whispered.

Cassell stood in the doorway, although they had not heard him approach. Behind him, in the corridor, stood two burly guards. Hovering in their shadow was a nervous secretary who entered only when Cassell made a motion of his hand. The trio had very obviously been told a number of things by their employer. Their faces still burned.

"Mrs. Days," Cassell said, "will you and the rest accept my apology for my outburst of temper?"

Sam had seldom seen a less apologetic-looking person, but Daisy did not appear to notice Cassell's manner.

"You mean," she said, "that you've found an explanation?"

Cassell nodded.

"Yesterday," he said, "I dismissed my secretary, Andrew, who has been with me for some time. The dismissal was justified, but Andrew resented it and made a number of threats. I ignored them. It now appears that he is carrying some of them out."

"Could it have been Andrew in disguise," Cherry asked, "who gave me those envelopes and things?"

"It undoubtedly was," Cassell told her. "I neglected —that is, Roberts, my new assistant here, neglected to inform my staff about Andrew's dismissal. Thus, when Andrew sent orders to them, at the train, to admit five guests of mine without question, they did so. Andrew also said something about tickets. That is why you experienced no difficulty in getting on the train. That—"

"I'm certainly glad," Cherry said, "to have that explained. So your dismissed Andrew was the doddering old man! Now I think of it, his voice was young for someone who doddered so. Where'd he get the tickets?"

"He had them printed—they're printed, by the way, on some of my own small cards! And the pink cards—they, of course, and the question you were to ask about gasoline, they were merely blinds. And now, I wonder if you will forgive my unpleasant words and continue as my guests—my real guests—to the Fair? I am going to the opening, although it is not my custom to attend such things. Andrew knew I was going. And it seems to me that the only way I can convince you of my very genuine regret is to beg you to come as my guests, and remain with me as my guests."

Sam and Daisy exchanged glances.

"That's all very well," Daisy said after a moment's hesitation. "It's very handsome and—er—de luxe of you. But, Mr. Cassell, why did your dismissed secretary pick five different types of people to have those tickets given to? And why? Why should he do a thing like that?"

"I'm glad," Cassell said, "that you have raised that point. That is another reason why I wish you would remain as my guests. If there is some plan on foot, we may be able to get to the root of it. Obviously, you would not have been enticed on my train without reason. There is something behind all this. And—"

"And you want us to walk into it for you, do you?" Madame Duplain inquired tartly.

"I can assure you," Cassell said earnestly, "that none of you will be in any personal danger whatsoever. Of course, I can understand why you well might say that this is my business, and not yours. I have not," his eyes closed again in that smile, "acted in any manner that would make you feel indebted to me. There is no reason for you to wish to aid me in the solution to my problems. But I should be greatly indebted to you if you would consent to stay as my guests, and assist me in getting to the bottom of this strange situation."

Whitty instantly rose to the occasion. Daisy wondered if he didn't rise almost too quickly.

"Sure, brother," he said, clapping Cassell fraternally on the back. "Why not? If you take us to the Fair, we owe you something anyway, and if we can find out what this guy Andrew is up to, why then we'll have paid off our obligations. There's no reason just because you got a lot of money, you can't fire a guy without he tries to get back at you with a lot of hocus-pocus. Sure, we'll stay and help you out!"

"Bigheart," Madame Duplain said. "Just as big as an ox, that's what. Oh, no," she added as Cassell looked at her questioningly. "I don't mean I want to stop being your guest. No. Not at the rate this train's going. If we can help, it's okay with me."

"Tell me, Mr. Cassell," Daisy said, "when we get to New York, do we go directly to the Fair grounds?"

"We'll go directly to the Fair in this train," Cassell said. "We remain on my private siding. No one knows about the time schedule. Intense traffic, you know, with all the specials. It annoyed me, but it can't be helped. We'll probably have a lot of waiting, and very likely they'll re-route us at the last minute. Have you the tentative schedule, Roberts?"

"The what, sir? I—I don't think I—that is—"

The secretary's sentence trailed off into mumbling sounds as Cassell glared at him. Privately, Sam gave Roberts just about two days at working for Cassell. A week at the most.

"Get Brand," Cassell said coldly. "Brand, in case you have forgotten, Roberts, is the steward. Brand appears to be the only individual in my service who is able to take orders. Brand will see about rooms for you all, Mrs. Days. And perhaps you'd like a rubber of bridge?"

"Bridge!" Whitty said with scorn. "That's no kind of a game. How's for some poker?"

50

"I'm sure," Cassell said, "that Mrs. Days will prefer bridge."

"As a matter of fact," Daisy said, "I prefer bed to either. Madame Duplain and the rest of you can take your choice. This has been rather an exhausting day, and with the Fair before me, I think I shall leave you to your poker and go to bed."

"I'll watch," Cherry said. "And, Mr. Cassell, d'you suppose Roberts or someone could find a spare toothbrush?"

"Brand will supply you with everything you need," Cassell said. "Both my aunt and my daughter often use the train, and I'm sure you and Mrs. Days and Madame—er—Duplain can all be outfitted from their things. My man can see to you gentlemen. And do let Brand take your suitcase, Madame Duplain."

"I'll keep it, thanks," she said. "I'll keep it right here with me."

"As you please," Cassell said, eyeing the suitcase curiously.

"You playing poker with us?" Whitty asked Madame Duplain.

She smiled faintly. "I might try."

Sam, getting ready for bed around one o'clock that night, chuckled at the memory of that smile. Madame Duplain could park in comfort at the Ritz for several weeks on what she had won from Cassell. And the old boy had taken his licking with more grace than Sam would have believed possible. It was amazing, Sam thought, how amiable Cassell could be when he wanted.

"But," Sam said to himself as he removed his property glasses, "I hate to think what would have happened to you, Sammy boy, if Mister Cassell had seen you without these shell-rimmed cheaters! If he'd recognized me—whee!"

In the next room, Daisy Tower divided her attention between Cherry's chatter and the queer sounds that apparently had no connection with the smoothly gliding train. She didn't mention the sounds, because Cherry didn't seem to notice them.

"Gert Duplain had wonderful luck," Cherry said, as she put her bobby pins into a sunken dish in the chromium dressing table. "There's nothing the matter with our luck, either, is there, Daisy? Such damn luxury! I'd forgotten there were such things as linen sheets."

"Mr. Cassell does himself very well," Daisy said. "Except that I wish he'd provided his train with Maxim silencers. The train itself isn't noisy, but there are more sounds! Oh, don't disturb my glasses, darling," she added. "They're my far-seeing ones, and I couldn't go to the Fair without them."

"Glasses? I don't see 'em anywhere," Cherry said rather absent-mindedly. She was fresh from a shower, and wrapped in rainbow towelling.

"They're right there," Daisy said.

Cherry pawed around among her own disorderly

array of compact, lipstick, wrist watch and cigarettes. That girl, Daisy thought, could make the shelf of an airliner look as if she'd kept house there for a year.

"They're not here, darling," Cherry said.

Daisy raised herself on her elbow and spoke in a wide-awake voice.

"Then I left them—I know where I left them. No, you can't go, Cherry. You'd take your death of cold. Just find me a bathrobe, or something."

"Cassell's aunty has an eye for color," Cherry murmured, bringing her a pansy purple negligée.

Daisy slid into it, and slipped on her own shoes. She even reached, automatically, for her cane, before she remembered that it wasn't necessary. She hoped that cane wasn't going to be a habit. She could walk miles without it, now that she was free of Elfrida and Eggy.

She thought of Eggy and what he'd done as she went out into the dimly lighted corridor. Eggy, she decided, had evidently had plenty of troubles that he didn't talk about, and as soon as the Fair adventure was over, she would have to take him and them in hand. She sighed. There were so many people whose troubles she'd rather cope with.

But she wasn't thinking of Eggy and his troubles when she came back. She was shaking all over.

Cherry, half asleep, turned and yawned.

"Find 'em, dear?"

Mrs. Tower did not answer. She did not even hear.

Sitting down stiffly on the edge of her bed, she closed her eyes. What she had just seen in the corridor had bewildered her to a point of forgetting everything, even her far-seeing glasses.

But she hadn't needed any glasses to be aware of the horrified expression on the face of Sam Minot, as he sneaked out of a room on her right, with something bulky clutched tightly under his coat.

The door to that room on the right had been ajar. It was a dimly lit, official-looking room. There might have been a desk in it, under that upright lamp.

And Sam had come sneaking out, clutching something. He hadn't even seemed to notice her. For her part, she had been so dazed at the way he looked that she'd continued on her way down the corridor, down to the end of the next car, to the oval room. And then she'd come back again, because Whitty was there, sound asleep and snoring, and fully dressed.

You would know, she thought irrelevantly to herself, that Whitty would snore. That button nose would be as inadequate as a terrier's when it came to the peak load in exhaling and inhaling oxygen during a deep slumber.

But Sam! What was Sam Minot doing, skulking around, hiding things, looking horrified and afraid and furtive! And in such a state that he didn't even notice other people passing by!

Daisy slipped out of the purple negligée and slid in between the soft linen sheets.

Sam's skulking was bad enough. So was that look on his face. So was the thing he had hidden under his coat. But none of them mattered as much as the door.

It was Fannie's influence, she said to herself. She never used to be the kind of person who went around twisting door knobs. But, on her way back down the corridor, she had tried the handle of that door on the right, and the door had been locked.

Why, she kept wondering. Why was the door now locked? And who, during the minute or two that she had walked down the hall, who had locked it so quietly?

And most of all, what for?

3

Daisy, standing the next morning at the smoking room window, turned as Brand entered.

"Isn't this Fair incredible!" she said.

"Good morning, madam." Brand bowed. "It is a very striking sight, is it not?"

"I never dreamed that it would be like this!"

"You should see *our* building, madam. Mr. Cassell's building. It's not large, but it's very effective. There's been nothing like it ever before, at any other fair. It represents a basic hourglass," he added. "It's been very highly spoken of."

"Hourglass?" Daisy said. "It seems to me I heard the newsreel man in the movies yesterday speaking about an hourglass building. Someone's spoken of it recently, I know, if he didn't. But I don't remember seeing a picture of it. Which way is it?"

"You can't see it from here," Brand said, "but probably Mr. Cassell will take you over it later, madam. He's very proud of his building. He was one of the

56

first to build—" Brand broke off. "Did you sleep well, madam? You look a little pale, if I may say so."

Daisy had tossed and turned most of the night until she had managed to rationalize, to some extent, Sam's actions in the corridor. But there was no need to tell Brand that.

"I slept like a log," she said. "Brand, have you seen Miss Chipman? Where can she have gone so early?"

"I've not seen her, madam, but I think she may have gone with Mr. Cassell. His car stopped to pick up someone. Oh!" Brand picked up an envelope from the floor near the table. "This is addressed to you, madam. I think it must have blown off from the table. I hadn't noticed it before."

"From Cherry," Daisy said, looking at the writing.

Her far-seeing glasses fell out as she tore the envelope open.

"Thank goodness!" Daisy said. "Now I can really look at this fair!"

She read Cherry's hastily scribbled note.

" 'Darling, here they are. What a shame you had to go roaming around last night without finding them. They were in the oval room. I'm off unexpectedly. More anon. Cherry.' "

" 'More anon,' " Daisy said, "is so beautifully indefinite. One of those phrases, like 'Old Age Security.' It rolls so nicely off the tongue, but it's so hard to define. Brand, may I have my breakfast here so I can see things?"

"I'll have a table brought at once, madam." Brand straightened out the blind and stood for a moment by the wide plate glass window. "Tonight is the official opening, you know, madam. With a pageant. A magnificent sight it'll be, from what Mr. Cassell says. But the crowds are already here."

"I've never seen such crowds outside of the rotogravure," Daisy polished her glasses and put them on. "They're like mobs massed in Red Square. Why, it's amazing, Brand. I've seen the pictures, but I somehow didn't understand it would be a colored fair. I saw a fair that had sort of tan buildings, once. But never anything like this!"

Brand looked gratified, almost as if it were his fair.

"I'll see to your table at once, madam," he said.

At the door, he stood aside to let Sam stroll in.

"Morning, Brand," Sam said breezily. "Hiyah, Daisy. How do you like Samuel in his new suit? That gentleman's gentleman of Cassell's brought it in to me just now. He said my things were being pressed, but he really meant cleaned. You're all dressed up, too. Very smart."

His flippancy and his breezy manner did not go well, Daisy thought, with the shadows under his eyes. He was trying to carry on with his usual airiness, but his attempt was not entirely successful. However gay and debonair Sam might try to appear, he was still worried and troubled and harassed.

Daisy suddenly changed her plan about buttonholing him and asking him point blank just what he was doing out in the corridor the night before, and just what was going on. There was no doubt in her mind that Sam would laugh off her questions, just as Boy had laughed them off when he was in a similar mood. The trick with Boy was to wait until he was off-guard, and then shoot questions at him before he had a chance to think. That always worked, and very likely it would work with Sam. One thing that increasing age brought, Daisy thought, was an appreciation of the value of patience.

"My clothes," she told Sam, "belong to the aunt of our host. More expensive than cook's outfit, but no better style. Sam, why do you keep on wearing those silly glasses? And can you get a Boston paper? I want to see if they've found anything in the horse pond they thought was me."

"I like these glasses," Sam said smoothly. "I think they give me a scholarly look. Sure, I'll try to get a Boston paper. And see here, you really ought to send your nephew a telegram!"

"I won't," Daisy said. "When I've thought Egleston over, I'll tell him what I think of him. I cannot understand what he's been up to. If he wanted money, why didn't he ask me? He has before. Either Elfrida's goading him, or it's the Foss blood coming to the fore. His mother was a Foss, and they were awfully strange about money. They— Sam, isn't that tall thing lovely? And the ball?"

"You mean the trylon," Sam said. "And the ball is the perisphere. And the circular ramp is the helicline. And that building you're staring at is the textile building."

"Why, Sam, you know all about it!"

"I'm practically a World's Fair authority," Sam told her modestly.

"Then sit right down. Brand'll bring your breakfast here, too, and you can tell me everything. How do you know about things?"

If she could manage to get Sam absorbed in the topic of the Fair, Daisy thought, she might be able to slip her question over on him.

"I began writing stuff about this years and years ago," Sam said. "Matter of fact, I got sent over to look at the place when it was an ash heap. One of my first jobs. But somehow I got sidetracked in New York and forgot all about it, so I rewrote Scott Fitzgerald's description of the dump from 'The Great Gatsby.' Made a big hit. The boss said it was as good as Richard Harding Davis."

"Point out things," Daisy said. "Tell me everything. What's that round building?"

"The Fair," Sam said, "is a mile wide and three and a half miles long. And the trylon's seven hundred feet tall, and the periphere's two hundred— Look, d'you really care?"

"Of course I care!" Daisy said. "And I resent your

yawning. Thank you, Brand. Sam, how can you look at all this and yawn?"

"Frankly," Sam said, "I haven't taken much interest in this fair since the preview they had just a year ago. I ducked it, and wrote a swell story from a publicity layout, and then it went and rained, and half the program was cancelled. You'll never hope to read anything more glowing than my description of those preview fireworks. It was a classic. They had the fireworks, too. A week later. But it didn't matter. I was working on another paper by then. Where's Cherry? And Whit and Duplain? Where's everybody?"

Daisy, watching the reflection of his face in the window, decided that those casual questions meant a lot to Sam.

"Cherry's gone out," she said. "Don't ask me where, because I don't know. She just wrote 'More anon.' I don't know where the rest are. I haven't seen them."

Sam frowned, and opened his mouth.

Then he closed it again.

Boylston Tower's mother was in his care. She came first. And Boylston Tower's mother would be happier if he kept his mouth closed. Everyone, in fact, would be happier if he kept his mouth closed. Even the police. And before he blurted out anything to anyone, he wanted to have a little more time around that corridor which led past that office. If he had to eat his way through that locked door, Sam intended to get into that office.

"Oh, here's Mr. Whitty!" Daisy said. "Come in, Mr. Whitty. You can see everything from this window. That freight train's in the way everywhere else. What do you think of the fair?"

"Say," Whitty said, "this is something!"

Mentally, Sam checked Whitty off his list. Then, after a moment's deliberation, Sam made another list and put Whitty on that. Sam had once known a man who looked like Whitty, and he had killed three women with an axe, buried the pieces behind his barn, and covered them with a silo.

"What's that tall thing and that round ball?" Whitty asked.

Sam smiled.

"That's the trylon, Whit. And the ball's the perisphere, and the girdle around it's the helicline, and that building you're staring at is the textile building."

"Fraud," Daisy said, "that's all you know. I suspected as much. You've never even been here before, have you? I thought you hadn't."

"What are they for?" Whitty demanded. "This pylon and terrisphere?"

"Trylon and perisphere," Sam corrected. "They're the theme. Both of 'em."

"They're which?"

"Themes."

"Why?" Whitty asked.

"To be any good," Sam explained, "a fair has to have a theme. This fair's got two themes, so it'll be twice as good. Hi, Madame Duplain. Join the throng."

Sam, Daisy noticed, didn't appear to be anywhere near as interested in her arrival as he had been in Whitty's. He seemed to expect her. Somehow he had not expected Whitty.

"Morning, everyone," she said. "Oh, you can really see it all from here, can't you?"

"The tall thing is the trylon, Madame Duplain," Sam said. "The ball's the perisphere—"

"And the ramp's the helicline," she said. "I know. I read about 'em in the papers."

"My public!" Sam said. "Did you sleep well after your triumphs at poker and everything?"

"Like a log." She set down her little suitcase. "Except when we got on that siding by the boiler factory."

"Wasn't that awful!" Daisy said. "There was one period when I thought that someone was engaged in target practice under my bed. Oh, Brand, is that a Boston paper you've got? Oh, it's Sunday, isn't it? I'd forgotten."

"Madame Duplain asked me to get it for her—"

"You can have it if you want," Madame Duplain interrupted. "I just wanted to see if a friend of mine had got her divorce. She was supposed to yesterday."

Whitty asked for "Orphan Annie."

"I always read her every day," he said. "Great girl, Annie."

Daisy agreed. "After watching what Annie copes with as a matter of course, my own lot seems so bright. Oh, can I have all these sections? Sure? I really just want to glance at the headlines. I—oh, Sam! Look! A whole—another holdup!"

Sam obeyed her peremptory gesture and leaned over her shoulder to look at the paper.

Together they digested the front-page story of the strange disappearance of Mrs. Boylston Tower. Aloud, at intervals, they commented on the pay roll holdup.

As he followed the story to page sixteen, Sam began to feel vaguely uneasy.

With an amazing display of intelligence, the police had decided that if Mrs. Tower was not at the bottom of a nearby pond, she must necessarily have been kidnapped. And while the page sixteen picture was not much more than a passport likeness of Daisy, there would be plenty of Boston newspapermen covering the Fair opening. They would be practically sure to spot Daisy, picture or no picture.

Sam looked from Daisy to Whitty and Madame Duplain, both wrapped up in their own reading.

Deftly, Sam marked around the picture with his thumbnail, and removed it. As he was about to thrust the little oblong of paper into his coat pocket, Daisy stopped him. Mutely, she pointed to the reverse of the oblong.

Sam turned the paper over and stared at the picture of Whitty.

Above it, in fourteen point Bodoni, was the double-line head, "Picture Thief Sought in America."

Madame Duplain glanced up.

"Have they found that missing woman yet?" she asked. "That Mrs. Tower?"

"Er—no." Sam said. "No. They haven't. Uh—no."

He was too busy blinking at the picture of Whitty to notice the slow wink Madame Duplain gave Daisy.

"I thought they wouldn't," she said.

Daisy smiled. She'd felt, when they first met on the train, that Madame Duplain had recognized her from that club meeting. It reassured her to know that Madame Duplain didn't intend to take any steps.

"Say," Whitty put down "Orphan Annie," "you got the section with the lodge news? I thought I'd look and see if any of my friends would be here. A lot of 'em plan to come, but I don't know just who's coming for the opening."

Daisy took off her far-seeing glasses, looked at Whitty's bland face and his button nose, and then put her glasses on again.

She hadn't thought, from the very first, that Whitty was a butcher, no matter how many picturesque little details he might contribute concerning the firm of Whitty and Glum. On the other hand, she had not expected him to turn out to be a picture thief.

She remembered his terrier-like snores the night

before. It was just possible, she thought, that those excellent snores might have been fakes. If Whitty were up to something and Sam had found it out, Sam's actions in the corridor might have a very logical explanation.

"Here's the lodge news," Madame Duplain said.

Daisy got up and walked over to the window.

"Sam," she said, "come look at this salmon building and tell me what it is. Isn't that a bizarre thing?"

"Colossal," Sam said in a strained voice. In her ear he added, "What shall we do?"

Daisy shrugged. "If we tell Cassell and show him the paper, he'll find out about me."

"But we ought to do something!"

"The pictures are all guarded," Daisy said. "And before we do anything, we ought to read the rest—get the paper again."

Sam turned to get the paper, but Madame Duplain was already gathering it up possessively.

"Where's Cherry?" she asked. "And Cassell?"

"Cherry's gone out," Daisy told her. "No one knows where. Brand could tell you about—oh, here he is. Brand, where did Mr. Cassell go? I thought he had some plans for us."

"He's at his building, madam. He has an office there, and even though it's Sunday, there are many things for him to attend to. He—er—we lost Roberts, you see, madam."

Daisy felt Sam relax.

66

"The secretary," he said. Sam had completely forgotten that rabbit-like secretary.

"Yes, sir. Roberts was—that is, sir, owing to an unfortunate disagreement, Roberts left. So Mr. Cassell has more details than usual to attend to. But I'm sure he'll make arrangements for you."

"So," Sam said with satisfaction, "so Roberts couldn't take it?"

"No, sir," Brand said. "Will you have more coffee now, sir?"

Sam declined the coffee and lighted another cigarette. At least, he'd found out that part. It was Roberts.

Before he finished his cigarette, Brand returned.

"A special Fair car has come, madam," he said to Daisy. "And a special guide. There is a message from Mr. Cassell. He hopes you will all avail yourselves of the guide and the car to see the Fair. He had intended to escort you himself, but pressing items have come up. He will join you later."

"Now, that's what I call white of him," Whitty said heartily. "That's darn white of him, to think of making arrangements for us, with him so busy and all. He's white, that guy is. He may have a lot of money, but he's just as kind and thoughtful as if he didn't have a cent. Why, he lent me a pair of his own silk pyjamas to sleep in, last night! And this is his own suit that I've got on. Yessir, he may be a wolf of Wall Street and all the rest, but that guy's a prince. Let's go!"

Sam tried not to look at Daisy. This Whitty, he decided, was even better than the man who had built the silo over the chopped-up ladies.

"We ought to wait for Cherry," Daisy said. "I can't think why she didn't tell me where she was going, or how long she'd be there. 'More anon,' forsooth! I yearn to see the Fair, but I think I'll wait for her."

"Aw, come on!" Whitty said. "She can catch up with us later."

"Look," Sam said as Daisy hesitated, "these guides probably have a routine. Suppose I find out where we go and in what order we take things, and then leave a list with Brand. When Cherry comes back, she can trail us."

For his part, Sam had no intention of viewing the Fair with a guide. He intended to stay on the train and do a little investigating. And he did not want Daisy to stay behind on the train. He wanted her away from the train and the mess he knew was coming. And Whitty couldn't get very far if he had both Daisy and Madame Duplain sitting beside him.

"By your system, Sam," Daisy said, " 'anon' will be two weeks from next Sunday. Being such an authority on the Fair, you forget its size. Brand, will there be someone at Mr. Cassell's office in the Fair building all day?"

"Undoubtedly, madam."

"And there's a telephone on this train?"

"Oh, yes, madam. But—"

68

"And of course there are phones at the building. Well, that's simple. We'll phone back here at intervals, and tell you where we are. When Cherry comes, and if we miss her, have her go to Mr. Cassell's building. You can tell us where she went, and we'll phone the office and tell her where we are, and wait for her to join us. There, that's settled. Give me the phone numbers, Brand. Sam, write them down—what are you sniggering about?"

"I can't help it," Sam said. "You sound so much like an article I wrote once called 'The Simplification of the National Debt and the Taxation Problem.' It was—"

"Hurry," Daisy said, "what *are* you stalling so for? Hurry up!"

She marshalled the group with such efficient speed that Sam had no chance to draw her to one side and talk with her. He tried again as they walked out to the olive drab touring car that waited for them by the tracks, but Daisy paid no attention to him. She was too delighted with the car and its orange and blue Statue of Liberty insignia and its uniformed chauffeur.

"And what are those orange and blue and white banners flying at the masthead, Sam?"

"Official World's Fair flags," Sam said.

Daisy nodded. "And that is the trylon and that is the perisphere, and so on. You guessed. I'm on to you!"

"You know what?" Whitty said. "I bet orange and blue are the Fair colors, huh?"

Madame Duplain looked at him and sighed.

"Either that, Porterhouse," she said, "or someone's good and color blind. It would take a man to think that all out."

"And a guide!" Daisy said. "How smart! Would you feel insulted, young man, if I asked you to turn around so I could inspect you?"

The brisk young man took off his gold-trimmed visored cap and gave his blue necktie a little pat. Then, obediently, he about-faced.

"Dark grey coat, Oxford grey flannels. Very smart turn-out," Daisy said. "Thank you, young man. You really should have seen the guides at the Columbian Exposition. Compared to you, they were just a bunch of postmen. And they chewed tobacco constantly. Now, how shall we fit ourselves in? Sam, you sit—"

"Look at the airplane!" Sam said rather desperately. "See, it's got orange and blue streamers—"

While the group watched the streamers, Sam whispered in Daisy's ear.

"Listen, send me back for something. Please! I can't go with you. I've got half a story here! And you watch Whitty."

Daisy looked from the streamers to Sam's face. Boylston had looked that way, often. After all, as she'd thought last night, no reporter ever had a better chance to get a scoop than on Cassell's private train.

You could hardly blame Sam for taking advantage of it.

Daisy took off her far-seeing glasses and thrust them into the depths of her pocketbook before the rest stopped gazing up at the airplane.

"Oh, my glasses!" she said in well-simulated despair. "Sam, my glasses! Sam, would you go back for them? I can't go to the Fair without my far-seeing glasses!"

"I thought you had 'em on," Madame Duplain said.

"I did," Daisy told her, "but I took 'em off when I put on my hat. They're probably in my bedroom, Sam. Or maybe the smoking room. Or did I leave them in the oval room, just now? Oh, dear!"

"I'll instigate a hunt," Sam said. "Tell you what, you three run along, and I'll join you at the peri-sphere in fifteen minutes. If I'm late, do your sight-seeing there, and I'll meet you when you're through. Anyway, I'll track down the glasses and bring 'em over."

"Say," Whitty said to Madame Duplain, "what you taking that suitcase for?"

"Get in," Madame Duplain returned, "and sit down. I'm carrying the case. You're not. How'll you get over to the Fair, Sam?"

"I'll manage it," he said. "So long."

He waved after them as they rolled off in the tour-ing car, and then turned back to the train.

If someone else didn't find out about this business pretty soon, Sam thought, he'd have to tell himself. It didn't seem possible that no one else knew. But there were no police about. Just a few Fair troopers, with their dark grey coats and Sam Browne belts and Stetsons with chin straps. And none of them had gone near the Golden Dart, except a tall one who paused to chat with one of Cassell's own guards.

Sam stopped at the car step to watch a cab coming down the platform to the train. At the sight of the single passenger inside, Sam made a sound under his breath, and revised his mental list.

It was Roberts, in the cab. The rabbit-like secretary. And he was alive and hale and as hearty as he was ever likely to be.

Brand and another servant appeared with luggage, which they loaded into the cab.

"No hard feelings, I hope, sir?" Sam heard Brand say.

"No, Brand. And thank you. You tried to give me good advice, and I didn't take it. I—I guess I'm just not suited for the job."

"You'll find your niche, sir," Brand said reassuringly. "Oh, thank you, sir. I'm sure you'll find your niche, Mr. Roberts. Only, you must learn to take orders, sir. Good-bye, sir. Good luck." He walked over to Sam. "Anything wrong, sir?"

"Just—er—my mother's glasses," Sam said. "When I find them, I'll join the rest at the perisphere."

"Yes, sir," Brand said. "If I may suggest it, sir, Mr. Cassell's own car is returning here from his building for some papers. Perhaps you'd care to take that when it comes? There might be a wait, but it would save you time in the end. Walking is not very satisfactory. The distances are deceiving, and there's an enormous crowd around the perisphere."

"Between you and me, Brand," Sam said, "what is this damn perisphere?"

"The perisphere," said Brand glibly, "houses the exposition's theme exhibit, a spectacular portrayal of the basic structure of the World of Tomorrow. That is where your party will be. In it."

"In it?" Sam said. "My God, how do you get *in* it?"

"From the side entrance, sir, fifty feet from the ground. You go up in a glass-enclosed escalator. Stepping within, you will find yourself seemingly suspended in space on a moving platform, gazing down at a vast panorama dramatizing the role of cooperation in modern civilization, and showing all the elements of society coordinated," Brand paused for breath, "in a better World of Tomorrow."

"Whee!" Sam said. "Did you mind it at all, Brand, being suspended in space and everything?"

"Oh, I haven't been there, sir."

"What? How do you know about it?"

"I've got a book," Brand said rather sadly. "I know it by heart. That was right out of the book, what I told you."

That he forgot to punctuate his words with the customary "sirs" was in itself an indication of his deep feeling about the Fair.

Sam looked out at the graceful white spire shining in the sun.

"It'll be fun when you go, won't it?" he said.

"Go?" Brand looked enviously at the trylon. "I'll never go. I'll never get there. If we stayed here six months, I'd never really get to see this Fair any nearer than this. Oh, I'd pass by the buildings. But that's all."

Sam asked why.

"Twelve times I've been to London," Brand said, "but I've never seen Buckingham Palace. I saw the Eiffel Tower because our rooms faced it. I could draw you the floor plans of any good hotel in this country, but I'd get lost a block away. But I keep my job when Andrews and Roberts lose theirs. I do what I'm told to do, and I don't ask why."

"Brand," Sam said, "could I take your Fair book if I'd be very careful of it?"

"Certainly, sir. I'll get it."

"Guess I'll walk along with you," Sam said. "I've got to get those glasses. This is quite a train, isn't it?"

"The only one of its kind," Brand said.

Casually, as they passed down the corridor of the next car, Sam pointed to a door on the right.

"What are all these rooms?" he asked.

"That one, sir, is Mr. Cassell's private office," Brand said.

"He doesn't seem to use it much."

"He hasn't used it, today or yesterday, sir," Brand said, "but he uses it constantly on long trips. Had Mrs. Days any idea where she left her glasses, sir? You know, I rather thought she had them on when she left."

"Brand," Sam tried to sound contrite, "I'm a fool! She did! Of course she did! D'you know what she's done again? She has put those damned glasses into her handbag and forgotten 'em. That's just what she's done. Oh, well, I'll wait here for the other car—will you get your guide book for me?"

Fifteen minutes later, armed with Brand's book, Sam allowed Cassell's private automobile to pick him up at the Golden Dart.

It had been a very profitable interval. Sam thought. He knew for sure that no one had gone into the office, and that no one knew, except himself, what was there. And, while Brand had got the book, Sam had hurriedly filched the key to the office from a keyboard in a closet. Brand's efficient tagging of keys had made the whole thing very simple and satisfactory. Sam regretted that Brand had returned before he had a chance to use the key, but the opportunity would arise, and when it did, Sam had the key smack in his pocket.

Sam felt pleased with himself.

As the car crossed the tracks, the cauliflower-eared chauffeur snapped on a radio.

"Good God, man!" Sam said. "What static—hey,

Stragg—is that your name? Well, Stragg, turn off that din, will you?"

The chauffeur turned the radio down, but he did not turn it off.

"Say, is that code?" Sam asked curiously.

Stragg nodded.

"Is it true," Sam said, "what I've heard about Cassell having his own wave-length and sending outfits and transmitters?"

"He uses radio a lot," Stragg said without turning around. "Yacht, country place, up in the mountains. Keeps him in touch."

"You wouldn't be getting orders now, would you?" Sam asked.

"Yeah. Got to drop you off up here, mister. Got to swing around to the Administration Building on an errand. You ain't far from the Theme, anyways."

"Okay," Sam said. "Thanks for the lift."

Stragg opened the door for him, and stood beside him while a band marched by.

"Okay," Sam said again. "Thanks. So long."

He realized, as he walked along toward the perisphere, that the distances were more deceptive than he'd imagined. How he was going to find Daisy and the rest, he had no idea. It was worse than a subway jam.

But Daisy spotted him.

"I'm so glad you've got here," she said, "now I can put on my glasses and see. I didn't see a quarter of the

Fair from the helicline, because I couldn't very well put on the glasses I'd sent you to fetch. Sam, I'm not going to bide my time any longer. What's going on? What were you doing in the corridor last night, with that thing hidden under your arm? What were you doing?"

Sam didn't appear to be at all disconcerted by her questions.

"That was Madame Duplain's suitcase I had," Sam said. "After I got to bed, she knocked on my door and said that someone had made off with her suitcase while she was having a bath, and would I find it. So I set out to ask Brand about it, and as I went down the corridor, I saw the suitcase sitting just inside that office door on the right. So I took it. I hid it under my coat, because it occurred to me that embarrassing questions might arise if anyone saw me with it. Funny, the way Duplain clings to her luggage, isn't it?"

"Very," Daisy said. "What else, Sam Minot?"

"You mean Whitty?" Sam said. "I don't know about Whitty. I don't get it. What do you think?"

"The more he seemed to be a butcher," Daisy said, "the more convinced I became that he wasn't. Now I know he's a picture thief, the more he seems like a butcher. Sam, I asked you what else!"

"Here's Madame Duplain and Whitty," Sam said. "Hey, over here—"

The guide, still talking, followed them.

"Tonight," he was saying, "this will appear as a

sphere suspended on jets of water, when the fountains are turned on. The sphere will be spotted with color from projectors, and there will be patterns of light—but you will witness the opening pageant, the real opening, as Mr. Cassell's guests, I suppose."

"Gee," Whitty said, "I hope so! Say, this *is* something, isn't it? But say," he lowered his voice, "say, guide, what about Sally Rand, huh? Where's that side of things?"

The lift of Whitty's eyebrows, Sam thought, was almost the equivalent of a frisky jab in the ribs.

"The Amusement Zone," the guide said, "is looped around the lakes, and—look quick! There's the Mayor! Quick, that way!"

Whitty was unimpressed.

"That fellow with the silk hat?" he said. "Why, he's no taller than I am! That's the Mayor, huh? Well, well, maybe there's a chance for me. I got the build."

Madame Duplain spoke softly in Daisy's ear.

"Don't look now, Mrs. Tower, but there are two men behind to your right, talking about you. They were pointing at you, back up on the ramp—look now."

"Dear me," Daisy said. "I think they're policemen."

"I know they are. Look at those heels. Sure, they're cops. I didn't say anything at first, because I thought they were after me—"

"After you? Are you being sought for too?"

"Little matter of a card game," Madame Duplain

78

said easily. "I can't resist cards. If it wasn't for cards, I might be a good singer. As it is, I'm being hunted for in a couple of card clubs—"

"They're hunting me in horse ponds," Daisy said. "Madame Duplain—"

"My friends call me Gert. I took Duplain off a crusty loaf of bread."

Daisy smiled. "Gert, what do you suggest doing?"

"I wouldn't know, dear," Gert said. "Ask Sam. Sam, we got a problem—"

"So've I," Sam said. "Bunky Unger's standing over there, just about to recognize you, Daisy. These glasses of mine have saved me, but—"

"Is he a reporter?" Daisy asked. "Oh, my. Two policemen and one reporter. Sam, we've got to do things. Is that guide following a route, do you think?"

"He's got a card he takes a peek at every now and then," Gert said. "All the buildings are numbered on it."

"I thought so," Daisy said, "and if we follow the route with him, we're going to be very easy to follow, in turn. We'll just have to lose that guide, that's all, and go around on our own. This place is vast enough so that we'll probably never see the police or that reporter again. What's the building across the way over there?"

"My God, I don't know!" Sam said. "Does it matter?"

Daisy walked over to where the guide was pouring statistics into the none too receptive Whitty.

"Guide," she said, "what is that perfectly beautiful building with the parallel lines?"

"The Consolidated Edison building, madam. We will come to that—"

"Isn't that the building that has that—oh, you know. That thing. You know what I mean!"

She was, she felt, on perfectly safe ground. Every building at the Fair was sure to have something as a feature attraction.

"You mean the diorama, madam? The largest diorama—"

"That's it!" Daisy said with enthusiasm. "The diorama. That's what you should see, Mr. Whitty. Didn't you hear that man on the ramp talking about it? He said it was splendid. Er—hot stuff. Don't you want to go there?"

"But, madam," the guide began.

"That's quite all right, my boy," Daisy said in her most impressive *grande dame* manner. "You may take Mr. Whitty there and show him the diorama. We'll wait here."

"Aw," Whitty said, "I don't know as I want to see any—well, whatever it is."

"Okay," Sam said. "If you want to wait till it's censored."

His attempt at a leering wink was not very successful, but Whitty got the idea.

"Oh," he said, "I see. I didn't get it before. Come on, guide—"

"But," the guide protested, "but—"

"Run along," Daisy said. "Take Mr. Whitty to the diorama, and we'll wait here."

She drew a long breath as Whitty and the guide, both visibly perplexed, walked off through the crowd.

"That worked," Sam said, "but what for?"

"The guide," Daisy said, "can show things to Whitty and supervise him as well as we can. And now we can take the car and leave those policemen and the reporters behind. I'm sure the guide would have been in our way—come on."

She beamed at the chauffeur, who jumped to open the tonneau door for her.

"There's been a change in our plans," she said. "Will you take us over there?"

"Yes, ma'am," the chauffer said. "Which way did you point?"

"That way. We want to go over that way. Beyond those gold buildings."

"Tomorrow Town? Yes, ma'am."

Sam looked admiringly at Daisy as the touring car drove off.

"Boy Tower," he said, "should be proud of you. Those flatfeet are just staring, and Bunky Unger still isn't sure of you. The special Fair car has 'em buffaloed."

"But if they ask the driver where he took us," Gert said, "they'll follow."

"I'll fix that. My," Daisy said, "this is rather fun, isn't it? And by the way, what *is* a diorama?"

"Might be anything from a Giant Baby Panda to a disease of the lung tissue," Sam said. "Whitty will hate it, anyway. Daisy, we should do something about him!"

"What?" Daisy said. "If we tell Cassell, we'll find ourselves in hot water too. 'Oh, by the way, Mr. Cassell, I'm Mrs. Tower who's supposedly kidnapped, and Sam is a reporter, and that man Whitty's a picture thief'—" she broke off. "Did you know he was, Gert?"

"No!" Gert said. "Honest? And Sam's a reporter?" She giggled. "What a lot of fun Cassell would have if he knew—is this Tomorrow Town? Say, it's a whole damn village by itself!"

"Quick," Daisy said, "before we stop. Think of the name of a building on the other side of the Fair, that won't be near the Edison place or the perisphere. Quick."

"Eastman Kodak," Gert said. "The guide pointed it out to me. On the Blue Plaza."

"Thank you," Daisy said as the car came to a stop. "Yes, you may leave us here, driver. Now, will you go to the Eastman Kodak building and wait for Mr. Cassell—you know him, of course? Wait for him there. Thank you!"

"Why did you throw in that about Cassell?" Sam

asked. "I understand why you want to keep the chauffeur from telling the guide or the cops where we went, but why drag in Cassell?"

"When you tell lies," Daisy said, "they should be convincing. I could just have told him to go to the Kodak building, but if I send him to wait there for Cassell, he'll never question anything. He's got both the answer and the purpose—oh, what a darling house! I'll never rest till I've seen every house on this street!"

Sam protested, but he was overruled. Against his will, Sam was taken on an intimate tour of two flat-roofed, glass-bricked, chromium-trimmed model houses. He rebelled at the third.

"I like the functional house," he said. "I like built-in laundry chutes and electric garbage choppers. But after all, Daisy, see one and you've seen them all. If you've got to coo over every house in Mr. Whalen's subdivision, I'm going to that little park and wait. Say, let me take your suitcase, Gert. No sense in your lugging that around."

"I'll keep it, thanks."

"I know it's none of my business," Sam said, "but why carry—"

"Listen," Gert said, "I don't ask you to carry it, do I? Yes, I asked you last night, but you didn't have to carry it very far. Why shouldn't I carry my suitcase if I want to?"

Sam shrugged. "Lots of people do, I suppose," he

said. "Like red caps. Don't tell me, Gert, that you're descended from a long line of red caps?"

"Go wait in the park," Daisy said. "Find a nice park bench and sit there and brood—"

"That's just what I intend to do," Sam said. "When your feet begin to sting, let me know."

But ten minutes later, Sam raced into a gleaming Monel metal kitchen of one of Tomorrow Town's houses, beckoned to Daisy and Gert, and led them hurriedly into a back hallway.

"Listen," he said. "I was sitting out there in the park, and two Fair troopers came along and hailed a third, and asked him if—brace yourselves, will you? They asked him if he'd heard the headquarters alarm—"

"You mean, the one for us?" Daisy returned tranquilly.

Sam stared at her.

"How did you know? How'd you find out about it?"

"We heard two women talking about it, and we asked them. They said there was a general headquarters alarm for a Mrs. Days, Sam Days, George Whitty and Madame Duplain. They'd even spelled the names out, like a brand name on the radio. We heard about that just after you left us for the park—"

"Why didn't you come tell me?" Sam demanded.

"We intended to. We were just starting. You see, it puzzled us at first, because Gert says she's just in a small mess in Boston, and there's no reason for her to

84

be wanted by headquarters here. And then I thought it might be Egleston, after me. By now he's probably got all the old Tories on my trail. And of course, anyone with a grain of sense who knows me will be sure to suggest that I've run over here to the Fair. I decided that those two policemen and that reporter, the ones at the perisphere, had probably gone to the Fair police. But that wouldn't work out, because they didn't ask for Mrs. Tower. They wanted Mrs. Days."

Sam continued to stare at her speechlessly.

"Then," Daisy went on, "we decided it was a trap."

Sam gulped.

"Did you?" he said.

"Yes, you see they used those names that Cassell knows us by. It just sounds as though Cassell wants us in a hurry. Probably they expected us to go to headquarters, and then I would be politely restrained as a senile incompetent, and you would be held as a kidnapper. But that was sort of far-fetched. And then, of course, we finally found out the real reason."

"Well," Sam said, "thank God you've found out the real reason, and I didn't have to tell you! I was wondering how to break the news."

"This other woman told us," Daisy said. "She told us about the pictures being stolen from Cassell, and then of course it was all as plain as the nose on your face. They want us for picture stealing. It's all that wretched Whitty! Why couldn't he have waited until we'd seen the Fair before he started stealing pictures and getting us involved!"

Sam leaned against the door jamb and drew a long breath.

So they were wanted for picture stealing, and not for murder.

Wasn't anyone, Sam wondered unhappily, wasn't anyone ever going to find that body over there in Cassell's private office on the Golden Dart?

4

Watching the expression on Sam's face as he leaned there against the door jamb, it occurred to Daisy that she had missed her cue by about thirty seconds. Thirty seconds before, she should have shot questions at Sam. Now it was too late.

"What do we do?" Gert inquired.

"Do?" Daisy said. "We do just what we came to do. We see the Fair. I've not stolen any pictures. Have you, Sam? What about you, Gert? Have you a couple of Tintorettos and a Titian in that suitcase of yours?"

"My God, no!" Gert said.

"Well, then! None of us has stolen any pictures, and I personally don't intend," Daisy said firmly, "to become involved with crimes I didn't commit."

"How about phoning back to the train," Gert suggested, "and checking up, sort of? Maybe we better make sure about all this."

"We can't phone. That would never do," Daisy said. "Brand expects us to call—oh, I've completely forgotten all our elaborate plans about Cherry, poor child! Anyway, Brand expects us to call the train, and it's a special, private number. And if they're really serious about involving us in picture thefts, they'd probably trace us as soon as we were connected. Oh, dear, I suppose we really should march straight to police headquarters. But I have this feeling that we'd be wiser not to. We'd better play safe."

"That is one of the quaintest definitions of playing safe," Sam said with an odd smile, "that I ever heard. What you really mean is, you think it would be more fun to be the object of a Fair-wide manhunt? With all these snappy troopers just burning to get their man?"

"But this Fair's so damn big!" Gert said. "And just look at the mobs. With half a million people milling around, how can they find us?"

"I don't see how they can," Daisy said. "If we just stay out of the clutches of the police for a while, they'll get Whitty themselves, and everything will be settled. There's just no need for our being mixed up with the picture business. I'm sure they'll never be able to find us—"

Sam motioned for her to be silent.

"People trooping into the kitchen," he whispered.

"Just more women admiring that sink," Daisy said.

But she found that she was unconsciously flattening herself against the wall of the little back entryway.

"What a beautiful sink! Oh, how I wish Herbert would give me a sink like that!" The nasal twang of the voice that floated out of the kitchen annoyed Daisy. "I think that sink's just about the nicest I've seen—what did that trooper want when he stopped you out there?"

"He was hunting people—didn't he have a funny nose? I don't think the guards here are as nice-lookin' as the guards we had in Dallas. We had fine-lookin' guards in Dallas. I come from Dallas. He was huntin' a fellow and two women."

"What for?"

"He didn't say. He just asked if anyone'd seen a tall young fellow in a tweed suit with glasses, and an older woman in blue with a cane, and another woman with a suitcase. He was sort of solemn about it."

"Bad news from home, maybe," Nasal Twang said. "Like when Herbert's sister died that time when we were in Kansas City. Let's go look at the bedrooms—"

"D'you begin to get the idea, Daisy," Sam said, "that the scope of this Fair doesn't matter? It's not just the troopers who will be watching for us. People like Kansas City and Dallas, there, they'll have an eye peeled for a young fellow in a tweed suit, and an older woman in blue with a cane, and another woman with a small suitcase. The—"

Sam broke off in exasperation.

He liked Daisy. She was a grand old girl. He had a lot of respect for her. But sometimes she goaded him. Sometimes she griped the hell out of him. Why, at this point, couldn't she keep her mind on things instead of staring at a Sealyham out in the next back yard?

"Daisy, have you heard a single word I've said!"

"Certainly," Daisy returned. "I'm not deaf. That dear little dog—oh, he's not lost. I see, there's the boy. Of course I heard what you said, Sam."

"Well, under the circumstances, do you still think you want to do what you intended to do, and survey the Fair?"

"I do," Daisy said. "It's very simple, if you stop and think. It's our clothes, principally. Your tweeds and my cane and Gert's suitcase. Our clothes and our accessories are the trouble."

"For my part," Sam said, "I don't feel that the troopers would be willing to accept a suit of tweeds and a cane and a suitcase and be satisfied to call the whole thing off. I do not!"

"Do you see that house on the next street, the one with the glass-brick bay window—no, Sam, don't be sarcastic. I've been watching people come out of that house. Here, look—"

Gert moved over to the little window and stared out.

"Say, guides!" she said. "Guides—I get it, Daisy! I get it!"

"Get what?" Sam inquired.

"There are a lot of men guides coming out of that house," Daisy said, "and women guides are coming out of the house next door. It's so perfectly simple. No one will ever notice us if we're guides. We can just be guides until they settle Whitty and the pictures, don't you see? Now, that guide we had told me they had some building where they dressed and rested their feet and ate. I forget which one, it doesn't matter. What does matter is that they've had such a call for guides, they've had to call out their reserves. And don't you see, they've taken over those two houses on the next street to cope with all the extras! Now, I wonder—"

She was getting a glint in her eyes, a glint that somehow made Sam feel a little uneasy. He was beginning to understand where Boy Tower got his reputation of never losing a single opportunity, and of producing a better one if he didn't entirely approve of what he had.

"Daisy," he said firmly, "we can't—"

"My dear boy, we can't stay here forever, any more than we could stay in that phone booth yesterday. If I could only get hold of Boy's editor—but this really isn't important enough to bother him with. You've got to get your outfit first, and then the rest will be simple. If only one of those tall guides would come over here and fall into a faint on the back steps!"

"That guy now," Gert said, "would do swell. He's just about right."

"Now, see here, you two!" Sam said. "If you've got any hairbrained notion that I'm going to follow that guide to some alley, and slug him and swipe his clothes, the answer is no. We've got troubles enough, if you'll only stop to figure them out. I'm not going to let you get mixed up with anything more, Daisy—Gert, where are you going! Gert, come back here! Gert—"

Daisy grabbed him by the arm and held on to him as Gert opened the back door, and, with her suitcase still in hand, walked out.

"You stay with me," Daisy said. "Gert'll get it."

"That's just what I'm afraid of!" Sam retorted. "She's going up to him—she's stopping him! Look, this has got to be stopped—"

His intended rush out the door was cut short by the tip of Daisy's cane, which neatly tripped him up.

As he fell, Sam's head hit the baseboard with a thud.

When he came to, a few minutes later, he opened his eyes, blinked, and closed his eyes again.

Things like that, he told himself crossly, did not happen. A lot of funny things happened in the world, yes. He had, in his varied newspaper career, seen a lot of them happen. The last twenty-four hours were a classic example of the world in a haywire state. But this was too much.

Cautiously, he opened his eyes again.

It was quite true. There was Gert, with that damn suitcase beside her, and that inscrutable look on her face. And a guide's uniform, complete even to the blue tie, hanging over her arm.

"She got it," Daisy said. "I felt sure she would, Sam,

I didn't mean to knock you out. That was an accident. Now, get up quickly and hurry down into the boiler room in the cellar, and change. Quick. Hurry up. Don't stop to argue. It's probably going to be for the best if we leave here as soon as possible."

Sam got to his feet, and looked from the uniform to Gert.

"You didn't—er—kill him, did you?"

She shook her head.

"Some day," Sam said, "will you tell me how you did it?"

"I'll tell you now. I asked him for the uniform, and he gave it to me."

Sam surveyed the little suitcase.

"I'd give ten years of my life," he said, "to know what sort of infernal machine you house in that. I would give—"

"Hurry and change," Daisy said. "Make a bundle of your own clothes. We mustn't leave them here for anyone to find. Hurry!"

He paused in the doorway.

"You know what burns me up, Daisy? There's no paper on God's green footstool that would even believe this story. There's just one person who'll even half believe it, and that's your own son."

Daisy looked her relief when Sam finally disappeared down the cellar stairs.

"I was almost afraid," she said to Gert, "that he wasn't going to—you know, people can say what they want to about the radical exuberance of youth, but it seems to me that young people are more conservative than they used to be. Cherry tried to stop me from taking the Golden Dart yesterday. Sam is very unhappy about all this. Gert, who took your suitcase last night? What for?"

"I don't know," Gert said. "Someone sneaked it out of my room while I was taking a bath. I suppose my carrying it around got Cassell curious, and he wanted to make sure I didn't have a bomb in it, or something. Maybe Brand took it. Anyway, I asked Sam to find it—"

"Why?"

"You should of seen the nightie I drew," Gert said. "And no bathrobe. I didn't want Brand or anyone to get any wrong ideas. Anyway, Sam found the case and brought it to me."

"How did he look?" Daisy asked.

"I didn't see him," Gert said. "He knocked on the door and said he had the case, and when I opened the door, he'd gone. He sounded sort of choked. Daisy, you know what I been thinking? If Whitty's picture was in the paper as a picture thief, why didn't Cassell spot him?"

"I wondered that, too," Daisy said.

"And Cassell bragged about pictures he'd bought in Boston," Gert said. "He talked about 'em while we played poker. I thought then, if I was him, I wouldn't go telling a lot of strangers about 'em. It kind of went through my mind that if anything happened to those pictures, we'd be the fall guys. In fact, if someone swiped a salt cellar, we'd be the fall guys."

"My own impression," Daisy said, "exactly. That is another reason why I think we will elude headquarters, if we can, for some time—oh, Sam, what a wonderful fit! Now, you go over to that other house, where the women guides are, and get *us* some clothes."

"Let's take it slowly," Sam said. "That tumble of mine did something to my ear drums. Rattled my semicircular canals. But it sounded just as though you said, go over to that other house and get us some clothes."

"I did," Daisy said gently.

"I'll go," Gert said. "Don't waste time with him. I can get 'em while he's pulling himself together!"

"That so?" Sam said. "Well, you watch! Hey, what sizes?"

"Thirty-eight," Daisy said.

"Thirty-six," Gert told him.

Sam squared his shoulders and tipped his visored cap to a jaunty angle.

"So long," he said. "Wait here for me."

The harassed looking woman in charge at the house on the next street asked him, with a grim politeness, what he wanted.

"Those two uniforms. Thirty-six and thirty-eight," Sam said.

"What two uniforms?"

"Didn't they phone you? They must have," Sam said quickly. "I was there when they called, ten minutes ago. From the publicity—"

"Listen, if it was for those reporters, those sob-sisters, I sent those uniforms out yesterday!"

"They never came," Sam grabbed at the straw. "And people are sore. You'd better get me something, before they start tearing your hair out for you."

In a low voice, poignant with emotion, the woman summed up her opinion of the World of Tomorrow.

"Check," Sam said. "And I say the helicline with it."

When he left, he carried two bright flannel dresses, and two orange jackets.

With considerable pride, he tossed them at Daisy and Gert, still in the back hallway.

"There, gals, pop down to the boiler room and slap these on. You'd ought to have hats, but hats are scarce. Yours are blue, anyway, and they'll do. Hustle."

Sam grinned when they returned.

"You look like a poster for Fascist youth," he said. "No, honestly. You look swell. What do we do with our own clothes?"

"I'm sure," Daisy said, "there must be a check room. That reminds me, why haven't we got a pro-gram, or a guide book or a map?"

"I had Brand's guide," Sam said, "but God knows where I left it. In the park, I think."

"We must get one," Daisy said. "And you'll check your suitcase, won't you, Gert?"

"No," Gert said succinctly.

"Well, we'll have to put a Fair sticker on it," Daisy said as they left the house by the back door. "We'll disguise it. Sam, call that boy back. Get him!"

To the boy was given the puzzling privilege of selling programs, maps and guide books to three Fair guides. It was an incident which stirred the boy's imagination, and worried him. Because it continued to worry him, he remembered it. That, in time, became unfortunate.

Holding their maps out before them, they found a check room in Tomorrow Town and deposited there their respective bundles.

"Your cane," Sam said to Daisy. "Where's that?"

"I left it in the boiler room. I don't need it. It's just to hail cabs with—"

"And trip up young men. Gert, here are some stickers. Plaster 'em on your bag. And figure out, Daisy, where you want to go next."

"It's all so clear when you have a map before you," Daisy said. "I like to have things in black and white."

"Look up, now," Sam said. "Now, tell me where is north?"

"I never understand directions," Daisy said. "I've tried all my life, but I can't tell north from south. East and west are all right if the sun's out."

"You," Sam said, "and Comrade Corrigan."

"That's one of the tiresome things about Egleston," Daisy said. "He always gives compass directions. Like, go east three blocks, and then turn due south. He knows what moss means on trees, even. Look, let's go to the textile building. Ready, Gert? It's just down here. That lopsided ladyfinger roof fascinates me. Oh, it's farther away than you'd think, isn't it?"

"Everything is farther away than you think in this place," Sam said. "Transportation's going to be a problem. That is, for us. We'd better just walk and be inconspicuous, but if we try to take in too much, you're going to have museum feet—"

"What are all those cars lined up over there?" Gert said. "Why couldn't we get a car? That would solve everything."

"Those are special Fair cars," Sam said, "like the one you started out in. For Visiting Firemen, Senators, and Captains of Industry. Looks like they're starting out on a grand tour—"

"Guides!"

The trio jumped self-consciously.

"Guides!"

There was something about the military bearing of the tall man who beckoned to them that made Sam stand to attention and salute, as their own guide had saluted them earlier.

He was glad that he had, because the man was clearly someone of importance. Rosettes and medallions dangled from his buttons, and in his coat lapel was a magnificent orange and blue flower.

"I've been waiting for you three for fifteen minutes," the man said sharply.

"Sorry, sir," Sam said, since the man paused for an answer.

"Somebody is going to be sorrier!" the man returned. "This is no way to cement foreign relations, keeping important delegates waiting! The tour's having to start without 'em, and they'll probably get offended and complain to the State Department. We've had enough trouble already, with those Japs and Chinese getting mixed." He looked curiously at Daisy's white hair. "You must be the interpreter."

"Yes, sir," Daisy said.

If a man like that said you must be an interpreter, she thought, there was little sense in disputing the matter.

"And that's their plates and stuff?" he pointed to the suitcase.

"Yes, sir," Gert said.

"Fine. Now, don't let 'em get jostled. Don't let 'em sit on leather. That's why they have the sedan instead of a touring car, because of the upholstery. They have their own chauffeur, too. You women'll have to ride in front, and you'll have to hang on the running board, fellow. I see you've got programs, but they won't need 'em. They've got de luxe guest programs. Now, remember about the milk. And their glasses.

But you've got your orders. Here's the special pass. Call me if the slightest thing goes wrong. We can't have another crisis. Go on, now. They're expecting you."

The man dismissed them with a nod, hurried over to a waiting car, barked some orders and departed.

"What'll we do?" Sam demanded. "He thinks we're bona fide guides for some special Fair guests! Well, the joke's on him. We're going to beat it—"

"We're not," Daisy said calmly. "It's too providential. We'll take the special pass, and we will ride around in the special sedan—"

"No!" Sam said. "We won't!"

"Better make up your minds quick," Gert said. "See what's coming."

Sam jerked his head in the direction she pointed.

Approaching them with a measured tread were two men dressed in flowing saffron robes. A little apart from them walked a heavily veiled woman.

"Merciful heavens!" Daisy said. "What are those things on the men's heads? Are those fezzes or tarbooshes?"

"For all I know," Sam said, "they're wimples. Or snoods—Daisy, let's get out of this, quick!"

"You better hadn't," Gert said. "That big shriner's got his eye on you, and he packs a hefty sword."

"What *are* they?" Daisy said.

The taller man pointed a lean dark forefinger at Sam.

"You," he said, "are ours."

"I think," Sam said, "there's been a mistake—"

"Come," said the man. "We go."

The impelling forefinger indicated a sedan, parked in the shade of a tree.

"We go," he said again.

"Go on, Sam," Daisy said.

The tall man beamed at her.

"Mother!" he said, and gallantly escorted her to the car.

"Er—I'll sit in front," Daisy said. "No, don't bother, Your Highness. I'll sit in front. Front!"

She hadn't the remotest idea of the language in which he replied, but the meaning of his staccato monologue was obvious, even if it had not been accompanied by explanatory gestures.

She was not going to sit in front. She was going to sit in back, with him.

"Mother," he said, as though that were sufficient.

The slightly ribald smile playing around Gert's mouth vanished when the tall man pinched her cheek affectionately and thrust her on the back seat, too. Then, planting himself down between Gert and Daisy, the tall man completed the seating arrangements. Sam was placed by the chauffeur, the other robed man was conceded a folding jump-seat.

"What about the girl friend?" Gert pointed to the veiled lady. "Doesn't she get a seat, General Sherman?"

As though she were quite used to it, the veiled lady curled up on the floor of the tonneau.

"Where to?" Sam inquired in a choked voice.

"I lof New York," the tall man said, patting Daisy's knee. "I lof de beautful voman." He pinched Gert's cheek again.

"Listen, brother of the Mystic East," Gert said, "let's not begin with any wrong thoughts. Let's—say, do you speak English?"

The tall man beamed, and nodded.

"I," he said, tapping his chest. "You," he patted her arm. "Mother." He stroked Daisy's knee. "Come. Go. No. Yez. I lof New York. I lof de beautful voman."

He leaned back proudly against the seat.

"I think," Gert said, "I can speak freely. Daisy, any ideas? Where do you want to go?"

"Isn't this going to work out well!" Daisy said. "Let's go to the foreign government exhibits, Sam. We'll take the midway later this afternoon. I want to see the French building—"

"No!" said the man with great firmness. "No French. No, no, no, no, no—"

"Belgium?" Daisy said tentatively. "That's got the lovely carillon tower we saw from the ramp. Belgium?"

"No!"

"How's for Italy?" Gert asked. "Italy—my God, man, take your hand off that sword! I didn't mean anything, that was just a slip of the tongue!"

"Maybe he's an Ethiopian," Daisy said, "but it seems to me they wore trousers, didn't they? How about—"

"You'd better drop the international aspect," Sam said. "How about the Ford building? You said you wanted to ride around the elevated drive. How does he feel about Henry Ford?"

The tall man apparently liked Henry Ford, because he nodded and said "Ford" several times, and held up five fingers. Then he consulted with his friend, and held up two fingers of his right hand.

"Does that mean he owns seven Fords?" Daisy asked, "or five Fords and two Lincolns. Dear me. I wonder what became of my lovely green Lincoln that Egleston disposed of. Well, let's go to the Ford place, Sam. It seems safe. Yes," she added as they started off, "I loved that green Lincoln. So did Cherry—we've simply got to do something about Cherry, Sam. Would you dare stop off at Cassell's building and see what you could find out? I think we should—oh, there's the cosmetic place that looks like a powder puff. Yes, I think we'd better stop there."

"Okay," Sam said. There was nothing that would suit him any better, he thought, than to go to Cassell's building and find things out. "Wait'll I get it pointed out for Bozo, here. Bozo's English is very shaky. We've used the index finger system so far. Let's see. Stop, Bozo?"

The car stopped with a suddenness that sent Gert bouncing off the seat on top of the veiled lady.

"Go," Sam said.

The car started up.

"That's peachy," Gert said, "but give us some warning next time. The lady on the floor packs a dagger, and she doesn't like being bumped. Say, what *are* these folks?"

"I can't imagine," Daisy said. "I've travelled a lot, but I never saw anything quite like them. If I could only find out what they wear on their heads! It's not a fez, and it's not a tarboosh."

"When you come right down to it," Gert said drily, "it's not a derby, or a beret. You know, it's nice goods in these robes. Nuh-uh, General Sherman. Don't get ideas!"

"Ready?" Sam said. "Braced? Stop, Bozo. Here. No! Go! Go!"

The chauffeur, following Sam's finger, swung them around a corner at a perilous rate, which he continued to maintain.

A trooper held up his hand, and the chauffeur, without waiting for Sam's command, made one of his rocking-horse stops.

"I'm sorry," Sam said quickly, before the trooper could speak. "Here, here's this outfit's pass. And," he lowered his voice, "you can't tell the Prince much, if you know what I mean."

"More international cement, huh?" the trooper

peered into the back of the car. "I see. Well, slow him down. He nearly made mincemeat of that rickshaw. Okay."

Sam pointed to the speedometer.

"Fifteen, Bozo," Sam said. "Hold it right there. No more."

"Why didn't you stop back there at Cassell's building?" Daisy asked.

"Did you see the cops? Fifty million, spread over the entrance. That wasn't the time to make inquiries about Cherry, or pictures, or anything else. Daisy, d'you realize that Cherry's name wasn't on the wanted list from headquarters?"

"You mean, you think they already have her," Daisy said. "I thought of that, at once. We're going to find out about her, and Whitty, after we've lost the Visiting Firemen at Henry Ford's."

But the Visiting Firemen did not turn out to be easily lost. In fact, they refused to be lost.

The tall man, on leaving the car, hooked one arm firmly in Daisy's and one in Gert's.

"We go," he said happily. "You. I. Yes!"

"Sam," Daisy said desperately, "this has got to stop. Gert, think of something. He likes you best."

"If you ask me, I think he loves mother best," Gert told her. "Honest, I don't know what to do! If he was a real shriner, I'd send him home with his tail between his legs. But this lad's tough. He doesn't take hints."

Daisy wrinkled her forehead. "If we could just *talk*

with them! If we just know what they were. That man said they mustn't sit on leather. Does that mean they're Moslems, or not Moslems? Sam, ask him where his home is!"

"From the way he's squeezing your arm," Sam returned, "his home is where his heart is. Probably they come from some place you only hear of in stamp albums. I think he's a lesser rajah."

"I used to be able to ask for hot water in Hindustani," Daisy said. "But that won't get us far."

"I know the Arabic numerals," Sam offered. "Or I could ask him about the cabbage of his aunt in French. I know a little Ital—whee, I nearly said that word. Well, I can ask for a streetcar in Florence. And I can tell a Munich waiter to hurry with the beer—"

"Yez!" said the tall man, with sudden enthusiasm. "Beer!"

Sam smiled. "I've got it. We put 'em back in the car, and then we pretend to go and fetch beer. Hein?"

"No," Daisy said. "We take them inside that building, and sit them down, and then we pretend to go get beer. In their car."

"In their car?"

"Certainly! You don't expect me to trudge these vast distances, do you, with a car at my elbow? Now, let's get them inside."

After a lengthy and elaborate pantomime, they got the Visiting Royalty to sit down on chromium chairs in the Ford building.

"Now," Sam mopped his face with an orange and blue handkerchief he'd found in his pocket, "I go. I get beer."

"Yez!"

"Mother," Sam said, "she go get beer."

"No."

"Yes, mother go too."

The tall man clapped a hand on the hilt of his sword and scowled.

"No use, Daisy," Sam said. "Wherever he comes from, its a matriarchate. Probably you'll lose face if you fetch beer."

"General Sherman," Daisy said crisply, "mother go! And mother does not wish to hear your opinions on the subject!"

Unexpectedly, General Sherman got up from the chromium chair, bowed low before Daisy, and then rather dejectedly resumed his seat.

"I guess," Gert picked up her suitcase, "mother goes. Okay, general. Gert goes too."

"No," the general said, leaning over and pinching Gert's cheek. "You no go. No!"

"General Sherman," Daisy ignored the interested little crowd that had begun to gather around them, "Gert goes too. Mother says so. Mother—oh!"

Daisy stopped short, and for the first time since Sam had met her, she looked agitated.

"Gert," she said hurriedly, "you'll have to manage.

Explain later. Outside here. Quick, Sam, come with me!"

She scurried out through the crowd, and Sam scurried after her.

"Don't stop," Daisy said breathlessly, as he paused. "I want to put just as much distance between that woman and me as I can. This way. Over here. Duck around the corner. There! It was that Mrs. Trimmingham, Sam. You must have met her. She runs every Woman's Club in Boston."

"Lizzie St. Clair Trimmingham? That woman?"

"Now you know why I fled. If Lizzie had seen me, she'd have marched me to the nearest policeman—she's the most forceful woman I ever knew. And so in the way. I had to hide from her yesterday, in the laundry truck. Let's go over there by the Motors Building and wait for Gert. Then we can take the car. I hated to run off like that, but Gert'll manage. She's efficient."

"*What* does she carry in that suitcase?"

Daisy shrugged. "I don't know. You carried it last night, you know more about it than I do. Sam, these crowds just grow bigger and bigger. And it seems to me there are more people around when you just stand still like this. I hadn't begun to notice the crowd, really, rushing around in cars. Where do those bands keep coming from, loud speakers?"

"For all I know," Sam said, "Mr. Whalen has hidden vast orchestras away in underground caverns, and

108

pipes them out like gas. I shouldn't wonder. The more I see of this, the less I wonder at anything. What's the din over there?"

"That's Railways," Daisy said. "I remembered that particularly when the guide pointed it out from the ramp, because I've simply got to go see the old-fashioned cars. I love old Pullmans. There's something about them that makes me nostalgic for the past. Is it tea time yet, Sam?"

He couldn't help grinning at her.

"It's just half past twelve. Didn't you hear the noon whistles and sirens, while we were with the sheik? It just seems like tea time. But remember, you left the train before nine. And if it'll make you feel any better, I'm going to lunch in ten minutes whether Gert comes or not. Here, let's get out of the way of this billowing herd. Something must be letting out."

"Guide!" said a voice.

"Don't turn, Sam!" Daisy said. "Remember what happened the last time. If anyone wants us to do anything, we're waiting for Comrade Ivetsky of the Soviet delegation."

"Guide, can you tell me—"

"We're engaged," Sam said in a loud, disinterested voice.

The man behind them paused, then slowly circled the pair until he faced them.

Daisy didn't believe her eyes.

It was Whitty. And at first, in their guide uniform, he did not recognize them.

"I want to know where—say, *is* that you, Sam? And your mother? How'd you get to be guides? It says in my book, they've undergone intensive instruction over a long period, and you just got here!"

Daisy looked at Sam, and then at Whitty, standing there with all those Sunday papers under his arm. He didn't look like a picture thief. He didn't act like a picture thief. He looked like a butcher, and he sounded like one.

"You been grilled yet?" Whitty said. "Say, didn't they grill you? For the murder?"

Something in Sam's throat began to pound against the collar of his khaki shirt. Daisy's fingers were biting into his arm.

"What murder?" Daisy asked in that frigidly calm voice which she'd used the evening before in summing up Eggy's actions. "What murder, Whitty!"

"The one on the train. Didn't you know they were hunting you for the murder on the train? I heard about it from a radio in that place with the diorama. They were sending out a general alarm for us. You and me and Madame Duplain. They said something about wanting us for picture stealing, but I know better. They want us for murder, that's what. Somebody was shot on the train, in Cassell's private office. They think we did it."

"Who was shot?" Daisy said.

"I don't know who. All I know is, it's a murder they want us for. Not picture stealing. I—"

"How do you know," Daisy interrupted, "that there's been a murder? How do you know about it, if they didn't say so over the radio?"

Sam's right hand gripped Whitty's wrist like a vice.

"If you didn't hear about the murder over the radio," Sam said roughly, "how do you know? And who was shot?"

"Look!" Whitty cried. "Look over there!"

It was an old dodge, but it worked.

Sam's attention wavered only for a split second as an impressive motorcade, with police escorts, rolled up in front of the Aviation Building.

But that split second was enough for Whitty.

Wrenching his wrist out of Sam's grip, Whitty disappeared into the crowd that surged like a tidal wave around the newly arrived cars.

5

Sᴀᴍ, grabbing wildly at Whitty, managed only to get his fingers on the newspapers under Whitty's arm.

"You can't catch him." Dàisy put a restraining hand on Sam's elbow. "Don't try. We'll just get separated. Don't race after him!"

"But that damned little rat!" Sam said. "That bland little butcher! That picture snatcher—standing there pretending to be so damned innocent! How'd he know about that murder, if—"

"You can't catch him, Sam," Daisy said, "so don't try. Sam, you knew there'd been a murder, didn't you? You knew last night. Who's been killed? Why didn't you tell me?"

"I don't know who!" Sam said. "Good God, I don't know who! I can't find out! Daisy, I don't know! I tried to use the process of elimination. I began at breakfast. But everyone's turned up, except Cherry and Cassell. And they're accounted for. I thought it was Roberts. He was the only person missing. But it wasn't. He came back to the train for his bags. I don't know who the hell it was!"

"Sam," Daisy said, "why didn't you tell me about this? I don't understand why you didn't tell me right away! Why didn't you tell everyone right away?"

"You think it out," Sam said. "Look at the spot I was in. Could I go to Cassell last night and say, 'By the way, I was just retrieving Gert's suitcase from that room on the right, and I happened to notice a body slumped in a heap in the far corner, and I think someone's been murdered, because my foot hit a gun and kicked it beyond the desk.' Could I go tell him that? And then go on to explain that I'm not Sam Days, but Sam Minot, a reporter, the reporter he kicked out of Mrs. Bottome's? And that you're not Mrs. Days, but Mrs. Boylston Tower, the one being hunted in horse ponds and suspected of being kidnapped? How'd you have crawled out of that one, Daisy?"

Sam paused for breath.

"So," Sam continued, "I took the case and left it outside Gert's door, and went back to my own room. Later I sneaked back out into the corridor, because I wanted to find out who the body was, but the door was locked."

"Why didn't you find out when you first saw it?" Daisy demanded.

"I had one impulse," Sam told her, "and that was to run; to run before someone nabbed me coming out of that place—"

"Did it occur to you," Daisy said, "that you had a scoop there, Sam?"

"It occurred to me in passing," Sam said. "But it also occurred to me that it was going to be a lot wiser to let someone else find that body. The people who find bodies, Daisy, get asked so many questions. And the minute we had to begin answering questions, you were in the soup. I was in the soup. So I didn't start any hue and cry."

"If you'd just told me last night," Daisy said, "I shouldn't have spent the night tossing and turning and brooding about you. Didn't you see me, in the corridor, when you came out with the bag?"

"Were you there? Did you see me? I just thought, when you asked me what I was doing, that you'd heard me. Were you—"

"So that's why you've kept wearing those glasses," Daisy said thoughtfully, "to keep Cassell from recognizing you. I see. Sam, this is perfectly awful! There was I, wandering around the corridor, and there were you, wandering around and hiding that silly suitcase. And there was Whitty in the oval room, snoring and pretending to be asleep. And for all we know, Gert—"

"For all we know," Sam said, "Gert was wandering around before she called me and asked me to get that damn suitcase. For all we know, she killed whoever's been killed, planted her suitcase in there, and then asked me to find the suitcase so that I'd be the one to find the body. She said she thought Brand or one of

114

the servants had taken it, but if pictures are gone—well, there's the little suitcase. Daisy, the best thing for you to do is to go back to Boston just as fast—"

"Sam, look at those," Daisy pointed to the Sunday papers he had grabbed from Whitty. "Let's look at that story about him. On the back of page sixteen in the *Herald*."

Sam found page sixteen in the *Herald*, turned it over, looked at it, and whistled.

"Daisy," he said, "we've done Comrade Whitty a great wrong. Look. It's the composing room again. That head goes with the next column, over the lead about the Mona Lisa. Whitty's picture's got its own column. He's just been inducted as Grand Leader of the Barambeba Lodge. My God, he spoke the truth about lodges—look at the mob of 'em he belongs to. He's a butcher after all. Well, that settles that."

Daisy glanced at the description of the festivities of the Barambeba Lodge, and nodded.

"It seems to settle it, but why did he run?" she said. "He can not be a picture thief and still be mixed up with the murder."

"That's true enough," Sam said, "but if pictures got stolen from that train, Gert took 'em. She took 'em and they're in her suitcase. Gert's the one who's responsible for that body—"

"Sam, why didn't you find out who the body belonged to? Who did it look like?"

"It looked," Sam said, "like any crumpled-up body

looks in a dimly lighted room, when somebody's been thoughtful enough to cover it with a voluminous over-coat—"

"Then it was a man?"

"It might have been a woman in man's clothes," Sam said. "I don't know. Daisy, I was too scared and shocked to do anything but grab that case and beat it. I tell you, I was scared! That sounds silly, but it's one thing to be sent out to view corpses in the line of business, and it's another to find yourself discovering one."

"I suppose so," Daisy said, "but I still wish you'd made a greater effort at finding out who the person is, Sam. Why didn't you do that this morning, when you stayed behind at the train, pretending to hunt my glasses?"

"I tried to!" Sam said. "I got as far as stealing the key to that room—its Cassell's own office, you know. Then Brand bustled me off in Cassell's car, back to the Fair. Say, Cassell gives orders by radio, did you know that? Stragg, that chauffeur, was getting instructions by radio. Pretty nifty, isn't it? Anyway, I've got the key to that room, but a fat lot of good it's done me. I intended to go back to the train while you and Gert prowled around Tomorrow Town, but things happened too quickly. I haven't had any chance since, God knows. And now, if the murder's finally been discovered, the key's no use—"

"How'd you get the key?" Daisy asked. "Where?"

"I took it from a board with a lot of tagged keys on

it, in a closet, while Brand went to get me a guide book. I know it's the right key, because it has a tag—"

Sam fumbled in his pockets.

"Daisy," he said, "I've lost the damn thing! I had it in my coat pocket in the car, I know that. But I've lost it. Must have been when I changed clothes in the boiler room. That bump on the head I got—"

"Did Brand suspect you took it?"

"Why should he?" Sam said. "We were just innocently discussing the Fair, Brand and I. They've probably got other keys to that office, if you're wondering about that angle. I suppose Cassell came back to the train, and unlocked the office with his own keys, and that's when they discovered the body."

"If Brand missed that key," Daisy said, "what would he do?"

Sam shrugged. "He might cluck his tongue, he might think Cassell had taken it earlier. I'm sure he'd never suspect me. He wouldn't have let me go, if he'd suspected anything. I probably lost it in that mob, before I got to the perisphere. Stragg got orders over the radio to go to the Administration Building, so he let me off at a corner, and there was a terrible mob there. I probably lost the key when I pulled out my cigarettes—now I remember. Stragg picked up my cigarette lighter. It'd dropped out of my pocket. There was an awful mob, and a band passing—say, what's that to-do over there?"

Daisy did not look at once in the direction Sam pointed.

She was toying with a fantastic thought. But Brand, after all, was an efficient man. If he had missed a key just after Sam had gone, Brand would probably do something about it. If Brand had phoned Cassell that one of his train guests had stolen the office key, and if Cassell gave orders by radio, it was entirely possible that Stragg, the chauffeur, had relieved Sam of that key.

It was a fantastic idea, but then, Daisy thought, Brand or some other soft-footed servant had always hovered in the background ever since they boarded the train. In a quiet, inconspicuous way, they had been under surveillance. Sam might think that Brand hadn't suspected anything, but Sam might well be mistaken.

"Look!" Sam said. "I think it's Shirley Temple—she was the one who came in that procession with all the fanfare and escorts. No, no, it isn't either. It's someone else—"

He jumped up and down several times as though he were bouncing on a pogo stick.

"Hey, Sistie!"

A man directly behind them had made a megaphone of his cupped hands, and he nearly cracked Daisy's ear drums with his bellow.

"Hey, Sistie! Hey! Hey, Sistie, hey, Buzzie! Hey, Sistie!"

118

"Is *she* there, Sam?" Daisy yelled. "She is? Oh, do lift me up so I can see—is she with them?"

"Hey, Sistie!" bellowed the man behind. "Hey, looky this way—aw, they've all gone and went!"

"Thanks, Sam," Daisy said as he put her down. "I always wanted to see her. I do so admire that woman's vigor. So does Boy. Sam, let's get out of this mob, the whole Fair's coming this way to see them. Have you still got General Sherman's pass? Wave it at that beach wagon and see if we can't get away in that."

The beach wagon driver was adamant in his refusal to give them a lift.

"I got to pick up a couple of Morgan partners at the Du Pont building, and get some Congressmen from Distillers, and take 'em all over to the Federal Building, the hell and gone beyond the lagoon. I can't do a thing for you!"

"But we've lost a Prince," Daisy said, "and I'm the only person in the Fair who knows his language!"

"You're no worse off than Kubelsky. He's lost a South American president—hey, let's see that pass again. Oh, boy, one of them? Okay, hop in. This'll get me by that police escort there. I'll take you as far as Elgin Watch, but that's all."

Daisy beamed at him as she got in and sat down on the back seat.

"We'll get you mentioned in dispatches, if we ever find that Prince," she said. "Yes, Sam, Boy admires her vigor, too. The last time he was home, he got an assignment to follow her for a week. He had acute appendicitis the second day, and I've always wondered if it weren't just an excuse. Sam, I think I know when that person was killed. When we were on that siding, and the noise was so terrible. When Cherry was taking a shower, or just before."

She waited for an orange and blue uniformed band to march past.

"Sam," she said, as the blare abated, "we've simply got to find out who it was. If pictures have been stolen, very likely it's someone who had something to do with pictures. If it was some one of the train staff, like the dish-washer, I'm sure they can't involve us. They simply can't, no matter how many queer things they find out about us, like the way we got on the train, and who we are, and all that. Sam, why aren't newsboys howling extras about that murder by now?"

Sam laughed shortly as he ducked a confetti spiral hurled playfully at him by an exuberant blonde.

"Well," Daisy said, "isn't murder on the opening day of the World's Fair a scoop? On a millionaire's private train on its Fair siding?"

"What do you think?" Sam said. "What—say," he called to the driver, "are we going to stay in this one spot forever? Can't you step on it?"

The driver said a number of things. Boiled down and deleted, his suggestions were simple. If Sam didn't like the way they weren't getting anywhere, Sam had two feet which he was welcome to use.

"Why isn't the murder being broadcast over the loud speakers?" Daisy said. "Why hasn't it got into the papers?"

"There hasn't been time enough for papers and extras, and it's Sunday, remember. And do you really think they'd let the opening get marred?"

"You mean, it might stop the Fair?"

"Nothing could stop the Fair," Sam said, "outside of a long-range bombardment from an enemy fleet. This murder of an unknown person on Cassell's train wouldn't touch the Fair. But it might leave a bad taste, and scare the timorous."

Daisy considered for a moment while another band and a company of color guards, with flags furled, marched past.

"But murders draw people—"

"They draw a certain element. But it's inclined to keep nice folks away. It's not nice publicity. So, I think the news'll be soft-pedaled until tomorrow. Funny, we were talking about this sort of thing at the office the other day. We decided then that the nicest scoop any man could get these days would be the scoop on no Fair."

"But there is a Fair," Daisy pointed out, "and it's opened."

"Well, officially, it begins with the pageant and hoop-la tonight. It's opened in the sense of being open, but tonight's the real fireworks. Yes, we tried to think of things that might stop the Fair—"

121

"And murder won't?"

"We couldn't see how," Sam said. "The murder or the death of some important personage might dim it, but there's really nothing that could stop this Fair. Fire is out, because the thing's been too well planned. Things are fireproofed, and all. An epidemic, like a big flu epidemic, might cripple it. Labor trouble might cripple it. But nothing could really stop it. It represents too much of an investment."

"In brief, the no-Fair scoop is one you'll never get?"

Sam nodded. "This murder on Cassell's train won't have any effect on the Fair. Nothing will. You could mow the whole top line Fair committee down with machine guns, and it wouldn't matter—why, look at the insurance angle alone!"

"Whose insurance?" Daisy asked. "What—dear me, it does seem that parade might stop! What insurance?"

"The insurance rates were tremendous at first, when the Fair was first proposed. Anyone who was going to invest money in the Fair, or in buildings or exhibits, wasn't going to take any chances of getting stuck if the Fair came a cropper. So they insured themselves and their buildings and things against there being a Fair. See?"

"Vaguely. Like London merchants insuring themselves against the weather of George's coronation."

"Or the coronation itself. Well, the rates were tremendous, but now they're nominal. But you see my point. You couldn't postpone the opening of this Fair because of a murder, or half a dozen murders. The insurance side of it alone is too huge. Cassell's building was one of the earliest, and he must have paid—"

"I've just remembered," Daisy said. "I've just thought of something I've been trying to think of since Brand mentioned it this morning. It was my nephew Egleston who talked about the hourglass building. He's in the insurance business, you know, and now that I think of it, he had something to do with Cassell's building. I do wish we could get along and get started!"

"You're getting that glint in your eyes," Sam said. "I don't like that glint. What does it mean, now?"

"What do you think it means? We've got to hurry and get started finding out who was killed, and who did it, and we'll never get anywhere if this vehicle doesn't hurry! We—"

"Say, bud," the driver turned around and called to them, "we'll be clear of this jam in a couple minutes. This parade's over—"

"Good," Daisy said. "Fine. You see, Sam, we really can't do anything else, can we? You can't get a job, I can't do anything about Eggy, or what he's been up to. Why, I can't even cash a check! And we can't begin to see the Fair properly if we're being hunted as murder suspects! You don't call what we've been doing seeing the Fair!"

"Is Boy Tower in China now?" Sam asked.

"Yes. Why? I'm sure he'd agree with me that we've just got to settle all this murder ourselves. Boy believes in taking the offensive. Like that Mexican revolution he was covering, the one that dragged on so. He got so bored with it, he planned a coup for the revolution so they won, and then he could get sent somewhere else. You've had some experience with murders, haven't you, on papers? Well, then!"

"I asked about Boy," Sam said, "because I thought I'd ship you off to him. Look, you don't really think that you and I could track down a murderer in the midst of this maelstrom, do you? With all this going on, when you and I are being hunted as suspects ourselves under a set of aliases, when you're being sought for as a missing person under your own name? And you don't even know who was killed! Daisy, I'm going to ship you back home, and—"

"I wish," Daisy said, "that you'd be still! You're talking so loud, that driver'll hear you! Oh, we've really started. That's a relief. I want—no, Sam, don't argue! Just you keep quiet while I think. I've got some ideas."

Ten minutes later they drew up in front of the circular Elgin building.

"Here y'are," the driver said. "My God, this driving here's something fierce. My nerves is shot."

Sam shook the driver by the hand.

"You don't know what nerves are," he said. "Compared to what I've got before me, you are in a state of benign calm."

"That Prince, huh? Want an aspirin?"

Sam took two from the little tin box.

"Thanks," he said. "If I live through the afternoon, it'll be because of you. Hey, give me back my pass! I need it."

"Now," Daisy said as the station wagon drove off, "we've got to settle the problem of who was shot—"

"Can't I distract you," Sam said desperately, "with thoughts of Cherry? Don't you think it would be nice to find her? Aren't you worried about Cherry? Come on, Daisy. Let's hunt her!"

"I'm going to do that too," Daisy said. "I've been thinking things over, Sam. We know the person who was killed wasn't one of us. Now, I don't think it could possibly be one of the train staff. If one of them was missing, they'd track him down. So," she ignored the lady in the feather turban who was pointing at her a cane that dripped orange and blue ribbons, "so, the person who was killed must have been a stowaway. If we got on the train so easily, someone else could have got on, back at the South Station. As far as I can understand, that train staff was pretty disrupted yesterday evening, with Andrew and his threats—"

"Guide," said the lady in the feather turban, "will you—"

"And his tickets," Daisy blandly continued. "I don't think anyone could have boarded the train en route, because no one could have known the route. Even Cassell didn't know it. And he said that there was no telling what changes would be made on the way—"

"Guide, I'm talking to you! You with the white hair!"

"Je ne suis pas un guide," Daisy said coldly in execrable French. "Je suis—er—d'liason brigade."

"Aw, she don't speak no English!" the woman said to her companion. "Wouldn't you think they'd had sense enough to get guides that spoke English—hey, mister, do you know what this building here is?"

Sam looked at it, and opened up the small guide book he had bought from the boy back in Tomorrow Town.

"This," he said politely, "is the Elgin Building, madam."

"What's that thing? That thing there?"

"Mmm. Let's see. Ah, that's a pier, or flying buttress, madam. Emphasizing the north-south meridian. In this building, madam, within these very walls, is unfolded a colorful chronicle of Time."

"Time?" The interest of the woman in the feather turban had begun to wane with the flying buttress, but now it revived. "Time, huh? I listen to that over the radio."

"Here," Sam said, "is Time, all right. Beginning with the prehistoric smoldering rope and the Egyptian slave gong, continuing down through water clocks and hourglasses to antique and modern watches, and ending with a glimpse of the timepiece of tomorrow. Then—"

"Do they act it out, like?"

"Well," Sam said, reading quickly, "the slave strikes a gong—"

"I know," the woman said, "and Time marches on. Let's go in, Bella."

Daisy shook her head as the two departed.

"I'm afraid," she said, "their conception of Time is going to be frightfully garbled from now on. They've got the wrong impression, entirely."

"Yes," Sam said, "but my fine feathered friend is terribly happy at my efficiency. Doubtless, as she marches along with Time in the World of Tomorrow, she will pause and recall that charming guide—Daisy, you'd better be pretty careful with that French of yours. You might find someone who can talk it."

"My French," Daisy said, "never fails to win friends and influence people. It sends them into hysterics, and the ice is broken at once. Sam, find me a phone booth. I'm going to call the Golden Dart."

"You said it would be fatal, when Gert suggested that," Sam said, "and, anyway, aren't you going to find Cherry, and then let me put the two of you on a nice train for Boston? And—"

"What seemed fatal a few hours ago is now routine," Daisy said. "I'm going to phone, and find out where Cherry is, and who was killed. There are lots of involved methods we could use to find out both things, but it just seems simpler to call and ask Brand."

"Daisy!" Sam said. "Daisy, won't you—"

"I'm going to pin my faith on Brand," Daisy said, "Brand and human nature. He was so kind and thoughtful and helpful that I gave him all the bills I had left in my purse to strew around the staff, and a little gold charm Boy brought me from China for himself. He seemed quite pleased and moved. Find a phone, Sam."

"But if they've given orders to trace any numbers that call the train—"

"I shan't say anything unless Brand answers," Daisy said. "I'll just hang up if it's anyone else. It'll be easy enough to tell his voice. It's so precise and controlled. We'll just have to take a chance with Brand. Find a phone—well, there's probably one inside here. And if this plan doesn't work, I've got another plan that should."

Her face, when she emerged from the booth a few minutes later, was glowing.

"Dear Brand!" she said. "Yes, he answered. Somehow I got the impression he was standing next to it, he answered so quickly. I said 'Brand, where is Cherry Chipman?' And that jewel of a man! He said, 'No, this is not the theater. You want the theater.' Isn't he a jewel?"

"I don't see why," Sam said. "You ask where she is, and he tells you the train isn't the theater!"

"Why, it's perfectly clear! Brand couldn't say, 'Hello, Mrs. Days, how are you, your friend Cherry is at the theater waiting for you!' But that's what he meant, don't you see? He told me without giving me away, or Cherry away. Probably people were listening to him. Anyway, Cherry's at the theater—"

"What theater? And did you ask who the body was?"

"He didn't know. I said, 'Brand, who was killed?' and he said, 'I don't know.' Give me that guide book, Sam. I'll find out what theater, and then we'll try my other plan for finding out who was killed. There's that Marine Amphitheater, that's just over there. But that can't be the one."

"Why not?"

"Too big. It seats ten or twelve thousand people—Sam, don't you know anything about this Fair, yet? I'll wager you don't know what the Four Freedoms are!"

"First cousins to the Flying Cordonas," Sam returned. "They fly through the air with the greatest of ease."

"They happen," Daisy said, "to be those four statues in the Central Mall. Freedom of Speech, Assembly, Religion, and the Press."

"I know," Sam said. "They're the four that George Washington is looking across at. Why wouldn't Cherry be at the Marine theater thing?"

"She'll have sense enough to know we could hardly

129

pluck her bodily from a group of ten or twelve thousand people, and there are things going on at that place all day. Now, let's see what the guide book says. Theater. Theater, Art of. Theater, History of. Theater, Tomorrow's. Theater, see Cinema Theater. Theater, see Punch and Judy—"

"Maybe she's joined an itinerant Punch and Judy show," Sam suggested.

"Don't be silly! And, Sam, keep your eye peeled for a lost child, will you? Theater," she resumed reading from the guide book, "see Community Arts Building. Theater—"

"What do you want with a lost child?"

"I need one," Daisy said. "Oh, they've got the Pantomimeteatret, that superb company from the Tivoli in Copenhagen. I didn't know they'd been brought over. I simply must see them again!"

"What do you need a lost child for?"

"I told you," Daisy said, "I had another plan— Sam, quick! There's a darling boy in a sailor suit over there, crying his eyes out! Go get him, quick! Oh, don't stop to ask questions! Go get that little boy, and bring him here!"

The little boy looked at Daisy, and stopped crying.

"Have you been lost very long?" she asked him cheerfully.

"Not very."

"Darling," Daisy said, "does your stomach ache?"

"No."

"Not at all?"

The little boy considered.

"It's sort of hungry," he said. "It's got a hungry ache."

"So it *does* ache some?"

"Daisy!" Sam said. "What are you—"

"Ssh, Sam. It aches a little bit, then?"

"Yes, but not like the time I went in the ambulance. That time it hurt awful."

"Did you like the ambulance?"

The boy's eyes shone.

"It was fine!" he said.

"Would you like to ride in an ambulance again? Really? Not to the hospital, just to the place where they'll find your mother. You would like to? Well, I see no reason why you shouldn't. Sam, call an ambulance."

"What!"

"Do as I say!"

"Daisy, I refuse to—"

"Get an ambulance quickly," Daisy said. "Tell the ambulance driver or the attendant that the boy is lost, but he has a slight stomach ache, so you thought you'd better be on the safe side and call them. And you go too, see?"

"Why? Why, in the name of all that's sane, should I go? Daisy, are you—"

"And find out from the ambulance driver, or the people at the first aid place, or the doctor, you ninny!"

Daisy said impatiently. "Find out from them, Sam Minot, who it was on the train!"

"On the train?"

"They had to have an ambulance to remove the person, didn't they? And where are the nearest ambulances? Right here at the Fair. Well, stop gawping and get to work. I'll wait here and figure out what theater Cherry can be in. Now, darling, will you go along with this tall man?'

The little boy hesitated.

"He's a guide," Daisy said, "and it's just his funny nose that gives him that stupid look. He's going to take you to your mother in an ambulance, because that will be quicker."

"Will it have a bell like the other one I went in?"

"If it doesn't," Daisy said, "this man with the funny nose will make sounds like it, which will be better than a real bell. Good-bye, darling. Hurry back, Sam."

Near the entrance to the building, Daisy found a place to sit down where she could see everything, and still not be too conspicuous. Then she set to work on the theater problem. No matter if there turned out to be a hundred theaters, she intended to find the one where Cherry was.

There was no doubt in Daisy's mind that Cherry must have returned to the train since the body was discovered. Brand, otherwise, would not have known where she had gone, nor would he have taken such

132

elaborate precautions. How, under the circumstances, Cherry could have managed to remove herself from the train Daisy couldn't guess. But Cherry was a resourceful girl, and very possibly Brand may have helped. And now, probably bursting with a number of vital and essential facts, Cherry sat in a theater. Some theater. Somewhere.

And she had to be found.

Daisy opened the guide book.

Half way through her intensive study of the index, a good-looking girl in guide's uniform sat wearily down beside her.

"I'm pooped," she said. "How are you bearing up?"

"I'm an interpreter," Daisy said promptly. "At the moment, I'm waiting for my rajah and his grand vizier to wash their hands."

The girl grinned.

"My party's washing their hands, too," she said. "My God, my feet! This is worse than Macy's housewares the week before Christmas. If I get home alive, I'm going to put my feet in a bucket of Epsom salts and let 'em soak for the next six months. Say, have you heard of the trap?"

"What trap?"

"They found out someone had pinched some guide outfits, and they're trying to get the people—say, think of anyone wanting to pinch a guide's outfit! They don't know what they let themselves in for. Seems some kid selling programs spotted 'em. He couldn't get over the joke of guides buying programs and guide books. It is kind of funny, when you think what we went through. Anyway, he told some troopers, and they got wise, so now they got a trap."

"I hope they don't trap me," Daisy said. "I've had trouble enough with my white hair. It seems they were hunting an elderly woman with white hair. They tried to snatch me away from the rajah, and nearly brought on an international crisis. The rajah has a temper."

"I wish I had a rajah," the girl said. "This party of mine is from Portland, Oregon, and they got all the lift of a bread pudding. Aha—there they are, all washed up and rarin' to go. Those men are dying to get off by themselves, and you know where they're going to get taken? To the Old English Village. They've got that sixteenth-century theater reproduction there, and they're going to do Shakespeare, and my ladies think it'll be nice. Well, hey nonny!"

"Good-bye," Daisy said. "I hope your feet bear up."

When Sam returned, she was beaming.

"There's a trap for us," she said, "and we'll have to be careful—Sam, I've found it. Where Cherry is. She'll be at the Old English Village. The sixteenth-century theater reproduction. The man who's running that is an old beau of hers—"

She stopped short and stared at him.

"Sam! Who is it! Did you find out?"

"I found out," Sam said grimly. "I saw him. He saw us get on the train, Daisy. He must have. He must have followed. Got on somehow. He—"

"Are you trying to tell me that it's Glue? Sam Minot, is it Glue?"

Sam nodded.

"It's Glue," he said. "Tie that one."

6

"S<small>AM</small>! Where—how did you see him?"

He sat wearily down beside her.

"They asked the little boy if he'd been sick to his stomach, and he misunderstood them and said, yes he had. So the ambulance whipped us to a hospital instead of one of the first-aid stations. And when we got there, they were carrying a stretcher out to a police ambulance. I asked one of the attendants what the matter was, and he said carelessly that it was just someone who'd passed out. But you know, they wouldn't be putting a faint into a police ambulance!"

Daisy nodded. "I shouldn't think so. But how did you manage to see him?"

"The body was covered, of course, but the blanket slipped and I saw his face. It was Glue."

"It can't be," Daisy said. "It's absurd! It can't be, Sam!"

"It's Glue," Sam said.

"Possibly the body you saw on the stretcher may

have been Glue, but you don't know that Glue was the body on the train, do you?" Daisy asked.

"Has to be," Sam said. "I said to the attendant, 'That's some faint!' And he said that faint was the story, and they were sticking to it, or words to that effect. Then I spotted Debbon of the homicide outfit. I've seen him up in Boston. He's plenty smart. He was talking to some Fair official, and he said that he was going back to the train. He said he didn't care how many dates Cassell had, or who he was lunching with, he wanted Cassell. And the Fair official said he'd have to wait, and that they couldn't ball things up. Debbon said the hell he couldn't. That's the gist of that. Then Debbon started to walk past where I stood with the boy, and I turned the kid over to a doctor, and left. There's no doubt about it, Daisy. Glue's the man who was killed on the train last night."

Daisy played with a button on her jacket.

"After yesterday," Sam went on, "I could pick Glue's face out of a million. Why, I dreamed about his eyebrows last night! I know it was Glue. Debbon wouldn't be out here unless it was something big. And he wouldn't be talking that way about the train and Cassell—"

"I'm disappointed," Daisy said.

"What?"

"Yes. I thought it would be someone important. A governor or a banker or a tycoon like Cassell. And to have it turn out to be that thug, Glue!"

137

"What thug?"

"Glue, of course!" said Daisy impatiently. "Sam, sometimes you're so stupid! Aren't we talking about Glue? Well! I said I was disappointed to have it turn out to be that thug, and I am."

"Glue wasn't a thug."

"He was a thug if I ever saw one. Beady eyes, shifty eyes, shifty face, that oily black hair—why, I remember thinking there at the news stand yesterday that he was a composite of all the gangster pictures I ever saw."

"Daisy," Sam said firmly, "Glue wasn't any thug."

"My dear boy, I saw him!"

"I'm beginning to wonder," Sam said, "if you did."

"You told me he had on a grey suit and a black hat. Well, he did. A grey suit with very padded shoulders, and a tight waist, and a sort of wide-brimmed black hat. And he was a thug. Someone you'd see around pool rooms or race tracks. What Boy calls the Dark Alley type."

"Glue," Sam told her, "wore a grey suit I'd be glad to own myself, and a black Anthony Eden hat. And before you interrupt me, let's figure out that you saw someone in a grey suit with a black hat, but he didn't happen to be Glue. Not my Glue. Didn't I tell you that was what puzzled me most?"

"No," Daisy said coldly. "What puzzled you most?"

"Didn't I tell you that Glue wasn't a cop? I know I

did. And he wasn't any private detective. He was—well, he was a gentleman!"

"Why," Daisy said, "should you sound so apologetic about his being a gentleman? Oh, I see. You mean you were puzzled that you should be trailed by a gentleman. It's odd how minds work, isn't it? I, personally, should be more curious about the fact of being trailed than the social status of the trailer. But I see your point."

"Look," Sam said. "I was puzzled because I was being followed. Relentlessly pursued. I was further puzzled because the man was well dressed, he looked like a gentleman, he did not seem to be the sort who would pursue a complete stranger on a moment's whim. Now, shall we drop that angle and go on? What happened at the station was that you saw somebody who roughly answered Glue's description, but he wasn't Glue. And while we nimbly boarded the train, convinced that Glue had gone, Glue was actually watching us. And, as you said, with the staff all worked up about Andrew and his orders about people with tickets, Glue somehow slipped on the train."

"How could he have got into that office?" Daisy said. "Sam, this is like those English cross-word puzzles with the enigma clues. Like, behead sixpence and add a gooseberry tart, and it turns out to be a word like pram. Don't you really know, Sam Minot, why you were being followed?"

"I don't. At first I thought it was some of the gang being funny. You know how reporters—"

"I've had intimate experience with their idea of wit," Daisy said. "Like that time some gay souls invited both Boston ball teams to the Louisburg Square house for dinner—in Boy's name, of course."

"What did you do?" Sam asked interestedly.

"I fed them, after incalculable rounds of drinks. I still get sent season passes. So you don't think you were being followed as a joke?"

"No, it was too pointless, if you know what I mean. Nothing happened."

"And if it had been the gang," Daisy said, "Glue would have rushed up to you at some busy corner and accused you of stealing his wife. Oh, yes, I know the habits of your tribe. Why were you fired, Sam? What had you done?"

"Nothing. I haven't the remotest idea why I got the sack. But I'm sure there can't be any connection between that and Glue. Why, Daisy, I thought I was doing swell."

"You said that Cassell kicked you out of Mrs. Bottome's," Daisy said. "What had you done?"

"Nothing at all. I was just trying to get an interview. So were a dozen others. We all got kicked out. I'd penetrated a little deeper than the others, so I got kicked harder. But that wouldn't be anything that Harris would sack me for! And besides, Harris fired me before I even had a chance to tell him I hadn't got an interview—"

"Guide!"

"This guide business," Sam said irritably, "has got to cease!"

"It has," Daisy agreed. "They've got a trap for us—"

"Guide!"

They were confronted suddenly by the military-looking man who had thrust them on General Sherman. Beside him were two Fair officials.

Sam swallowed. Then he saluted.

"Oh, I know you," the man said. "I know these two, Dick. Everything all right with His Highness? Where is he?"

"At the Ford Building, sir." Sam, without pausing to consider the consequences, automatically told the truth. "At the Ford place."

He knew that he ought to continue and present a reason for Daisy's and his presence there, but to save his life, Sam couldn't think of any adequate explanation.

"His Highness," Daisy said, "ordered us to come here and have the crystal on his watch repaired. He insisted that I come along," she made an appealing little gesture and smiled a fleeting smile, "so that I could interpret. He feels I have to interpret everything. I wanted to stay with him, of course, but—well, his orders were very definite. We got someone to fix the watch as a special favor to His Highness, and now we're waiting for him—"

"I see, I see. He's happy, is he? Well, keep him happy. Do anything he wants. The way things are, he matters very much. Keep him happy. Come along, Dick."

Neither Sam nor Daisy took anything in the nature of a full breath until the three men disappeared from sight.

"That was close!" Sam said. "And orchids to you. The watch crystal was genius. My mind got clogged. I couldn't think of a thing. Anyway, we're safe now."

"Until we hit the trap," Daisy said. "That wasn't any trap just now, that was just expert supervision. Sam, we must get to Cherry and find out what she knows. Let's see that map. We've got to get from here over to the Old English Village—merciful heavens, that's miles and miles away! If we had the time, I'd say we should go back to the Ford place and get General Sherman's car—"

"I meant to ask you, what about him, and what about Gert? And Whitty?"

"Gert will be safe enough with the General," Daisy said. "He'll never let her get out of his clutches, and he's not going to be too hard to find. There's nothing inconspicuous about that entourage. After we've got Cherry, we'll find them. The General is going to be very valuable, Sam. With his pass, and his car, and the costumes—why, the man amounts to a safe-conduct! As for Whitty, he's probably gone with the wind. Well, let's start wending our way to the Old English Village. We'll have to put on different clothes pretty soon, too. Sooner or later, we're going to get caught—"

"Guide! Hey—"

"This way, Daisy," Sam said. "Slip past—"

A pompous-looking elderly man buttonholed Sam.

"Didn't you hear me call? Well, why didn't you stop? What're you two trying to run away for?"

"Sir," Sam said, "I thought you were calling that guide over there. We're engaged—"

"I'm going to report you," the pompous man announced. "I'm going to report the whole lot of you. Call yourselves guides! I've asked a dozen of you a simple question, and not one's answered it. I'm going to ask you. And if you don't answer me, I'm going to march you back to the Administration Building and demand that steps be taken!"

Sam couldn't think of anything to say, so he kept quiet. His silence seemed to make the pompous man even more annoyed.

"Whyn't you say something? What's the matter with all you fellows? Now, here's the question I want answered. Where—now, mind you, if you laugh or look as if you didn't hear me—back you go! Where is the trylon?"

"Sir," Sam said, *"there* is the trylon. It is seven hundred feet high. That ball is the perisphere. It is two hundred feet high. The ramp, sir, is the helicline."

"That thing there is the trylon?"

"Yes, sir."

"Huh! Whyn't someone tell me?"

"There's something," Daisy said weakly, "that watches over fools and children—let's start out before anyone else stops us. The thought of that walk appalls me, but maybe we can pick up a ride."

Sam, remembering her gold knobbed cane, became solicitous.

"Do you think you can—"

"Of course, I can make it. I'm not lame. I just hate to walk—what in the world are those men marching by?"

She pointed to a company dressed in scarlet trousers and gold-frogged, gold-braided white tunics. The faces of the men were almost invisible under enormous bearskin busbies.

"They can't be Fair," Sam said, "there's no orange and blue. Look at that band! Daisy, I've never seen so many bands! I didn't know there were so many. Where do they come from?"

"If sound is any criterion," Daisy said, "they have all been hibernating since the Columbian Exposition. Oh, that lovely man with the bass drum on his rump —if he doesn't hurry, he's going to be left behind in Charleston while the rest go marching through Georgia."

"They're stopping," Sam said. "They're not going to march through Georgia, anyway. They're going to bivouac by Harding Boulevard—say, the front end of that drum needs a good bivouac. He's dripping under that bearskin."

"You mean dropping," Daisy said. "He—why, he's unhitching himself and marching over here! Sam, he looks truculent. I think he's mad because we've been laughing at him."

Sam took her arm.

"Come on," he said. "After all we've gone through, I'm not going to get arrested in a brawl with the front end of a bass drum—my God, he's running after us!"

"Guide! Hey, guide!"

"If I ever return to civil life," Sam said as they hurried along, "I'm going to shoot the first person who uses that word in my presence. Turn—"

"Guide!"

"Wait!" Daisy said suddenly. "Stop, Sam! I think I recognize that voice! It—it *is* you under that thing, isn't it, Whitty?"

The bearskin nodded.

"Did we scare you, when we shot those questions at you before?" Daisy said. "I'm sorry, but—"

"Thought you were going to arrest me again," Whitty said, puffing heavily.

"Did they arrest you? They did? Take off that thing, and cool off," Daisy said, "and get your breath, and tell us—"

"I can't take it off," Whitty said. "It's my disguise. Yup, they got me once, but they can't arrest a free-born American citizen like that. No, sir! I beat it. I thought you wanted to arrest me again, when you grabbed me, Sam. That's why I beat it then. I was sorry I ran, afterwards, on account of I've got things to tell you—"

"Whitty, those trucks!" Daisy said, pointing. "Where's this band going?"

"Over by Meadow Lake. Going to give concerts there all day."

"Whitty," Daisy said, "I want to go over that way. We're going for Cherry. Can you wangle a ride for us, and tell us things on the way? You see, Sam and I are trying to make sense of things."

"That's why I tried to find you again, after I ran away," Whitty said, "but there was too many crowds. That's why I been trying to find you since. I said to myself that you'd get to the bottom of this, Daisy. I knew you wouldn't let 'em arrest you. That's why I was sticking with this outfit. I figured it would be a good way to look around for you. Stay right here while I fix it up with my friend to give you a lift."

"What *is* this outfit?" Sam asked.

"Grand Loyal Order of the Sons of Liberty," Whitty said. "I used to belong. Boy, was I glad when I saw 'em! I marched right over and give 'em the grip. I give 'em my cousin's name. He used to be National Wing Commander. So they asked me to join 'em. Seems some of the boys got lost from last night, and they wanted to make a good show. But I figured the drum was safer than just marching. Wait here—and say, I got plenty to tell you!"

"I bet," Sam said, as Whitty bustled off, "I bet he's a Mason, and a Bison, and an Elk, and—"

"And I bet," Daisy said, "that he can fix up rides with any of 'em. You can laugh at him if you want to, but I think he's coped rather well with things. Should we tell him what we thought he was, or shall we just keep silent over the picture-thief fiasco? Oh, Sam, he's got a camp chair for me to sit on in the truck. And, Sam, I see lunch baskets!"

How she accomplished it, Sam couldn't figure out. But before the trucks started up, Daisy had been served a regal lunch by the Liberty Boys.

"What are you grinning about?" Daisy asked him.

"Something I was told once about your son," he said. "Harris said, 'Boy has a certain charm. It's not his smile nor his manner, but there's something about him that makes people enjoy doing things for him. It makes 'em feel good. He never seems to manage or wangle, but people do exactly what he wants, and they love it.'"

"Boy is like that," Daisy said. "I've always wondered how he did it. Grab Whitty, Sam. We're starting. Whitty, come tell me things. When were you arrested?"

"Way back there, in front of the diorama—"

"What was it, by the way?" Sam asked.

"It was swell," Whitty said. "It wasn't what I expected, but it was swell. A relief map, like, of New York. Forty feet high and a couple hundred feet long, and the lights go off and on. And there I was, looking at it and minding my own business, and I heard that announcement about us being wanted, over the radio. And then this pair of troopers come and grab me and tell me to come quickly. They wanted me for picture stealing! I tell you, I was mad!"

"So you beat it?"

"I sure did. I was so mad, I could of run away from Glenn Cunningham. I went straight to Cassell's building, but he wasn't there, and then I took a rickshaw back to the train. I didn't know about the murder then, but something told me not to go down to the train. So I stayed up by the platform. I thought the cops had made a mistake, and I wanted Cassell to do something about it. Then, when I seen that bunch of cops going down to the car, and the troopers all around, then I was glad I played my hunch, I tell you! I knew then there was real trouble. Then when I heard 'em talking about a body, I knew there'd been a murder. And say, I didn't know what to do. I said to myself there wasn't anything to run away from. But on the other hand, that business of the tickets and getting on the train, that's going to sound crazy to the cops, I said."

"What did you do?" Daisy asked.

"Well, while I was thinking, I was chewing on a cigar, and I tipped my hat on the back of my head,

148

and I had my thumbs stuck in my vest—you know how I mean. And there's some suspender badges I wear of a lodge up home, and I guess they showed. Because this trooper comes up to me and looks me over, and asks if I'm one of Cassell's guards. I said sure I was, and started talking with him."

Daisy nodded as Whitty talked on. She knew just exactly how Whitty had proceeded. In his bluff, hearty manner, without even bothering to act, he would have pumped the trooper dry.

"And when he got to this murdered man's eyebrows," Whitty continued, "let me tell you, I sat up and took notice. Because I stood outside that train gate a long time yesterday before I made up my mind to go. I didn't make up my mind till I saw you and Sam and Cherry. I said to myself, you were nice-looking folks, and I decided to chance it, right there at the last minute, like. And say, I saw this fellow the trooper described. He was outside the train gate home in Boston. You couldn't make any mistake about that. Grey suit, black hat, and the rest."

"Did he follow us down?" Sam demanded.

"No," Whitty said. "I didn't see him follow you, or get on, but he was hanging around the gate. And do you know what? Madame Duplain knows him!"

Sam whistled.

"This," he said, "begins to percolate. Gert and her suitcase—"

"That always bothered me, that suitcase," Whitty

said. "And the way she plays poker—say, I never seen a woman to touch her! Well, sir, she stood outside the gate there, too, just like I was standing. And when she saw this fellow in the grey suit, she kind of moved away, down to the next track. You know how you kind of edge out of sight of folks you don't want to have to talk with? Like that. After she saw him go, she sort of strolled back. She watched you folks, too, and she got on board when I did. She was looking over her shoulder, too. I think she was watching for that man. What do you think of that?"

"I think," Daisy said, "that it's very interesting. Very. How about Cassell, Whitty?"

"Cassell," Whitty said, "there's somebody I don't know what to think about. If you'd asked me early this morning, I'd of said that guy had a heart as big as a wash basin. But what do you suppose he had the nerve to tell the cops?"

"I'm willing to wager," Daisy said, "that he disowned us, publicly."

"That trooper told me that Cassell said that we were all conspirators in a gigantic plot against him!"

"What a lovely ring that phrase has!" Daisy said. "I suppose he said that Andrew was at the foot of it?"

"Andrew and business rivals," Whitty said. "And picture thieves. He told those cops, Cassell did, that he'd accepted the bunch of us at our face value. He thought we were nice folks that'd got bamboozled. But now he realized that he was the one that got bamboozled, instead. Why, say, to hear that trooper tell what Cassell said about us, you'd think we were a dirty bunch of crooks—well, here we are. I guess that's where we're to play, over at that stand. Now, I can't leave right off—s'pose you meet me over beyond that roller coaster, huh?"

Daisy thanked the Liberty boys for her lunch and for her ride.

"And I'm coming back for your concert tonight," she added. "And don't forget, you promised to play 'The Pink Lady' for me!"

As she and Sam started off toward the roller coaster, Daisy watched Whitty bustling about in his ill-fitting scarlet trousers and gold-bedecked tunic. Every few steps he reached up and grabbed at the busby to keep it from toppling off.

"Well?" Sam asked quizzically. "Have you heard enough ramifications to feel that the solution of all this isn't something you toss off in an afternoon? Are you discouraged yet? Are you willing to be put on a nice train for Boston?"

She didn't appear to hear him.

"A great deal more has been going on," she said, "than I had the wit to realize. Boy says it's easier to report a war a hundred miles away from it than in the front line. And we've not only been in the front line, but we didn't know we were there. We really are in a most absurd position."

"And you want to take a nice train—"

"If anyone finds out about you," Daisy continued, "and about Glue following, it could be assumed that you were being followed for a purpose. And that you, in order to escape some possible consequences, killed him."

She paused.

"Oh, don't mind my feelings," Sam said. "Go right on with your theorizing—I hope it *is* theorizing! I shouldn't like to have you think I'm a murderer."

"I don't," Daisy said, "but a very good case could be made against you."

Sam smiled.

"When you come right down to it," he said, "everyone has a good case, probably. Some of Cassell's staff find an intruder, say, and shoot him. Take Cherry. How do we know she isn't mixed up with Glue? How do you know she didn't shoot him? No, don't gasp and don't interrupt. How do you know? You haven't seen her for a long while. You don't know what she's been doing, do you? You—"

"I'd sooner think of suspecting you," Daisy said, "than Cherry! If—well, if someone like Eggy were found shot, that might be different. Cherry can fly off the handle when she's mad. But—merciful heavens, Sam, we were together, Cherry and I!"

"Please don't get so worked up," Sam said. "I only wanted to show you what a swell bunch of suspects there is. Take Gert. Take the way she plays poker. Whitty says she knew Glue. Take that suitcase. You've got a lot right there, Daisy. And then Brother Whitty. Whitty may be the Elks' left ear and the Masons' right eye, but he still looks like the man who built the silo over the chopped-up ladies. Hadn't we better stay right here and wait for him?"

Daisy sighed. "Yes. Sam, it seems a million years since I saw Egleston kissing Fannie behind the door."

"I thought her name was Elfrida."

"If you mean his wife, it is. But Elfrida's not the type who gets kissed behind doors." Daisy sighed again and shook off the memory of the Early American house, with its smell of dichloricide and beef tea. "Now we'll have to find General Sherman and Gert, after Cherry—"

"Daisy, how did she get this uniform of mine away from the guide?"

"I thought she simply bribed him. She disappeared into the garage with him, and when she came back, she had the uniform. But—well, I don't know."

"If you just start pondering on what she might have done," Sam said, "it'll send shivers loping along your spine."

Daisy nodded.

"I'm worrying about Cherry," she said. "If whoever hired her to distribute those tickets should find out that she—is double-cross the word I want? Well, if that man should find out, it's just possible that he might be angry enough to take steps concerning her. After all, if there were plans behind that ticket business, she certainly spoiled them by giving the tickets to us. And then there's that gun of Whitty's."

"What?"

"Don't yell, Sam, people will look at you and start asking where places are. Yes, he carries a gun, didn't you notice? I didn't last night, but I did notice it just now, while he was bustling about. Those trousers of his do fit so badly. It's in his hip pocket. Oh, yes, I'm sure it's a gun. Once during prohibition, Boy was being pursued by bootleggers—that was a trying period! I learned then how to look for guns. In shoulder holsters, and coat pockets, and all. Of course, the gun may not mean a thing."

"No, of course not," Sam said. "Probably he's just carrying it to quell that bearskin. Or shoot a few squirrels with. Didn't Boy ever tell you that people don't carry guns for fun? Say, maybe that's what Gert has in her suitcase!"

"I don't think so," Daisy returned. "It doesn't rattle. I lifted it once when she wasn't looking. Where is that man Whitty! Sam, tell me about Mrs. Bottome's yesterday, and all that."

"You keep harping back to that so!" Sam said. "First I chased around with the rest of the boys, and got nowhere. Then I had a swell idea. I posed as a guy from the picture dealer's. But I didn't get to first base. Daisy, lean toward me and cover your face with your hand, and look out over the lake as though you were watching the speed boats—that's right. Hold it."

"Who," Daisy said resignedly, "is it now?"

"Lizzie St. Clair Trimmingham," Sam said, "with a delegation of lady culture lovers, all set to ride roller coasters after a bout with the World of Tomorrow."

"What do they look like?"

"Oh, they've each got two legs, and two arms—"

"What have they got on?"

"There's one in a natty brown bombazine, and another in that nasty shade of green. Cabbage green—"

"Sam, this is no time for whimsy! If that is a crowd from some club I belong to—have they any distinguishing features?"

"None," Sam said. "I never saw a less distinguished group. They have little pink feathers stuck on their hats. Would that mean anything?"

Daisy shuddered.

"It's the Women Consumers," she said. "They fuss about labels on cans and the tensile strength of sheets. I don't belong, but Elfrida does. Oh, Sam! Maybe Elfrida—of course, she never said a word to me about it, but she wouldn't have. She'd have known I'd have made a fuss about going along with her. Sam, with me in a horse pond, she'd never have left. But suppose they finally guessed I'd popped over here! Sam, I'm in agony! Of course if Lizzie came, Elfrida would come. She always does things that Lizzie does. Sam, is there a tall statuesque blonde in that group? Are they near? Can I look?"

"No, they're almost on top of us. Keep looking at

the boats. No, I don't see any tall statuesque blonde, but maybe we'd better leave. We can always find Whitty with the Liberty Boys. Daisy, take this handkerchief and hold it to your face. You've got a toothache. Now, I'm going to put my arm around you, and we're going to make a sharp right turn. Don't you dare let your curiosity get the better of you and look at 'em! They're already sufficiently interested in you. Now, start—"

As they swung around on the sharp right turn, Mrs. Trimmingham detached herself from the group of women and stalked over to them.

"Take my purse!" Daisy spoke with difficulty from under the orange handkerchief. "Initials on it!"

"Guide!" Mrs. Trimmingham said in her major-general voice, the voice usually described as being audible to the farthest corner of the auditorium. "Guide, we want—"

"I wonder if you'd excuse me, madam?" Sam said, standing between Daisy and Mrs. Trimmingham. "Miss Flint has a badly ulcerated tooth, and I'm taking her to a first aid station. She's in severe pain."

"That's too bad," Mrs. Trimmingham said. "We want a woman guide. If she's in pain, young man, she should not hold that dirty handkerchief against her face like that. The dirty handkerchief probably contains germs, and clutching her face will only accentuate the pain. I think I'd better help you take her to the station."

"That's very kind of you," Sam said, "but that would make you miss the governors and Mr. Whalen, and you have such a fine vantage point. But if you don't mind missing—"

"Missing them? What do you mean?" Mrs. Trimmingham snapped at the bait.

"They'll be here," Sam looked at his wrist watch, "in eighteen minutes, madam. Didn't you know? The governors, and their suites."

"It doesn't say anything about it in the program. I've read the program thoroughly, and I know there's nothing like that in it!"

"Surprise visit, madam," Sam said promptly. "If you'll look down there, you'll see where that band has formed to meet them. See them, in the scarlet trousers and white coats and bearskins?"

"Well," Mrs. Trimmingham said, "they certainly look as if they were waiting for someone, and we do have a fine place to see everything. Are you sure you can manage alone, young man? And don't let anyone try to pull that tooth until the swelling has gone down, and the area x-rayed by a competent person. What did you say the name of this woman is?"

"Flint." Sam made a prodigious effort of memory.

"Well, Miss Flint, if you recover to the extent of being able to resume your work, please ask for me at the Consumers' Building. Mrs. Lizzie St. Clair Trimmingham. And the first aid station is *that* way!"

Obediently, Daisy and Sam went that way.

Then, after elaborate circlings, they turned and set out toward the Old English Village.

"Now," Daisy said, "we've got to find Wecker."

"Who?"

"Wecker Jacobs."

"Is that Cherry's beau?"

"One of 'em. For a while he practically lived at our house. He's—er—a brilliant youth, and if he's saved Cherry from the police, we must be nice to him. Don't make any suggestions if he needs a haircut or a clean collar, Sam. He's—"

"He's above such things. I see," Sam said. "I shall be very polite to him, Daisy. Where do we go, or don't you think this is the place?"

"It's the only thing that looks even remotely Old English," Daisy said. "It must be. Yes, there's the theater, that circular open air thing to the left—"

"Daisy!"

Daisy recognized Cherry's voice before she recognized the girl herself in her costume of farthingale, stomacher and plumed cap.

"Daisy, I've been waiting for hours! I've been nearly crazy worrying for you! Did you get back to the train? Do you know what's happened?"

"We didn't get back to the train," Daisy said, "but we know."

"D'you know everything? Have you seen Elfrida yet?"

158

"Elfrida? Oh, how perfectly horrible! Is she here, after all? Oh, isn't that awful!"

"I saw her," Cherry said. "D'you know everything?"

"Yes. Sam saw Glue."

"Saw who?"

"Glue. You know. That man who was following him yesterday. Didn't you know that it was Glue who'd been shot?"

"Glue?" Cherry said in a small voice. "Glue? Oh! Oh, then you don't know! Oh, this—this is simply ghastly! It wasn't Glue, Daisy!"

"It is," Sam said. "I saw him. It's Glue, the man who was following me."

"Look," Cherry said desperately, "I was with Cassell on the train when he unlocked that office and went in and found the man! I know! I know who it is, Sam. And it isn't Glue! Oh, I don't know any way to break it to you gently, Daisy!"

"My dear," Daisy said, "if you have anything to break, break it. Nothing is as bad as being kept on pins and needles like this! Who is it?"

Cherry swallowed.

"It's Egleston," she said.

7

Good God!" Sam swung around and stared at Daisy. "Your nephew Egleston? The fellow you were running away from? But it couldn't be! Not unless there's two of him!"

Cherry's elbow dug into his ribs.

Daisy had winced and closed her eyes at Cherry's news. As Sam stepped closer to her and took her arm, he saw that her face was set and immobile. But she wasn't going to faint. Boy Tower's mother wasn't the fainting kind.

When she spoke, she spoke in that calm, icy voice that had frightened Sam a little, the few times he'd heard it. A lesser woman would be having hysterics, Sam thought. And perhaps hysterics might be easier to take than that silent calm.

"Poor Egleston!" Daisy said. "No matter what sort of hole he was in, he didn't deserve this. It *was* Egleston, Cherry? You're sure?"

Sam frowned as Cherry nodded. Cherry knew it was

Egleston, and he was equally positive that the body was Glue. But they couldn't be the same.

"He must have been mixed up in something perfectly frightful," Daisy went on in that calm voice. "Why didn't he tell me? Why didn't he let me know? I've helped him before. I could help again."

"First," Cherry said, "I wondered if he'd followed you and me onto the train, and then I realized that was impossible. He'd have been stopped, and he'd certainly have had us stopped. And then I decided that we were right yesterday. Eggy's in a money jam again, and he was running away."

"Like that time he phoned us he'd gone to Quebec and was going to shoot himself because he owed Frank Hogarth all that money," Daisy said.

"Yes. And you talked with him till I got the hotel on another phone and warned them, and then got Frank—"

"It's the Foss blood," Daisy said. "His mother's family were so erratic. Cherry, that must be it. He'd just lost his grip and was running away, and he landed on Cassell's train, and whoever or whatever he was running away from just caught up with him. He must have got by the guards, and stowed away."

She didn't sound, Sam thought, as if she really believed that. She sounded more as if she wanted to believe it. More than likely, if it had been Egleston, he had recognized his aunt in the station and followed her on the train to get money from her.

161

Daisy seemed to read his thoughts.

"The case that could be made out against me," she said, "is rather staggering, isn't it? Eggy was at his wit's end for money. He followed his wealthy aunt on the train. Wealthy aunt is seen wandering around the corridor, presumably in search of her far-seeing glasses, and later, her nephew is found murdered in a room off that corridor."

"My case is better," Cherry said. "You resented Eggy, but you tolerated him. I disliked him intensely. After the year I've put in, I've got a motive for shooting Eggy. I had just as much opportunity as you— look, Daisy, don't you want to sit down, or something?"

"I'm not grief-stricken," Daisy said. "I think this is awful, and I'll confess I'm nervous—it's enough to make anyone nervous! But I'm not shattered. Cherry, you're positive it was Egleston, and Sam knows it was Glue. So—"

"Let me describe Glue," Sam said. "You never saw him, Cherry—"

"Yes, I did. Daisy pointed him out to me yesterday when he was rushing for a cab. There's not a thing alike between Glue and Eggy except they both wore grey suits and black hats. They aren't a bit alike."

Sam pulled Cherry and Daisy a little farther away from the mob that was surging about the entrance to the Old English Village.

"Listen to me," he said. "The person you and Daisy

saw and thought was Glue, he was just some man who happened to have on a grey suit and a black hat. The real Glue, the man who followed me, had light brown hair, eyebrows so light that his eyes seemed bulgy, a thin upper lip, and a sort of thick underlip that gave him a sulky expression—"

"But that's Egleston!" Cherry cried out.

"If only I'd thought!" Daisy said. "You talked about Glue's eyebrows, and so did Whitty—if only I'd thought to ask you more! But Egleston never entered my head, any more than I'd have thought of Boylston if you'd said that Glue had a pug nose."

"Why should you?" Sam asked. "Why should you have guessed? You couldn't have. But it's shot your theory of Egleston running away from his money troubles—by the way, is it a habit of his, to bolt at intervals?"

"He only did it once. That time he went to Quebec. He'd borrowed a lot of money to cover his losses, and he'd brooded over everything so much that he lost his grip. He just cracked. It wasn't his business, but his own personal affairs—"

"Anyway," Sam said, "it shoots your theory of his rushing off in a frenzy. Shoots it into a cocked hat."

"Why?" Cherry demanded.

"Because," Sam said, "out of this infernal mess, just a few things emerge. Egleston was Glue, and it was Egleston who was trailing me like a leech yesterday."

"Why? Did you know Egleston?" Cherry asked.

163

"Well, if you didn't know him, what in the world would he be trailing you for? Why should Eggy trail *you?*"

"That," Sam said gently, "is what I've been asking myself wonderingly since yesterday afternoon. But he was trailing me. Me, and not you and Daisy. He'd have stopped you two——"

"The sight of me alone would have been sufficient," Daisy said. "He'd have led me home by the ear. Cherry, did you say Elfrida was here?"

"Yes, darling. With Trimmingham, and a bunch from some club. I couldn't believe my eyes. I thought she was back in New England dragging horse ponds for you."

Daisy sighed.

"I know what happened. Elfrida wanted to come to the Fair because Lizzie was coming, and when someone suggested that I might have run off to the Fair, Elfrida jumped at the chance to combine business and pleasure. So she came over with Lizzie and the others, no doubt consoling herself that with accommodations so scarce, it was better to come with them. She's probably been told about Egleston, and that's why she wasn't with the rest of the group when we saw them, Sam."

"I don't think she knows," Cherry said.

"What!"

"I'm sure she doesn't. She didn't look like a bereaved widow when I saw her. She looked vivacious—as vivacious as Elfrida could ever look. And—"

"She doesn't know!" Daisy said. "But of course she must! You don't suppose she thinks that Eggy is just off on his usual week-end fishing trip!"

"But no one knows," Cherry said. "No one knows who he is. At least, they hadn't found out up to the time I got away from the train—Daisy, as I live and breathe, there's Lizzie headed this way, with her lady delegates! They *would* come here, wouldn't they? We'll have to beat it—here, follow me in—"

Hurriedly, Cherry led them around to a side entrance of the village. After a briefly heated discussion with doormen, she ushered them into a tiny dressing room.

"Now," Daisy sat down on a green stool, "tell us everything. What do you mean, no one knows that it's Egleston? Why not? He always carries dozens of licenses and identification cards in his wallet."

"There wasn't a thing, Daisy. Labels all taken out of his clothes, no wallet, no papers, no cards, absolutely nothing. You see, I'd come back with Cassell, and Brand told me you had some plan for finding me, and while I was getting to the root of that complicated phoning and re-phoning business, Cassell went into his office and found the body. And I rushed in and looked, and gasped—I was so shocked and startled that I couldn't talk. Which was terribly fortunate for me, because if I'd said that it was Eggy—well, it's just too awful to think about. And Brand asked who he was, and Cassell said he didn't know, and for Brand to find out. And Brand called the police, and then came back and sort of gingerly hunted for a wallet, and there wasn't any—"

"Should they have touched him?" Daisy asked Sam.

"As long as they didn't move him around," he said. "After all, they had every right to find out who the man was. Cherry, didn't you tell 'em?"

"I couldn't," Cherry said. "I simply couldn't. I know it was wrong of me, but—how could I stand there and say that was Egleston Tower, and the person Cassell knew as Mrs. Days was Egleston Tower's aunt, and I was the aunt's companion that Egleston had fired—how could I go into all that? With Cassell ranting around the way he ranted last night. And that business of the tickets, and our being on the train!"

"I understand," Sam said. "I know just what you felt. You weren't in the ideal position to make any disclosures of a startling nature."

"I was not. My first thought was to get hold of Daisy, and to get out of the place before the police came and started asking questions. So I slipped out of the office—"

"Wait now," Daisy said, "where had you gone with Cassell that you were coming back with him?"

"I waked up early," Cherry said, "and got dressed. I didn't wake you, because you were sleeping so happily. And I went out, and met Cassell, and he asked me if I could type. I said certainly, could I do any typing for him? And he said that Roberts had been fired. He said it more nicely, of course. Something about dispensing with Roberts' services. Anyway, Cassell needed some work done, and I said I'd be glad to do it for him. I wasn't glad to at all, but under the circumstances I thought I ought to sing for my supper, and the trip. So Cassell champed around on the platform while I had toast and coffee, and then we rushed over to his office—doesn't that building of his look like a mashmallow with an hourglass on top?"

Daisy nodded thoughtfully. "What did you do for him?"

"Took dictation, wrote letters, did some filing, tidied up his private office, put flowers in vases, got his radio put up just where he wanted it, tracked down a delivery man who had books for his bookcase, mended a tear in his coat pocket—"

"Little Miss Fixit," Sam said.

"Was I ever! I was dying to look at the Fair, and I barely got a chance to look out the window. It rather annoyed me, because there seemed to be other girl secretaries there, for all it's Sunday. I know why his secretaries leave, his own personal ones, I mean. It's not the amount of work, or the fact that he tells you a string of things to do at once, but he just gives orders without any explanations. It's not, 'Put that radio there because it looks better,' or 'Tell the man to put those cartons of books by the bookcase and we'll unpack them tomorrow,' but 'Put that there!' 'Put this here!' 'Move this around!' It made me feel like a gear being shifted. But I can see how he's got ahead in the world. He knew just exactly what he wanted done, and he began having me do it the minute his hat was off."

"I can't see why he should take you," Daisy said, "if he had some of his office staff there. Hm. Was the office on the train locked when you and Cassell returned?"

"I think so. It seems to me Brand unlocked it. I wouldn't know."

Daisy looked at Sam, but he didn't seem to notice what Cherry had said. If Cassell had had a key to the office, he would have given it to Brand, and Cherry probably would have remembered that. But if Brand just unlocked the office, Brand had a key. Perhaps her fantastic thought that Stragg had taken that key from Sam's pocket was right.

"Did you get away before the police came?" she asked Cherry.

"No, but Brand smuggled me off—"

"Brand?" Daisy said. "Brand did?"

"It's all because of that gold charm you gave him," Cherry said. "And the trylon I bought—"

"You bought the trylon?" Sam said. "The way people used to buy Brooklyn Bridge?"

"Haven't you seen those little models of the trylon

and perisphere that people are selling? Why, where've you been? They're all over the place."

"We've hardly had the time, my dear," Daisy said, "to delve into the souvenir angle."

"Well, neither did I. I just grabbed it before Cassell and I started back to the train. I thought I'd give it to you as a present, because I'd ripped off without telling you where. But Brand looked at it so hungrily, I gave it to him instead. He seemed very moved. I think Brand must lead a dog's life, Daisy. I'm sure he must, after my experience as secretary. Probably he's used to being given huge tips, but these thoughtful, personal little gifts just moved him."

"So he helped you get away before the police came, did he?"

"Oh, no, they'd come. In the first frenzy of excitement, I was sort of thrust into protective custody in my room. But after a few minutes, Brand came in and unlocked me, and said he was sure I hadn't stolen pictures or committed any crimes. I came out, and he locked the room again—"

"That's probably why her name wasn't mentioned as one of the hunted," Sam said. "They thought they had her tucked away. How'd Brand get you away?"

"He sneaked me off the train, and I slid around engines and tracks, and tracks and engines, and we fixed it that when you phoned, he'd suggest theater to you. He said it was a shame that you and I should get mixed up in this—"

"Did he say anything about Sam, or the rest?" Daisy asked.

"No. He was upset, Brand was, but it was decent of him to help me out."

"Did you know Wecky was going to be here?" Daisy asked. "Did you know before we started, I mean?"

"Lord, no, I thought he was painting in Taos. But in Cassell's office, during a breathing spell while Cassell was telephoning about pictures and boxes of books, and writing out memos and orders for his other offices, I relaxed by reading a guide book. And there was Wecky's name. I called him at once on another line—Cassell glared, but after all, I was pinch-hitting, and he couldn't complain. Wecky was overjoyed. He said to come over with anyone I could find, because his cast was shot, and he needed a Romeo and a Juliet. The ones he had got ptomaine, or ran away, or something. I couldn't follow."

"What is this Wecky?" Sam demanded.

"He's one of the artistic left wing," Cherry said with a grin. "I can't find out why he's succumbed to Shakespeare, but probably his salary's got something to do with it. I've a feeling he'd put on *Captain Applejack* if someone paid him enough."

"I see," Sam said. "Left wing, but susceptible to occasional capital gains. What *is* that costume you've got on?"

"This is no costume, this is atmosphere," Cherry smiled as she put her arm around Daisy. "If we didn't

170

have this awful business of Eggy," she added, "we'd have a field day here. They wanted someone to stroll around and be atmosphere, and I jumped at the chance. It was ideal. Somehow it never seemed possible that you'd actually ever get here, but I wanted to be visible if you did. Wecky wants—"

"Does this Wecky know about Egleston?" Sam asked.

"Wecky is putting on a show," Cherry said. "That's the only thing that matters to him right now. You could tell him about twenty murders, and he'd never hear. He—"

Someone banged on the dressing room door, and strode in without pausing.

"My God, Cherry, I've hunted high and low! It does seem you might show me some consideration—is that your Romeo?" He pointed to Sam. "Are you her Romeo?"

"I could be," Sam said. "The question's never arisen before, but since you bring it up, I think that possibly—"

"My God, hasn't she told you the rehearsal's in fifteen minutes? Here, take these!"

He slung an armful of clothes at Sam, who automatically caught them.

"What are these things?"

"French slops. French slops! And don't start yelling for trunk hose, you won't get 'em. My God, French slops are what Shakespeare said, and what he meant, and the hell with Marlowe and Sothern! For once the public gets a Romeo in French slops. You the nurse?"

He pointed to Daisy, who nodded.

"Where've I seen you before? Don't tell me, I know. Boston. That's it. Well, Cherry'll find you a costume. My God, Cherry, find her a costume, will you? Will you do something constructive? Will *some*body do *some*thing constructive?"

The door slammed behind him.

Sam surveyed the clothes with distaste, and dropped them on the floor.

"Pick them up," Daisy said, "and put them on. We've got to get out of these guide outfits, and we might as well take what—"

"Daisy," Sam said, "I don't know what French slops are, but I draw the line at wearing them! The sound of 'em is enough to make a man throw up!"

"Nevertheless," Daisy said, "you retire behind that screen and put them on. Hurry, Sam, please! We've got so much to do, and it's almost three o'clock! Sam, hurry! Cherry, what about the gun? Did you find out anything about that on the train?"

"Didn't I tell you? Oh, I forgot. There's been so much to tell about, and ask about, and worry about, I can't think very consecutively. That gun business seemed to infuriate Cassell as much as finding Egleston. You see, there wasn't any gun."

Sam, forgetting his state of undress, swung around and walked over to them.

172

"No gun? You're crazy! I know there's a gun!"

"Egleston was shot," Cherry paused and glanced at Daisy. "He was—"

"I wish you wouldn't try to spare me details," Daisy spoke in her calm voice. "Go on."

"He was shot through the heart. At least," Cherry made a gesture, "in the left part of his chest. He was shot twice—"

"Twice?" Daisy interrupted. "That sounds as though someone were making very sure, doesn't it?"

"You—well, you could see," Cherry said. "But there wasn't any gun in the office."

"There was last night," Sam said. "My foot hit it. Daisy, what do you make of that?"

"Probably the same person who removed the labels, and the papers and the wallet, and all the things that might have identified Egleston at once, probably that person also removed the gun. Sam, finish changing and get Whitty from the Liberty Boys and bring him here."

Sam's eyes narrowed.

"Look," he said, "you don't think that the gun you thought he had in his pocket—well, if it was a gun, certainly you don't think it's *the* gun?"

"If I'd shot anyone," Daisy said, "I personally would have tossed the gun out of the window at once. Or I'd have hurled it into Meadow Lake this morning. I'd have disposed of it, anyway. But a gun is missing, and Whitty has a gun, and there's no harm investigating."

"Suppose," Sam said from behind the screen, "that Whitty never meant to meet us. Suppose he just intended to beat it—"

He struggled with the slops, and won.

"Take it from the other side, Sam," Daisy said. "If Whitty were a murderer, would he still be here at the Fair, carrying bass drums, getting us lifts in trucks, playing around with the Liberty Boys? It doesn't seem that he would—good Lord, let me see you! So those are French slops! Well, Sam, I can positively assure you that nobody will pay any attention to your face. And I'd take off the Harold Lloyd glasses, I think."

"Don't laugh at him, he looks fine," Cherry said. "You have nice legs, Sam, and those slops just set you off. And don't be afraid anyone'll run after you and make wisecracks, because there are really much funnier costumes running around. And have that doorman give you a pass—"

The door slammed behind Sam with more violence than it had slammed behind the temperamental Wecky.

"There goes a man in a dudgeon," Cherry said. "Daisy, I can't be gay and casual about this a minute longer. I'm frightened to death! It seems to me that everyone I've seen all day long has been hunting for me, waiting to grab me—it's ghastly!"

"I know," Daisy said.

174

"And it's worse for you—oh, we've always laughed about Eggy, but after all he's your nephew—"

"One of my few consoling thoughts," Daisy said, "is that he isn't. There, I've said it, and I've wanted to say it for years. But he never looked or acted like the Towers, and even though I'm casting aspersions on the wife of my own brother—what a mercy he's not alive to know about this! Well, Cherry, the Foss family were an unprincipled lot. That sums it up. But Egleston's paternity isn't the point now. The point is that he's been murdered, and I've got to do something about it."

Cherry took off her plumed cap and played nervously with a broken feather.

"Obviously, Eggy needed money," Daisy went on. "That's why he rented my house and sold the cars. And he must have needed money for something that wasn't entirely honest or proper, or I would have been asked to contribute. In short, he was mixed up in something shady. And he was following Sam. If only I could get some connection—Cherry, what do you think of Sam?"

"He seems pleasant enough."

Daisy nodded. That meant, she knew, that Cherry thought Sam was something very special indeed. If Cherry hadn't thought so, she would have gone into the matter at some length.

"I thought so, too. Cherry, I want a phone. I want to find out why Sam was fired."

"What's that got to do with things?" Cherry asked.

"I don't know. But he was fired, and shortly after, he was followed, and even if he doesn't think that the two are connected, I don't see why they shouldn't be. Hurry, child. Where's a phone?"

"What are you in such a rush for? You rushed Sam, you—"

"Because," Daisy said, "I learned from Boy, long ago, that it is unwise to discount the police. Sometimes, like Wecky, it looks as though they did their best to take the hard way. But very shortly, if they've not done so already, they'll find out who Egleston is. They'll find out I'm missing. Someone will put two and two together, and turn Mrs. Days of Cassell's train into Daisy Tower, Egleston's aunt. So we've got to hurry, because we've got to beat the police to it. We've got to find out who killed Egleston."

"How are you going at it?"

Daisy thought for a moment.

"There's only one thing I know very much about," she said. "That's human nature. And I admit that I still get fooled by it now and then, even after sixty-seven years. But there's one thing I'm not often fooled about. I know when a person lies. There are remarkably few good liars in this world. Boylston is one. You, on the other hand, lie badly."

"I can lie—"

"But not well, Cherry. A good liar has to have more than just imagination and inventiveness. Having told

176

one lie, he must bolster it up with another, and he must continue to bolster and pyramid. And he must be able to get the past straight as well as the future. He has to revise fact as well as to create it. And above all, he must create the illusion of reality."

"You mean, local color," Cherry said. "I think I do grand local color, Daisy!"

"You do too much, dear. That's where you fell down when you told me about the hall bedroom you were living in. Where have you been living, now that we're on the topic?"

Cherry walked over to the window.

"In a select home for lady derelicts," she said. "Thirty-three to a layer, two layers to a room. Uppers and lowers, canvas on racks. I've killed Eggy Tower in my mind every night for months. Where did I go wrong on the hall bedroom?"

"The steel engraving, dear. If a boarding house had 'The Stag at Eve,' it would be in the front hall, or the living room, or maybe even over the sideboard. And the upright piano would have a green cover. Don't think about all that, Cherry. It's over with. Sam's a bad liar, too. He dries up in the middle, or else he goes completely pixie. Dear, what is that thing hanging on the hook?"

Cherry removed the shapeless garment.

"A sort of dirndl," she said. "I'm sure I don't know what it's doing here."

"Give it to me. And have you a wig?"

"I've got a bonnet with false side-curls," Cherry said. "It was too big for me, but it'll do beautifully for you. So you're going to figure out who's lying?"

"I'm going to try. After I've done some research on the things people would like to lie about."

"Haven't you got to jump to a lot of conclusions?" Cherry asked as she helped Daisy off with the guide's dress.

"No," Daisy said, "I think it's better to say that we haven't time to explore side roads. We've got to assume that someone on that train killed Eggy. It's possible that's not true. But facts like the train schedule not being known, and the doors being locked, and Cassell's guards being around—all those things have got to outweigh the possibility of an outside murderer. Twitch that hook into the eye, will you?"

"I suppose you can rule out the servants," Cherry said. "Eggy wouldn't know them. And that leaves us. I—Daisy, I didn't. I—oh, damn, I pricked my finger!"

"There's a handkerchief in my purse," Daisy said, "and please don't start crying. You'll start me crying, and we'll never get anywhere. Speaking of local color, Cherry, does it occur to you that we've had local color since we stepped on to that train? Think it over. And have you any money? I want to phone, and I haven't a cent."

"Neither have I," Cherry said, "but Wecky has. He jingles with money."

While Cherry went out to relieve Wecky of some

of his jingling cash, Daisy sat before the dressing room mirror and looked thoughtfully at herself.

Those fantastic thoughts kept running in and out of her mind, and they bothered her. They frightened her.

"I'm going to call Standish," she said when Cherry returned. "Not that editor of Sam's."

"Standish? That darling old duck with the wing collar and spats who lived on Lime Street? Why call him?"

"He owns that paper. No, you'd never think it to look at him, but he's a malefactor of great wealth and a distorter of public opinion. Where's the phone booth? Has it got a chair? I may be some time."

Mr. Standish, aroused from his Sunday afternoon nap, was inclined to be irritable until Daisy convinced him of her identity.

"No," she said, "of course I'm not calling from a horse pond! I'm at the World's Fair! Well, if you thought I would be, why did you let people print that trash? All right, but not till tomorrow. I'll give you a beautiful story, but not till tomorrow. Now, you can have that pewter jug of mine you covet so, if you'll promise on your word of honor to keep quiet about me, no matter what you hear. Yes, I thought you would. Now, be a dear and find out for me why your man Harris fired a reporter named Samuel Minot. M for Minot's Light."

Laboriously, she spelled the name out.

"He's a friend of Boy's—oh, you know him? You know all about that? Oh, you had him fired? Why? Operator, don't cut—all right, all right, wait till I find my change!"

She dropped most of it on the floor twice before she managed to pay for her extra time.

"All right, Standish," she said. "They took so much time getting you to the phone—now, let me get this straight. Cassell called you, himself. And you fired Sam at his request. You fired him at once, because you didn't want any trouble with Cassell before his advertising contract was renewed. I see. You think that Sam is able? What a lovely way you took to show him! Oh. You mean to hire him again after Cassell's advertising is set. I see. Why do I want to know? My dear man, I wish I had the time and the money to tell you! Of course I will. You'll get that jug just as soon as I get home. Good-bye."

Daisy sat for several minutes in the phone booth after replacing the receiver. Then she counted her change and called Standish again.

"Yes, me again," she said. "Why would my nephew Egleston Tower be following that reporter, Sam Minot?"

Standish's laugh irritated her, and so did his counter-question.

"No, I am not at the bottom of any horse pond!" she retorted with asperity. "And I asked you, why

180

would Eggy follow that reporter? Why would he be trailing Sam Minot?"

His answer was identical with her own conclusion, that Egleston had probably done no such thing.

Daisy sighed as she hung up.

"I thought you were there for life," Cherry told her when she came out of the booth. "But really, it didn't take you so very long. Did you find out anything?"

"I found out that Sam was fired for the plain and simple reason that he punched Cassell's secretary, and tried to steal some papers yesterday while he was trying to get an interview with Cassell. At that Bottome woman's. They threw Sam out, and Cassell found out what paper he was from, and called Standish, and told him all about it, and suggested that the reporter be fired. And Standish promptly called the paper and said to fire the reporter who annoyed Cassell. Later, Standish found out it was Sam. That disheartened him, because he thinks Sam is able. But Standish is going to wait till Cassell signs some advertising renewals before he rehires Sam. Standish said that under the circumstances, he would gladly have fired his whole staff to keep Cassell happy and kindly disposed, and in a good humor."

"I don't get it," Cherry said. "Why didn't Cassell recognize Sam? Why didn't he recognize Sam right away, on the train? Why didn't Sam guess why he'd been fired?"

"Sam had on those glasses," Daisy said. "The ones

181

I bought as a disguise to get him past Glue. Cassell didn't recognize him. I can understand it. Those glasses changed him enormously."

"But why didn't Sam guess why he was fired?"

"I suppose that Cassell phoned Standish, and Standish phoned Sam's editor, and he was waiting with Sam's marching orders long before the time Sam called his paper—"

"You mean," Cherry said, "that Cassell actually phoned Standish and told him to have a man fired, and Sam was?"

"Exactly. It seems to me Sam should have got the connection. I think I should have, in his place. But I suppose he was thrown off the track when his editor said that even if he'd got the interview, he was still fired. I should have guessed. On the other hand, I remember Boy once thinking it was queer he was fired, when he blacked his editor's eyes. Both of 'em. He kept saying indignantly, that was a personal issue, and had nothing to do with his work. I suppose Sam felt that punching Cassell's secretary was a matter of similar unimportance."

"In short," Cherry said, "Sam wasn't lying when he said he didn't know why he was fired. But why was Egleston following Sam?"

Daisy smiled, but her eyes were grave.

"Sam claims he doesn't know the reason for that, either. Cherry, don't mention those Boston calls, please. Be sure—I see him coming along the corridor.

182

And he's got Whitty! Whitty, whatever became of you!"

Whitty took off his bearskin and mopped energetically at his dripping brow.

"Gee, Daisy," he said, "I'm glad to get to see you again. When I got over by that roller coaster, you'd gone. I was just telling Sam, I was saving the most important thing for the last, and when I didn't find you, I was sorry I hadn't told you about the gun—whew, it's hot!"

Daisy pointed to the door of the little dressing room. She was hot, too, and tired. But she was not going to let Whitty get away again.

"In there," she said. "Go in, Whitty. You too, Sam and Cherry. Get seated—shut the door, Sam. Whitty, what gun?"

"I got it in my pocket," Whitty said. "My hip pocket. I think it's *the* gun—"

He struggled a moment with his white tunic, and then removed a gun from the pocket of his scarlet trousers.

"Here," he said. "I think it's *the* gun, all right. I'm sure it is. Want to look at it, Daisy? Say, don't you want to look at it? I thought you'd be real interested in it." He sounded hurt. "Isn't it going to mean anything?"

Daisy answered in her calm voice.

"Yes, Whitty, it's going to mean something. But I don't need to look at it. You see, it's my gun."

8

Yours?" Sam asked incredulously. "What makes you think it's yours? How can you tell? How in hell could it be yours anyway? What do you mean, Daisy? Your gun!"

"I do wish," Daisy said, "you'd let me get a word in edgeways, Sam! Where'd you get the gun, Whitty?"

"From the train's garbage pail," Whitty told her. "While I was talking there with that trooper that thought I was one of Cassell's guards, somebody came out with this garbage pail—"

"Who came out?" Daisy interrupted.

"I don't know who. I just saw the man out of the corner of my eye. I didn't dare turn, because I didn't want to be recognized. Anyway, I didn't think anything about it until the light struck something in the pail and it .kind of glittered. You know," Whitty added parenthetically, "I always have to keep my eye on the pails at the store. My partner's awful careless.

184

He keeps losing things in the trimmings. Once he let my best gold pencil—"

"Yes, yes," Daisy said, "you have a habit of scrutinizing garbage pails. Hurry up!"

"Well," Whitty said, "there was this thing catching the light, and the trooper'd said something about a missing gun. So, a few minutes later while he went off to talk to another trooper, I edged over, and there was this gun under some potato peelings. So, I sneaked it out and put it into my pocket and went off with it."

The simplicity of the process struck the group with fully as much force as had Daisy's announcement that the gun was hers.

Whitty mistook the reason for their silence, and became a little apologetic.

"Gee," he said, "maybe I shouldn't have taken it, but if that trooper'd only looked, he'd have seen it himself. Anyone who was near that pail could have seen it, if they'd just looked. Whoever come to collect the garbage couldn't have missed seeing it. Why, if the person that put the gun there wanted someone to find it, he couldn't have put it in a better place. It almost seems like the person who put the gun there wanted it to be found."

"It does," Daisy said. "It does indeed."

"I hope I haven't gone and ruined all the fingerprints," Whitty said anxiously.

"You've probably just added more," Sam said. "Fingerprints are—"

"Fingerprints," Daisy said, "hardly matter to us. We couldn't do anything about fingerprints even if the gun crawled with 'em. Sam Minot, will you stop gaping at me? And don't, please, start asking if the gun is really mine, and how on earth, and all that sort of thing! It *is* mine. It's got my own initials on that little silver plate. See them? It's that Smith and Wesson, Cherry, that—"

"I remember it," Cherry said. "It used to be on the mantel of the library downstairs in the Louisburg Square house."

"Yes. It's the thirty-eight Russian that Boy gave me in Morocco, during the Riff business. I'd gone over to see him, and he insisted that if I insisted on travelling around with him, I had to have a gun. No, no, Sam, of course I don't know how to use a gun! They frighten me. But Boy thought that if anyone saw me waving that thing, they'd very properly rush away and hide behind a rock and decide to kidnap someone else instead of me. Yes, that's my gun. And the last time I saw it, it was on my library mantel. That was over a year ago, the morning of the accident."

"Egleston supervised having the house closed," Cherry said. "I know he did, because he was there when I came to get my things—"

"And he supervised letting it," Daisy said. "And obviously, at one time or another, Egleston took the gun. Cherry, he must have been in a frightful state of mind to be carrying it. He must have had it with him on the train, too, because otherwise the person who shot him would have thrown it away. Yes, that's all clear."

Whitty scratched his head. "I don't get all this, Daisy."

"Don't you see," Daisy explained, "if a gun can't be traced to you, then you don't have to take the trouble to throw it away. If I, myself, had killed someone with that gun, I should throw it as far as I could send it. I'd bury it. I'd get rid of it. But if another person commits a murder with my gun, then they don't have to bother disposing of it. It won't lead anyone back to them. And of course the danger of throwing things away is that people go to such lengths hunting for them. You couldn't ever be sure they wouldn't turn up something else in the process."

"Think," Cherry said rather hysterically, "of what they must have turned up while they hunted you in horse ponds!"

Daisy nodded.

"Exactly," she said. "Now, let's straighten this out. Eggy took the gun from my house. He had it with him on the train. That means Eggy was terrified, because while he's a good fisherman, he's also the world's worst shot. He was so bad he demoralized the local skeet club—remember, Cherry, they asked him to stay away? He flinched, and they claimed he always closed his eyes before he pulled the trigger. Really, this gun throws more light on things, Whitty! It's better than a

187

dozen shreds of Harris tweed, or blonde hairs, or cigar ashes, or any of the clues they always have in books. This really gets us somewhere!"

"I don't get it," Whitty said in his patient chant.

"Eggy," Daisy said, "wouldn't carry a gun because he expected to shoot anyone. He carried this gun because he was afraid. He wanted to have it to protect himself. To wave at anyone he was afraid of. And someone goaded him into waving it, and whoever he waved it at took him seriously, and took the gun away from him, and shot *him* with it. And then the person laid the gun in the garbage, after a while. That," Daisy added, "is very interesting, that garbage pail business. Someone isn't obstructing justice, you see, by removing the gun entirely from the scene. They intend that the gun shall be found, but not at once. If you stop and think, removing the tags from Eggy's clothes and the papers and licenses from his wallet— that was done for the same purpose. The police will be sure to find out who Eggy is, eventually, but removing means of identification will delay them."

"But," Whitty said, wrinkling his forehead, "if someone put the gun in the garbage, and it got found, then—"

"Then," Daisy said, "there are those five unexplained strangers on the train. The ones with that crazy story of tickets. You can be sure it'll be clear to Cassell that one of us, or all of us, put that gun in that pail. You can hardly blame the police for agreeing with him. Yes, the person who is behind all this didn't care if Eggy was identified, or if the gun was found. But they don't want it found out right now. Cherry, Whitty needs to be sewed up, there on the side. Take a needle and patch him up, will you? Sam, we've got to go back and find out about that train."

"I'm glad," Sam said, "that you're finally ready for your nice train to Boston, Daisy. Because you couldn't be referring to the Golden Dart. You *do* mean you're going home, don't you?"

Daisy looked at him, and then she sighed.

"Boston, nothing! Go find some overalls or something to cover up those silly pants, because you and I are going back to the train to investigate, while Cherry and Whitty find Gert and Ali Baba. I think I'll do, with my bonnet and curls and dirndl, but those slops are just too silly—"

"The minute you go near that train," Sam said, "you'll be arrested—"

"Does it occur to you," Daisy asked crisply, "that if Cassell had really gone into action, we would have been arrested by now? Think it over, Sam. Brand let Cherry go. Brand obeys orders. You heard Cassell say as much to Roberts last night. Brand had Cherry, and he let her go. He even told us over the phone where we could find her. All Brand had to do was to tell Cassell or the police to pick us up here. In fact, he could have kept Cherry and laid a trap for us. He could have told us she was at some one spot, and the police could have been waiting for us when we got there. Cassell has a system of giving orders by radio, you said. With that, with trooper, police—why, Sam, we should have been found hours ago, even if we disguised ourselves!"

"I thought that once or twice," Sam said slowly, "and then I decided I was crazy. But don't you think, Daisy, that Cassell still feels there's a plot going on against him, something engineered by that Andrew? And don't you suppose he's asking the police to soft-pedal, so they can get to the root of everything?"

"Cassell may feel that way," Daisy said. "He may think that way. But the fact remains, as long as we are free, we are suspects, and anything that happens is our fault. We're the fall guys, to borrow Gert's phrase. I want to find out why. Maybe we *are* being tools in some plot that Andrew has manufactured against Cassell. Maybe we're being kept dangling at the end of a leash so that Cassell and the police can find who's holding the leash. That's all very well—"

"But if they don't find who's holding the leash," Sam said, "we'll be in a worse jam."

"We certainly shall. Yes, Sam, we're being a string of red herrings for someone, and I've had enough of it. So you and I are going back to the train and investigate. We've pulled ourselves out of a number of holes, today, and we've risen to a number of occasions. I'm sure we can continue. Go find a pair of overalls."

Sam turned, and then paused at the door.

"There's another angle, Daisy. If we were warned that we were being sought for, we wouldn't go back, would we? It's like Whitty running when I grabbed his arm. He didn't really have anything to run for, but he was afraid—"

"I'll say I was," Whitty said. "Aren't you nearly through, Cherry? And go easy with that needle. You're sewing me, not the cloth."

"Yes," Daisy said. "Cherry would tell us, even if we hadn't heard in any other way."

"Suppose," Sam said, "that Comrade Brand has joined up with this Andrew lad and the two of 'em are ganging up on Cassell—"

He stopped short as the door opened and Wecky Jacobs came in. Compared to his previous bombshell entrance, this one had less force than a sheet of tissue paper falling on a snow bank.

Walking over to the window, he sat dejectedly on the ledge and buried his face in his hands.

"What's gone wrong now?" Cherry asked. "There, Whit, you'll hold together now. What's the matter, Wecky? Who's walked out now?'

"I am through," Wecky said, in the sort of voice he might have used to announce the death of his entire family. "The wrong costumes have been brought from the train. Our costumes are on Track Ten. I have given up. Our wardrobe mistress is lost. She knows the cases. The tags on the cases are lost. The truck driver's gone to lunch. I'm going back to Taos."

Sam looked at Daisy, but she had already reacted.

"How soon," she asked briskly, "do you need the costumes?"

"In an hour. But don't give it a thought. I'm going back to Taos—"

"If you'll get Sam some overalls to cover his slops," Daisy said, "Sam and I will get your costumes. I'll know them," she added reassuringly. "I used to be wardrobe mistress in Boston, you know."

Cherry frowned, but Daisy felt secure in that bit of fiction. If Wecky had not recognized her as Mrs. Boylston Tower before, she thought, he certainly wouldn't recognize her in his present frame of mind.

"Overalls in the wings," Wecky said in a tired voice. "Pass in the truck. They had so damn many pictures stolen, all trucks have to have passes." He stood up suddenly. "Look, you don't really think you can get 'em, do you?"

"Certainly," Daisy said.

"Come along," Wecky said to Sam. "I'll get overalls. Come along, come along, hurry up!"

Pushing Sam ahead of him, Wecky left in a spirited flurry.

"In ten minutes," Cherry observed, "he'll stare at you blankly if you mention going back to Taos. Daisy, I was so busy stitching Whitty, I didn't hear half what you and Sam were saying. But you don't mean to go back to that train, do you?"

"Yes. You and Whitty have got to find Gert and Ali

Baba. You can't miss 'em." She described the saffron robes, and the headgear that was neither a fez nor a tarboosh. "You've got to find 'em. Take them over by the Liberty Boys—Whitty knows where they are, over near that modernistic roller coaster near the shore of the lake. Hang on to Gert and Ali Baba. And the car. Now, Sam and I will take the truck and go to the Golden Dart. Then we'll get Wecky's costumes, bring them back here, and then join you. See?"

"It sounds swell," Cherry said. "It sounds pretty efficient, Daisy. But it seems to me there's plenty of room for things to go wrong. Suppose we don't find Gert? After all, how *can* we, Daisy? She and the visiting royalty may be inside the perisphere, for all we know. They may have gone to Atlantic City—"

"If I know Gert," Daisy said, "she's here, and you can find her. Now, you stay with Whitty, and hang on to Gert and Ali Baba, and whatever happens, we'll meet you over by the Liberty Boys. You'll be safe with them. You—there's Wecky yelling for me to hurry—now, you do just what I say, Cherry. Goodbye. Take care of her, Whitty!"

Sam, in greasy overalls, was already behind the wheel of a truck in the courtyard at the rear.

"Don't help me up," Daisy said. "I can make it. There's a visored cap there on the floor, Sam, you'd better put it on. I'll sit on this pile of burlap bags behind you—"

"Are you sure," Wecky asked, "that you'll get back

in time with the costumes? You've got to! You must get back!"

Sam looked at Wecky's quivering nostrils, and grinned.

"Comrade," he said, "you're right. We must get back. And if we do, we'll have the costumes. So long!"

Sam backed the truck out of the courtyard and down a service drive that ran along the rear of the buildings.

"D'you really mean to get his costumes?" he asked Daisy.

She smiled enigmatically.

"The train," she said, "is my first thought. If it should happen that the costumes fit in our plans, all right. If not, I dare say Wecky will manage. Sam, there's something here that's missing—"

"If you mean in this truck," Sam said, "I think those are just natural noises. Something inherent."

"I mean about Egleston," Daisy said. "I've not noticed the truck. There's some connection that I can't think out. It's like remembering a name. Don't you know how often you have names on the tip of your tongue, but you can't say them? Well, that's my trouble. There's something on the tip of my tongue— well, maybe if I think of something else, it'll come to me."

They drove on perhaps three hundred yards when Daisy yelled in his ear, a piercing yell that sent Sam's foot jamming down on the brake.

"Have you remembered—"

"Sam, look over there!"

He followed the direction of her finger, and picked out two saffron-robed figures from a crowd around the rear entrance to a shooting gallery.

They were Gert and General Sherman. There was no mistaking his tall figure, or the suitcase in her hand. That damned, omnipresent, ubiquitous suitcase.

"Pull the truck in this alley," Daisy said, "and go get 'em. Bring 'em here!"

Two minutes later, Gert climbed breathlessly into the truck.

"Daisy," she said, "you'll never know how glad I am to see you. I'd almost given up hope. Ali's a nice lad, but he wears you down—"

"Ali what? Have you found out his name?"

"Ali something," Gert said, "but I call him Al. He's a real prince, Daisy. And he's got oil in them thar hills of his back home, and that's why he's rating all this service. People are after oil contracts. I pumped that much from some Fair official that stopped and chatted with us. I had to explain that the other guide and the interpreter were off doing errands. That was before I changed into Al's spare dress," she pointed to the robes she wore. "Al thinks he'll be gypped on the oil, and I wouldn't be a bit surprised—come on up, Al. Here's an old friend."

In climbing up to the truck, Al was hampered not

so much by his robes as by his trophies, which included a Kewpie doll, two woolen koala bears, several beribboned canes, half a dozen plaster miniatures of the Theme Center, an imitation Hudson Bay blanket, and an ormolu clock.

"Al," Gert said, "is a swell shot. We've been to all the galleries. Help him, Sam. There. Now, sit down, Al—"

"Mother!" Al said joyously, and heaped his trophies at Daisy's feet.

"There," Gert said, "that's the kind of lad Al is. Generous. He bought me a swell lunch—"

"Where are the other two?" Daisy demanded. "And the car? Oh, Gert, where *is* his car? We're in need of that car!"

"Sister Jane and Butch—I couldn't make out their names—they've settled down in the Temple of Love," Gert said.

"The what? Gert, you mean there's one of those things in the World of Tomorrow?" Daisy said.

"Streamlined," Gert said, "and doing a good business. Sister Jane and Butch got on, and they wouldn't get off, so we left them, and we left the car there. We can get it for you, easy. Daisy, I'm so glad I thought right. I decided you'd make tracks over here, because it's easier keeping in the crowd and out of sight in this part. There's so many costumes, no one pays much attention to 'em. Daisy, you didn't run away from that woman a second too soon, back there in the Ford building. She marched over to me and asked what your name was. I said you were a Mrs. Murphy, I thought."

"Sam told her Flint," Daisy said. "You—"

"Did you know," Gert went on, "that pictures have been stolen sort of left and right, Daisy? Not just on Cassell's train, but from his building, and other buildings? Is that all Whitty's work?"

Daisy explained about the mistake she and Sam had made about Whitty's picture.

"So he's no thief, he's just what he said he was, a butcher, and the senior partner of Whitty and Glum. Gert, have you heard about the murder?"

Gert nodded. "We heard, but no one knew who."

Daisy looked at her.

"It's the man," she said slowly, "you saw at the train gate before you got on the Golden Dart last night. The man you avoided."

"You don't mean Egleston Foss!"

"Egleston Foss Tower," Daisy said. "My nephew."

Gert whistled under her breath, and then she winced.

"Are you sure?" she said. "Egleston Foss is a medium-sized fellow, with very light eyebrows, light hair, a sort of peevish face. He had on a grey suit and a black hat yesterday. I was ducking him—this sounds crazy! I was ducking him because he owed me money. The last time I asked for it, he went into a fit. And at the station, I had my own troubles, and I didn't want any fuss raised that would call attention to me. Besides, I knew Foss hadn't any money. He hadn't paid up Tom Mike, and Tom Mike was giving him twenty-four hours to pay."

"If Tom Mike," Sam said, "was giving him twenty-four hours, I can see where he was in a state. Foss gambles, I take it."

"Foss," Gert said, "is the lousiest poker player I ever knew. He's the biggest sucker. But this is bad for me, Daisy. A lot of people heard me promise to give Foss the works if he didn't pay me. And say," she looked at Sam, "was my suitcase—yes, I bet it was. I can tell from the look on your face. Well, that's that. They got a nice case on me!"

"How much," Daisy asked, "would you say Egleston owed?"

"If he owed Tom Mike," Sam said, "he owed plenty, didn't he, Gert?"

She nodded. "Someone told me more than fifty grand, but I wouldn't know for sure. He only owed me five hundred. That sucker! No wonder his wife beats him up and throws electric light bulbs at him!"

Daisy blinked.

That did not sound like Elfrida to her. But if Egleston had another name, very likely he might also have another wife to go with it. It was entirely in keeping with the Foss tradition.

"Is his wife," she asked Gert, "a tall, statuesque blonde, named Elfrida?"

198

She almost knew what the answer was going to be before Gert opened her mouth.

"His wife," Gert said, "is a little redhead named Fannie. She's got the temper of three fiends."

"Fannie," Daisy said, "is the housemaid of his official wife. Hm. I see. I see lots of things. I think I even understand why Egleston never seemed to be weatherbeaten from his fishing trips. Fishing trips! Well, Gert, you've settled a lot of things. We know that Eggy desperately needed a large sum of money, and that he was probably carrying a gun because he was afraid of the people he owed. We know that Elfrida was an injured wife—so it was Fannie who went prowling through my desk! Yes, Gert, you've helped clear up a lot of sundry items. Isn't it amazing! I thought that to solve a murder, you had to have material clues. Things like shreds of Harris tweed, and scraps of paper, and hairpins of a peculiar color and size. But think what we've pieced out, just from odds and ends! If only I could settle you, Sam. Why Eggy was following you, I mean."

"I've told you some ten million times," Sam said, "that I don't know why he was following me! I can't think why. All I know is, he followed me. My God, how he followed me!"

"Can't you connect him with your being fired?" Daisy asked plaintively.

"I can't connect anything with that," Sam said. "Look, you don't want me to go through that again, do you? On my word of honor, Daisy, if I knew the answer to Egleston's trailing me, or to my being fired, I'd tell you. But I can't see that they have anything to do with this business of Egleston being killed—"

"Mother," Al said. "Toots."

"I see, Gert," Daisy said absently, "that Al's vocabulary has increased."

"He's picked up quite a bit," Gert admitted. "Al's not dumb—"

While she went into detail on the topic of Al, his quickness on the uptake, and his ability to pick up a phrase, Daisy sat back on the burlap bags and considered the data she had been storing in her mind.

Sam, she thought, was telling her the truth. He hadn't lied about anything. He had kept back the murder, but that was more because he wanted to shield Boy Tower's elderly mother than anything else. He'd even brushed aside a scoop and the chance of a new job.

Gert was telling the truth. She made no attempt to hide her acquaintance with Egleston. She had made no attempts to gloss either her own life or her own past. There was that suitcase, of course. Daisy would have liked to know the contents of that mysterious suitcase. But that didn't alter the fact that Gert told the truth.

And Whitty told the truth. He was a butcher, and nothing else, unless you counted in his numerous fraternal affiliations.

And Cherry told the truth.

"Gert," Daisy said with a sudden briskness, "which way is Al's car? There? Well, start for it. On your way, see if Cherry and Whitty are in that Old English Village, in the theater part. If they are, take 'em with you, and wind up at the Liberty Boys' bandstand near the roller coaster. If they've gone, get the car and go to the bandstand and wait for me."

"Check," Gert said. "What do the Liberty Boys look like, and what'll we do with Sister Jane and Butch?"

"Leave them on the Temple of Love," Daisy said. "At least, you'll know where to find them, and they might conceivably crowd us, if we have to travel en masse. Tie a tag around their necks—who is paying for this extended tour in the Temple?"

"Al. He left bills with the man."

"Leave more bills," Daisy said. "Now, you take Al and get along. We've got to be on our way."

Al, having found Mother, did not wish to leave her again, nor could he be persuaded to part with all his trophies. But Gert finally won him over, and he strode off at her side, bearing the ormolu clock and the Kewpie.

Sam backed the truck out of the alley, and started off again.

Despite the crowds, the service drive was comparatively clear, and Sam did not have to stop until he reached a fabulous chromium cafeteria, outside of which troops and troops of Boy Scouts were lining up, with their drum and bugle corps.

"What cunning little boys!" Daisy said. "That one there reminds me—"

"Quiet!" Sam said. "Duck. It's Lizzie Trimmingham and—"

"Not again!" Daisy said, ducking behind Sam's seat.

"And—I hate to break this to you," Sam pulled his visored cap down over his eyes, "but she's got all the lady members with her, including a tall, statuesque blonde—"

Daisy peered cautiously over Sam's shoulder.

"Elfrida? Sam, it is. The blue coat, and that awful blue and white print dress, and that hideous hat!"

She ducked as one of the women turned around.

"Shall we try to get through the scouts?" Sam asked. "Because Liz and her gals are going to pass smack by us."

"Stay," Daisy said. "Wait. Maybe we can hear something. Besides, you can't get through those boys. The trooper's stopping cars on the other end, too."

The Lady Consumers started past the truck.

"Yes," one of them said brightly, "there's a brand new use for Tootsy-Wheetsy. You put it in cake. They say it makes the cake much fluffier and lighter—"

"I'm going to that reception!"

Daisy poked Sam. "Elfrida," she whispered. "That is Elfrida speaking."

"I'm going to that reception," Elfrida repeated. "I see no reason why we all should not go. The program gives it five stars, and we'd be in a wonderful place to see the opening pageant."

Someone suggested the matter of tickets.

"I'll see to those," Elfrida said. "I can get those. I'll go see him, myself. Right away. Yes, it's that rather startling building—"

"Educationally speaking," another voice drowned out the rest of Elfrida's sentence, "I feel it is beyond price. Definitely beyond price—oh, can we get across now? Hurry!"

Sam grinned as he watched the group scuttle across in front of the truck.

"Say, Daisy," he said, "what do you know? That startling building Elfrida pointed at was Cassell's. It seems he's the one who's holding the five-star reception. I gather Elfrida wants to go, and she seems to think she can wangle it."

"I'd give my bonnet and my false curls to hear her try to wangle her way in past Cassell's underlings," Daisy said. "She'll put on her My-good-man-you-don't-know-I'm-Mrs.-Egleston-Tower air, and—Sam! Why, Sam Minot, what—"

She nearly bit her tongue in two as Sam unexpectedly started the truck forward with a jerk.

They proceeded at a terrific pace to the boulevard, where another parade held them up.

"But this won't be long," Sam said. "There's the

end, over there. Daisy, were you saying something to me back there when we started up? I couldn't hear."

"There?" Daisy said. "Oh. Way back there."

Sam stared at her quizzically.

"Way back there? Why, it wasn't far. What did you start to say?"

Before Daisy could answer, they were hailed frantically by a hatless young man.

"Hi, Sam! Hi, Sammy Minot! Hi there, Sam!"

Sam looked at him, and tried to start off before the hatless young man could reach them. Bunky Unger, of his own late paper, was one of the last people whom Sam wished to meet at that point. But Bunky's long legs caught up with the truck, and he swung himself into the seat beside Sam.

"Sam, I see you've got a railroad pass sticker, will you give me a lift to my car? It's being fixed down by the tracks. Sammy, I thought I saw you over by the perisphere this morning. Fellow there with glasses on, and he looked just like you. Nearly spoke to him, but I wasn't sure—Sam, what're you doing over here?"

"Oh, driving trucks and stuff," Sam said. "When did you come over?"

"Last night. Plane. Sam, you might have dropped around before you left."

"I was told not to," Sam said. "Say!" he had a sudden inspiration. "Say, Bunky, you see the lady in the rear? She's my aunt."

Bunky turned and respectfully surveyed the dignified woman in a satin bonnet, sitting calmly—almost meditatively, he thought—on a heap of burlap bags.

"Er—how do you do?" he said.

Daisy inclined her head, but she didn't trouble to speak. She had too many things to get figured out before they got over to the Golden Dart. Now that they were approaching the train, she was conscious of a certain nervousness.

"My aunt," Sam said, "is not going to leave me her money. She's cutting me off without a shilling. All because I got fired, and I can't tell her why. She thinks I went off on a big drunk and don't remember—"

"He didn't," Bunky told Daisy. "He got sent to interview Cassell, and he punched Cassell's secretary and tried to make off with some papers, and that got Cassell sore, and he pulled a lot of wires, and got Sam fired."

Sam pulled the truck to the curbing and stopped.

"I never did!" he said. "Listen, I had a card saying I represented an art gallery dealer, so I got into Bottome's. And Cassell came into the room and took one look at me and said I was no art dealer, and he had me booted. But, Bunky, he booted the whole gang out! Who told that yarn about the punching and the paper stealing?"

"Harris," Bunky said. "He broke down. He was sore. I didn't understand the business, myself. I phoned Carey at the *Gazette*, and he said that you'd got as far as a sitting room for two seconds, on the strength of a fake card, but that he didn't know about the secretary and the papers business. He said he didn't believe that. And he said he didn't see why Cassell should be any sorer at you than at the others. You didn't get anywhere either. It's a dirty deal, Sam. If I didn't know Harris so well, I'd say he was making it up out of whole cloth. But he claimed that's what Standish told him."

"Then Standish," Sam said hotly, "is a damn liar!"

There was one thing, Daisy thought to herself, that she could be sure about. That was Standish's veracity. If anyone was lying, it most certainly was not Standish.

"Well," Bunky said philosophically, "it'll probably all blow over, and they'll yell for you to come back."

Sam started the truck.

"The hell with it," he said. "It's a crazy mess. Bunky, what's news? I keep hearing about a murder."

"That damn murder!" Bunky said. Remembering the lady in the rear, he turned around. "I mean, it's a—"

"Don't mind my aunt," Sam told him. "She has a son who's a reporter. Speak your mind. What about this murder? You can speak freely. I'm not professionally interested. I'm just curious."

"It's haywire," Bunky said. "Nobody knows much about it. Cassell gave a statement, and some of the fair boys gave a statement, and Hank Bradley said that Debbon—remember Debbon? Brad said that Debbon just choked over 'em. Brad saw the body. He bribed someone on the ambulance, and Brad said he looked like a fellow he used to know in Boston. Some insurance man. He tried to check, but he got squelched and told to mind his own business, or else. They said that Cassell didn't want anything to go out until there were fresh developments. Cassell claims there's a big plot going on against him. So they're nursing things along easy, trying to get to the bottom of things. You can drop me off over by that flagpole, Sam. My car's down that way."

"What about pictures?" Sam asked. "All this picture business?"

"Some of 'em seem to have been taken before they got here," Bunky said. "Fakes substituted, and all that. Some got cut from the frames. Funny, they're not the most valuable ones at all. Cassell's had the worst of it, in his own gallery in his building. As far as that part goes, it looks as if there was a plot against him. It sounds like the work of some crank. After all, it's crazy to snatch pictures. You couldn't get rid of 'em easily, after all this publicity. They'll be too hot to handle. And if someone wanted to snatch pictures in a big way, whyn't they grab the Mona Lisa instead of two sheep in a meadow? Okay, Sam, you can let me out right here. I'll see you later. What's this outfit you're with?" Bunky looked at the lettering on the side of the truck. "My God, the Bard of Avon Little Players!

In the English Village? Well, I'll drop over later and quaff a tankard with you when I get my car—"

Bunky waved politely at Daisy, and left.

Sam started the truck again, crossed over the tracks, and stopped beyond the Golden Dart.

"There you are," he said. "There's your train, Daisy. What now? How do you expect to get on? Say, see all those official cars lined up near the entrance. Looks like Cassell had guests."

"We'll wait till they go," Daisy said.

Sam turned and looked at her. She had that glint in her eye again, and it looked as though she'd had it for some time.

"Daisy," he said, "what were you starting to say to me just before Bunky dropped in? And by the way, I'm glad to know they had some reason for firing me, even if it wasn't true. I don't understand that. Look, was it something important, to put that glint in your eyes?"

"It was and it is important," Daisy said. "I've remembered what was on the tip of my tongue. I should have remembered it before. But I wasn't living with Eggy when it happened, and he just mentioned it casually at the time. When I was sick, and living with them, I paid as little attention to what he said as I could. Egleston insured Cassell's building—"

"There," Sam said, "is the connection between Egleston and Cassell! Eggy wanted money, he hears Cassell is in town, he sneaks on the train with some

208

idea of getting a million-dollar life policy from Cassell, so he can get the money he needs for Tom Mike. But he gets killed en route. So—"

"Very likely," Daisy said, "that's the gist of it. But you've missed the big point, Sam. If Egleston had all that insurance with Cassell, my son Samuel, why didn't Cassell recognize Egleston at once? Why did he pretend not to know who the body was?"

Sam whistled. "That's a point," he said. "But maybe Cassell never saw Eggy. Maybe he didn't know. That's possible."

"No, it isn't," Daisy said. "That's what I've been trying to figure out. I'm positive that Eggy has been to New York to see Cassell. That's why Elfrida was so sure she could get into the reception at his building, don't you see? Because her husband was a personal friend of Cassell's. We didn't hear her say that, but you can guess it from the way she was so positive. Cassell lied, Sam. He knew it was Eggy. Cassell started lying back there on the train, when he put on that mad act for us, and then swung around and became so sweet and benign and apologetic. That act wasn't genuine. I thought he was lying. I know he was. And he's so quick, and he walks so quietly—don't you remember how he popped in on us at dinner, and later when he came back with the guards? The person who closed that office door and locked it, during the time I went to the oval to get my glasses, that person had to be quick, and quiet. Then—"

"But—"

"Then," Daisy continued, "there's that business of your being fired. Standish wasn't lying, Sam. He told me the same story when I phoned him a while ago. If you didn't punch any secretaries or steal any papers, then Cassell himself made up that yarn. He's the one who's lying. He's lied all along. And he's the only one who has lied."

Sam looked at her. "Maybe that's so," he said, "but look over there."

Out of the train and down the platform came Cassell with a group of men.

Daisy put on her glasses.

There was Cassell, and the Fair director. An admiral in dress uniform, a couple of cabinet members, an ambassador, two movie stars, a famous banker. It seemed as though a rotogravure section had come to life.

There was certainly nothing furtive or suspicious about Cassell. He was being the genial host, and he was being treated with deference and respect.

Daisy wavered for a moment.

"You see what I mean," Sam said. "Maybe you're right. But what are you going to do about it? Cassell is above suspicion. He—"

"Sam," Daisy said, "do you know Boy's publisher?"

She had just spotted Boy's publisher, behind a famous radio crooner.

"No," Sam said. "I don't. Do you see what I mean, Daisy, Cassell is above—"

"I want you to go phone him," Daisy said. "Here's the number." She fumbled in her pocketbook and wrote it down on a calling card. "You leave me here in the truck, and go phone him. Ask him to come here to the Fair, and arrange a place to meet him. Get him if it takes you all night."

"That's the sanest idea you've had so far," Sam said. "You'll promise to stay right here? What're you doing with that Golden Dart notepaper!"

"I'm going to write things down," Daisy said. "I've got to a point where I've got to put things on paper, and this is the only paper I've got. Go on, Sam. I'll wait."

Daisy, as she had told Cherry, was a good liar. It never occurred to Sam to doubt her. Swinging down off the truck, he departed in search of a phone.

Daisy smiled. It was a dirty trick to send the boy off on a fake errand, but Sam didn't concur in her opinions concerning Cassell, and this wasn't the time to argue with him, or to try to convince him that Cassell could be above suspicion and still be guilty of murder. And Sam would never permit her to go on at this point with the plans she had in mind. He'd feel it was his duty to protect Boy's mother, and keep her from any such rash excursions.

Boy's publisher and another man had strolled quite

near the truck while they waited for the official cars to be filled with the more important guests.

"Quite an effort for Cassell to make, coming here," Carter said to the stranger. "Handshaking around. It's phenomenal. I sometimes wonder if he doesn't like publicity and limelight, for all he fusses about it."

"Nasty business on the train," the other said. "I didn't want to mention it there, but what's the story?"

"I was talking to Debbon," Carter said. "Seems that five people got on the Dart with fake tickets. Motley bunch, I gather. Cassell wanted to throw 'em off, and then he considered the publicity angle, and let 'em stay. He thinks his ex-secretary has a plot up his sleeve, and these people have something to do with it. I think that's nonsense, myself. I know that secretary. Harvey Bolling's boy, Andrew. He's no plotter. I told Cassell so. It's all a mess, with the Fair people all worked up, and the police rushing around, and those five people still loose—"

"Good God, haven't they nabbed them?"

"They got a man, and a girl, but they both got away. They don't even know who the murdered man is. Probably someone was after Cassell as well as the pictures. That's what Debbon thinks. He thinks someone is still after Cassell, but Cassell wouldn't stand for police guarding him."

Daisy nodded to herself. Of course he wouldn't. It would hamper him too much.

"Here's our car," Carter went on. "Let's get started. My feet are dead."

"Did you hear anything about Boy Tower's mother being missing up in Boston?"

Carter laughed. "Yes, I knew if anything happened to her, Boy would tear China apart, so I called Standish. He said not to worry. I wasn't worrying, really. Ever met her?"

"No. Is she anything like Boy?"

"More so," Carter chuckled. "The two of 'em together are dynamite. Standish said once that life with that pair was like living with the Marx brothers in a den of lions—"

Daisy sniffed as their car went off. She would settle later with Carter and Standish for that crack.

A few minutes after the last guest had gone, Brand came down the platform and hurried away on foot.

Daisy smiled, and put the finishing flourishes on the letter she had been writing. Then, adjusting her bonnet and false curls, she rose from the burlap bags, got out the rear end of the truck, and walked around over to the guard at the entrance to the platform.

"I'm the decorator," she said pleasantly. "Mr. Cassell sent me to see about those chintz drapes."

"Sorry, lady, you can't get on the train without a pass."

"Oh, I've got a letter." Daisy took it from her pocketbook. "Mr. Cassell said to give it to the guard."

The guard was visibly impressed by the letter, and

it did look official and genuine. The Golden Dart stationery alone was imposing, and she had made a magnificently swirling signature. She doubted if any guard would question that writing, and this one didn't.

"Okay, lady," he said. "Want me to call one of the servants?"

"I just spoke to Brand," Daisy said easily. "He told me just what the matter was. May I have the letter back?"

"Sure," the guard said. He made a mental note to ask his wife what a decorator was when he got home. It must be something pretty arty, he decided, from the way this one was dressed.

Daisy's throat pounded as she went down the platform.

Two troopers stopped her, but the letter satisfied them. It even satisfied the headquarters man in plain clothes.

Drawing a long breath, Daisy stepped on the train.

9

Once on the train, Daisy's throat stopped pounding, and that shaky feeling left her legs.

Pausing for a moment in the corridor, she closed her eyes and listened. Somewhere ahead was a clatter of dishes and glasses and pans. That, she thought, would be the waiters and the galley staff cleaning up after the departing celebrities. Considering the number of guests, the galley staff should be safely occupied with their work for some time to come.

Cautiously, with frequent pauses, Daisy started up the corridor toward the office and the observation car.

It seemed to her that there should be a trooper or a policeman on the train somewhere, but she couldn't hear anyone. It was quite possible that the police had finished their work in the office before the body had been removed, and then, having locked the office, taken up their duties of guarding the train on the outside.

She had never really felt that the dismissed secretary Andrew was plotting against Cassell, and now, after hearing Carter's opinion, she felt doubly sure. If any plot existed, it was Cassell's own, and Daisy intended to find out, somehow, what it was.

She was convinced that Cassell himself had killed Egleston. Why, she did not know. If only the situation were reversed, she thought, it would be so simple. There were any number of reasons why Egleston might have killed Cassell. In his frenzied search for money, there were probably no lengths to which Egleston would not have gone. But Cassell would never kill anyone for money. She couldn't think of any reason why Cassell should kill anybody, unless, of course, the person was thwarting him, getting in his way, keeping him from getting something Cassell wanted.

And, Daisy thought with a sigh, she couldn't imagine a weakling like Eggy thwarting Cassell. She couldn't imagine a weakling like Eggy thwarting anyone, least of all Cassell—

A noise outside interrupted both her thoughts and her progress along the corridor.

Standing a little to one side of a window, so that she could not be seen by anyone on the platform, Daisy peered out.

A rickshaw had appeared beside the train.

Getting out of the vehicle, with the assistance of a perspiring, unhappy-looking youth, was Elfrida.

A sound of annoyance escaped Daisy's lips, and a

frown settled on her face. She would have preferred almost anyone, even Cassell himself, to Elfrida in a militant mood. And Elfrida was militant. Daisy knew that by the way the feathers bobbed back and forth on that awful blue hat. Daisy had never achieved the comparative seclusion of her room in the Early American house that Elfrida, wearing that particular outfit of blue coat, blue and white print dress, and that awful hat, hadn't poked her head into the room and asked what Daisy did. Daisy would not have minded telling her, but she resented the monotony of that question, "What are you *doing*, Aunt Daisy?" And besides, Elfrida never gave her a chance to answer. She simply used that question as a springboard from which to jump into a recital of the woes of the particular club she happened to be returning from.

The guard from the gate, the headquarters man in plain clothes, and two troopers, all surrounded Elfrida and the rickshaw.

"Lady," the guard was panting, "I told you not to come in! I said you couldn't come in without a pass. As for you," he turned to the rickshaw boy, "I'll see you're fired—"

"She made me," the boy said unhappily. "She made me. I didn't want to come, but she had a hatpin in her hand and—"

"I want Mr. Cassell," Elfrida announced.

"Mr. Cassell isn't seeing people," one of the

troopers told her. "He never sees people. You'll have to leave here, lady, right now."

"How absurd!" Elfrida said. "I want to see Mr. Cassell!"

The headquarters man gave it as his opinion that a lot of people felt the same way.

"But you can't see him here, lady," he wound up. "If you want to stay outside the gate and look at him when he comes back, okay. But not here. Now you just climb back, lady, and—"

"It's ridiculous!" Elfrida was losing her temper. "My husband insured Mr. Cassell's building. He knows Mr. Cassell. Of course I can see him, and see him here! There's a reception right now, over at his building, and I want Mr. Cassell to get me tickets for myself, and my friends. They're waiting for me over there. I simply must see Mr. Cassell!"

"Lady," the trooper said wearily, "this train is being guarded, see? No visitors are allowed. Not unless you got a pass. You got to get back on your rickshaw and leave, see?"

"It makes no difference to me," Elfrida said loftily, "whether this train is being guarded or not. I've got to see Mr. Cassell. I want a pass to his reception, and furthermore, I want his aid in finding my husband's aunt."

"Oh, you do, do you?" the plainclothesman said. "You do, huh?"

His irony sailed over the feathers on the blue hat.

218

"I do," Elfrida said. "She's simply ruined my trip here. Running off like an inmate from an asylum, wearing the cook's clothes. Why, we even dragged ponds for her. Why—"

"Listen, lady," the guard said, "you go back and drag ponds. You go back and drag! Say, I listened to a lot of half-baked excuses from people trying to get on this train today, but yours takes the cake, yours does! You want a pass to the reception, and you want Mr. Cassell to find your husband's aunt! What do you think, he's going to drag ponds for you?"

"My husband's aunt," Elfrida was misguided enough to assume her broadest "a", "my husband's aunt is here at the Fair. We guessed when cook told us about the clothes. I want Mr. Cassell's aid in finding—"

The guard took her elbow.

"Lady, you climb back into—"

"Take your hands off me!" Elfrida said angrily. "If my husband were here instead of on that silly fishing trip, you wouldn't dare touch me! You wouldn't dare address me in that tone of voice! There's no reason, my good man, why I should not enjoy the privileges of my husband's position as Mr. Cassell's insurance man, and I'm sure Mr. Cassell will agree with me. Call him at once!"

"Lady," the trooper said, "let's get this straight. Nobody is allowed here without a pass. Nobody. Not the Fair director himself. You ain't got a pass. You got that far? Okay. Now, Mr. Cassell ain't here anyway. He's at his building."

"I've been to his building!" Elfrida retorted. "They're getting ready for the reception, and he is *not* there!"

"If you should ask me, lady," the guard said, "you're not all there, either. Now—"

Elfrida's large upper lip curled.

"My good man," she said, "you will hear from your arrogant impudence, mark my words!"

She turned to her rickshaw boy, who was standing first on one foot and then on the other.

"You! Take me back to Mr. Cassell's building, at once! Quickly! And when I get there, I shall demand a personal interview with Mr. Cassell. And before I ask his help in finding Aunt Daisy, I shall—"

"There's a bureau of missing persons," the headquarters man said. "Thought of that?"

"Indeed!" Elfrida said. "I shall tell Mr. Cassell that it has never been my misfortune to see a less cooperative group than the persons guarding his train! Now, hurry up, you, boy! And can't you possibly make this thing stop jiggling so?"

From the look on the face of the rickshaw boy, Daisy decided that Elfrida was going to be even more aroused and agitated before she got to Cassell's building.

The headquarters man shook his head as Elfrida departed.

"You know what that dame made me think of? Suffragettes. Used to tie themselves on railings and sit down on the station steps, all to get arrested so's they could fuss about getting the vote. My God, I hate that kind of dame! You can't tell what that kind'll do when they get worked up."

"Think we ought to have held her, maybe?" one of the troopers inquired. "You know what Debbon said. Suppose she gets to Cassell and starts some sort of a row, and it comes out she was here, and we let her go?"

"Cassell's all right," the headquarters man said. "He's got plenty of protection. She'll never get near him. They'll sidetrack her. Debbon's got a bunch posted just to sidetrack people like her. Come on, let's—"

A third trooper hurried over to them.

"Say, who's this guy coming?"

"He's all right," the headquarters man said. "That's Brand. He's the head servant on the train."

Daisy looked around the corridor and tried a door handle. The door was locked. All the doors were locked.

"What's he got under his arm?" the trooper asked.

"Curtain shades," the headquarters man answered with a chuckle. "It's okay. I know all about them. Seems something's the matter with the shades on the train, and he's in a stew getting them fixed. He brings down one batch, and they fit, but Cassell don't like the color. He brings down some more, and they're the right color, but they don't fit right. He's been stewing around all day long with those damn window shades—"

Daisy stiffened.

Perhaps, after all, Sam had been right about Brand. Perhaps she was on the wrong track entirely. Window shades—she couldn't think of a better way to conceal pictures than to roll them up in window shades.

"Just the same," the new trooper persisted, "hadn't you ought to take a look at 'em? We were supposed to look at every single thing that might be a rolled up canvas, no matter where it was or who had it."

The headquarters man shrugged.

"Go ahead and look, if you want to," he said. "Brand—hey, Brand. Unroll those shades, will you? This guy wants to take a look."

Daisy, forgetting for a moment the danger she was in, moved nearer the window.

"Certainly, sir," Brand said, and unrolled the shades.

To Daisy's disappointment, the shades were quite all right. They were genuine, bona fida window shades, and no stolen canvases slid from them.

The headquarters man grinned, and Brand looked a little aggrieved as he rerolled the three curtain shades.

Daisy moved from the window and started hurriedly down the corridor. She wondered why Brand had not been told of her presence, and then she remembered her own casual explanation that Brand had told her what drapes to fix. Those men on the platform all thought Brand knew about her. That was a help, but it didn't alter the fact that Brand was about to enter the train, and she had to get out of his way.

The long draperies in a sitting room which she had seen only in passing, the night before, seemed to offer a solution. They had to be a solution, because the other rooms appeared to be locked.

Daisy slipped in behind them.

Somehow, in her eagerness to get on board the train, she had neglected to consider the problems, like this, which might arise after she actually was on board. She could only pray that her dirndl was out of sight.

Brand, whistling morosely, paused just outside the sitting room door.

There was a jangle of keys. Daisy, peering through the drapes, could see that Brand was taking his white coat from the hanger in a cupboard out in the corridor. She hadn't noticed the cupboard before. Probably it was partially concealed by the panelling.

Brand changed into his white coat, picked up the three window shades, and went off in the direction of the observation car. He did not bother to lock the cupboard behind him.

Holding her breath, Daisy slipped from behind the draperies and tiptoed out into the corridor.

It was the cupboard she hoped it would be. The one Sam had mentioned. It was the cupboard with all the keys.

Daisy had to pinch herself to keep from making a noise. She wanted to crow. She wanted to dance a jig. Because there was a key with a tag that identified it as belonging to Cassell's private office on the Golden Dart. That was the key Sam had taken, and she had been right about the manner in which he had lost it. Stragg had taken it from him, and here it was, back on the board.

Her eyes lighted on a large key ring, labelled, "Mr. Cassell. All Master Keys."

With sudden inspiration, Daisy picked it off the hook and put it in her bag. Then she started off toward the observation car. She told herself that she ought to take the keys and run. She ought to go to Cassell's building and see the man himself, and bluntly accuse him of murdering Egleston. She ought to raise a terrific rumpus, and see if Cassell could cope with the burden of defense. If her own position became too awkward, she could always call for Carter. Carter was around, and he would get her out of any difficulties.

That was what she should do. She should go and accuse Cassell. But such an accusation would probably react on both police and bystanders as Elfrida's at-

224

tempt to see Cassell had reacted. She would either be sidetracked by Debbon's sidetracking squad, or she would be arrested as a crank.

Daisy continued on toward the observation car.

If she wanted to accuse Cassell, she had to have a lot more to back up her accusation than the fact that Cassell had lied on several occasions.

Brand was in the observation car. She could hear his morose whistle.

She stood for a moment by the car door. It was dim in there. The curtain drapes had been drawn.

Brand stood on a table. He was taking down a shade.

Shivers chased each other up and down Daisy's spine. Even in the dim light, she could see that there was something rolled inside the shade he was taking down. It was a canvas! A picture!

Daisy put one hand against the door jamb to steady herself. She felt weak, as she watched Brand remove another shade, in which another picture reposed.

The window shade story was all a blind. The whole window shade story, all this going and coming with right shades and wrong shades was all to cover up the removal of stolen pictures.

Brand took down a third shade, and then set to work putting up the three shades he had been carrying under his arm out on the platform.

Daisy tried to figure it out.

Those shades that Brand had were all right. These

shades in the windows had pictures in them. That might mean that someone else had inserted the pictures in the observation car shades, and that Brand was just bringing more shades for more pictures. But however that worked out, she was sure that the agitation about shades that the headquarters man said had been going on all day was simply a neat method of getting pictures to the train, and, for all she knew, off the train as well.

Daisy ducked to one side of the door as Brand finished with the shades and got down from the table. But she needn't have made the gesture, for Brand never turned around. He seemed to feel secure in his knowledge that no one would be allowed on the train.

Picking up the rolls with the pictures, Brand stopped his morose whistling and stared for a long time at the telephone. Then he removed the receiver and dialed a number.

"Mr. Bolling, please," Brand said. "Mr. Andrew Bolling. Thank you, I'll wait."

Again Daisy wavered. Sam was perhaps right. Andrew and Brand were ganging up in a plot against Cassell. After all, why in the world would Cassell be stealing his own pictures? On the other hand, Carter said that Andrew Bolling was all right.

"Mr. Andrew?" Brand said. "Yes, this is Brand, sir. I'm going to take your advice and leave. Yes, sir. Do you still think you could get me that position at your club? That's fine, sir. I hate to, after fifteen years, and of course the pay won't be the same, but I don't see any other way out, sir. I—I don't know, sir, what *is* going on! I don't understand any of it. Did you hear about the murder? Oh, have the police been to see you? But you were in New York—I see, you satisfied them on that account. Well, sir, he put that business of the tickets off on you. But it was Mr. Tower that did that for him. Yes, Mr. Egleston Tower. I got that from Stragg—"

Daisy gulped. Cherry had said that the doddering old gent of the tickets had eyebrows like Egleston's!

"He's the man that was shot," Brand continued. "I don't know how he got on board, sir. I don't understand any of that. This morning when I unlocked the train office for Mr. Cassell, there was the body on the floor. He looked at me and said, who was the man, he'd never seen him before. I didn't dare say anything. You know how he can look at you, sir!"

Daisy's tongue seemed to be sticking to the roof of her mouth.

"Pictures, sir? I don't know, sir, I don't understand! Stragg has been bringing pictures here all day, and I've been getting them from him in window shades— yes, Mr. Cassell is taking them. He says it's to protect himself, but, sir, I don't understand what he—tell the police? Oh, sir, you know I can't! Mr. Cassell has that old check of mine, and he knows about Leavenworth. He'll have me arrested. It'll be just as bad if you tell, sir! How can you prove you didn't have anything to do with the tickets, and that message to the train to let those people on?"

There was a pause while Andrew Bolling talked at some length.

"Those people on the train were all right, sir," Brand said. "The old lady was a real lady, and the girl was nice. I let her get away. I'm not sure about that young fellow. He took a key, but I called Mr. Cassell and he spoke to Stragg in the car, and Stragg got it back. That was before I knew about the murder—yes, Stragg knows more than I do, but he doesn't care what's going on as long as he gets paid for it. Sir, please don't do anything about the police until I see you! I'll meet you at the club, and we'll talk it all over. I'm supposed to go to the building with Stragg in half an hour, but I'll take the subway into New York at once and meet you at the club. Good-bye, Mr. Andrew!"

Brand put down the receiver and looked at the window shades on the floor at his feet.

"Club be damned!" he said harshly. "I'm going to take the first boat I see! I'm not going back to Leavenworth!"

Beside Daisy out in the corridor was a small table, and on it was a small but heavy cut glass vase. Almost absent-mindedly, Daisy gripped the vase and waited.

Brand could not take any boats now. Not until he'd told everything he knew to the police. His was the first real evidence she had, and she was not going to let

228

it slip out of her fingers on any boat! Andrew would stay at his club, waiting for Brand. She could be sure of finding Andrew. But Brand was not going to take any boats. And Daisy felt that it would take more than mere verbal persuasion to change Brand's mind on that point.

Lifting the vase, Daisy swung it as Brand came through the door.

He slumped to the floor so quietly that Daisy was almost afraid he was dead until she looked again. She remembered Boy saying that sometimes a little blow in the wrong place would kill a man.

But Brand was alive. He was breathing.

Daisy knew that she ought to feel shocked and appalled at what she had done, but instead she felt a distinct thrill of elation. Not every woman of sixty-seven, she thought, could wield a vase with such devastating effects!

Kneeling down, she unhooked Brand's suspenders, and unbuckled his belt. Brand wouldn't stay unconscious forever, and it was wiser that she tie him up before he started protesting.

She lashed his ankles together with the suspenders and tied his wrists tightly with the belt. There would have to be a gag, too. She reached for the handkerchief whose corner protruded from the pocket of Brand's white coat.

"Stick 'em up, lady!"

The man who had crept up behind her was a

stranger to Daisy, but she knew from his uniform and from Sam's description that this was Stragg, the chauffeur, who was standing there, pointing that ugly little gun at her.

"Get up, lady!" he said. "Stick up your hands, I said! Get up from there!"

Slowly, Daisy got up from the floor, and slowly, she raised her hands.

That gun would have terrified her more if she hadn't had the benefit of all that experience in being held up, back in the days when Boy was writing those articles on Happy Mosello, when rum-runners and hijackers lurked in every shadow of the Louisburg Square house.

Boy's advice, so often dinned in her ears, came back to her.

"Take things slowly, mother. If you go slow, they'll go slow. If you fly off the handle, they're more apt to shoot. Look scared to death, and then pretend to faint. There isn't much anyone can do when a woman faints."

It had worked before, Daisy thought. There was no reason why it should not work again.

Daisy made her hands tremble, then, closing her eyes, she gave a little moan and crumpled to the floor.

There was a moment of silence except for the noise of the trains outside.

Stragg was apparently perplexed.

Daisy forced herself to breathe evenly. If only Stragg would stay perplexed!

"Well, lady, whoever you are," Stragg said at last, "I'll just do you up with Brand's suspenders and cart you over to the boss. My God," he added wonderingly, "how the hell did you get here!"

Daisy felt him step over her. After a few seconds, she cautiously opened one eye.

Stragg's back was to her as he knelt beside Brand. The ugly little gun was by his side.

Inch by inch, Daisy's hand crept out. It hovered over the gun, drew it back towards her.

Gripping the gun, Daisy wondered just what she ought to do next. It would be simple enough to order Stragg to put up his hands, but Stragg was a big hulking brute. If he decided to jump at her instead of obeying her, that would ruin everything. Then there was the problem of tying him up, too. She could never tie him and hold the gun at the same time. And she couldn't shoot the man in the back, even if she wanted to. A shot would bring guards and troopers and the galley staff rushing to the scene.

Daisy transferred the gun to her left hand, and with her right hand cautiously picked up the cut glass vase again.

Aiming with great care, Daisy swung the vase with all her force.

Stragg went over like a log.

Daisy took her first full breath in minutes, and set

to work binding Stragg up with the tie-backs from the curtain drapes. Then she tightened Brand's bonds, and gagged both men.

"Dear me!" Daisy murmured to herself, as she surveyed the two trussed figures on the floor, "I feel like Pearl White in 'The Iron Claw'! Whatever would Elfrida say!"

At any rate, she had evidence, and that was all that mattered. Now she had to think of some way to keep the evidence.

If only there were someone to watch over the two men in the observation car, while she got hold of Carter and took him with her to Cassell.

There was Sam, of course! She had almost forgotten about Sam and the truck. She would have to get Sam.

Closing the door of the observation car, Daisy walked back along the train to the door through which she had entered—how long ago had it been? Probably not over half an hour, she decided, but it seemed like several years.

Patting her false curls in place, Daisy smiled sweetly at the headquarters man, lounging out on the platform.

"Hasn't my helper come yet?"

"Oh," the man smiled back. "You're the one about the drapes. I forgot you. What helper was coming?"

Daisy described Sam.

"Overalls and cap?" the man said. "Say, you'd ought to have told us, lady. There was a fellow like that hanging around outside the gate a while ago, but he didn't say anything about being your helper. He hung around, and then he went off. He didn't say he was after you."

"That stupid boy!" Daisy said. "He knows perfectly well he's got to change those fixtures, and I'll have a frightful time with Mr. Cassell if the whole business isn't in order when he gets back. You see, now that he's got those shades changed, he wants the drapes changed, too."

"Kind of a particular man, ain't he?"

Daisy shrugged. "Yes, but he keeps me busy, and he pays me well. I can't complain. Oh, dear, what can have become of that fellow! You wouldn't want to go up to the gate and yell 'Sam' in a loud voice, would you?"

"Let's go up and take a look around," the headquarters man offered. "If you see him, I'll yell."

"That's awfully good of you! You can't think," Daisy said with perfect truth, "how badly I need him!"

There was no sign of Sam at the gate. There was no sign of the truck, either.

The headquarters man discussed the situation with the guard.

"That fellow in overalls, the one with the badge on his cap—didn't he go away just after that dame went off in her rickshaw?"

"I think so," the guard said. "He looked like he was waiting for someone. He worried around here—"

"He ought to look worried!" Daisy said. "He'll look more worried when I'm through with him!"

Probably, she thought, Sam had seen Elfrida leaving, and had followed her. Or else he had decided that she had gone back to Whitty and Cherry and the rest, over by the Liberty Boys.

"I don't know what to do," Daisy forgot herself and thought aloud. "If only—"

She stopped short, but neither guard nor headquarters man seemed to notice what she had said. They were watching a small roadster approaching the gate.

Daisy recognized the hatless youth at the wheel, and her eyes began to gleam.

"If only," she continued, "if only—oh, there he is! There's Mr. Unger with the samples, and he can see to the fixtures! Mr. Unger!" she yelled at him as the car stopped. "Mr. Unger!"

Bunky looked at her and blinked.

"Mr. Unger," Daisy went on hurriedly before he could speak, "come here quick! Have you got those samples? Sam was supposed to bring 'em, and change the fixtures—oh, don't you dare tell me you haven't got those samples!"

"I've got 'em," Bunky said promptly.

He hadn't the faintest idea of what she was talking about. He had come to the Golden Dart only because it occurred to him that with Cassell holding that reception at his building, it might be an opportune time to do a little pumping there at the train. He never expected to get past the gate. But if he could get inside by playing up to Sam Minot's obviously crazed aunt, Bunky was perfectly willing to play up.

"Got 'em in my pocket," he added.

"Oh, but you haven't a pass!" Daisy said. "Oh, dear! But my letter will cover him, won't it?" she appealed to the guard. "It says to admit Mrs. Flint and representatives of Flint and Company—won't that do for him? D' you want the letter again?"

"It's okay," the guard said, and let Bunky pass.

"Oh, thank you!" Daisy said. "Hurry, now, and see if the samples match. If they don't, I'll have to rush back into town—"

Daisy kept up a constant stream of chatter as they passed down the platform, pausing only long enough to explain Bunky to the troopers.

"D' you want my letter again? It covers him," he concluded.

"Okay," one of the troopers said.

Both of them responded to her infectious smile as she followed Bunky into the train.

"Don't ask questions!" she whispered in his ear. "Just come along and listen carefully. I'm Boylston Tower's mother. Sam and I were two of the people who got on the train with those fake tickets. If you want the scoop of your young life, come into this observation car and watch over these two men here—"

She opened the door.

"My God!" Bunky stared at the two trussed-up figures.

"You stay here," Daisy said, "and you keep this pair here, and keep everyone else out. Stay here till I return, or Sam comes. These men are my evidence—"

"You—you mean, about the murder?"

"Exactly. The murdered man was my nephew. Here. Here's a gun to wave if you have to. I took it from that chauffeur."

Bunky looked from the hulking figure of Stragg to Daisy, whose head barely reached the lapel of his coat. There was almost something reverent in his manner as he took the gun from her.

"You don't look a bit like Boy Tower in that rig," he observed, "but this all sounds enough like him. Okay, I'll cherish your evidence for you, Mrs. Tower. Er—did you knock 'em both out with your bare hands?"

"I used that vase," Daisy said. "I had to. Look, you take this letter, too, in case anyone questions you. I wrote it, but everyone thinks Cassell did. Stave people off with that, hold these two here with the gun, and wait till I get back—"

"What are you going to do now?" Bunky asked respectfully.

"I hope," Daisy told him, "to make a Garrison finish. Oh, I'm going to take your car, by the way—did you leave the keys in it? You don't mind if I use it, do you?"

She did not wait for him to answer.

"Mr. Unger brought the wrong colors entirely," she said to the troopers as she got off the train. "I'm going to have to go back into town. And Mr. Unger's got to refit all those fixtures, too. Lord knows how long that'll take, even with Brand and Stragg helping!"

The troopers expressed their sympathy.

"I suppose it can't be helped!" Daisy said with a wry smile.

She hurried down the platform, explaining about the wrong samples and the fixture-fitting to both the headquarters man and the gate guard. If they were told something, she thought, they wouldn't start poking around and investigating.

Then, with a friendly wave of her hand, she got into Bunky's car.

She had not driven a car since her accident, and she had some trouble finding the starter. In her cars, the starter had always been on the floor. In Bunky's, the starter was an inconspicuous little button on the dash.

The guard waved back at her as she finally drove off. He agreed with the headquarters man that she seemed like a nice woman, in spite of that funny outfit she wore.

Daisy eyed the trylon and turned the little car toward it. There was a press card on the seat beside her, and she thankfully stuck it on the windshield with a little rubber suction cup. If anyone stopped her, she would say that she was a reporter. She looked as much like a reporter as she did like anything else.

Even if she had wanted to go over and get Cherry and the rest, she couldn't have gone. Barriers had been put up, she noticed, over the road that led to the amusement loop. Besides, joining Cherry and the rest was not as important now as getting to Cassell's building, getting hold of Carter, and getting things done.

Her eyes were on the crowded road ahead, but her mind was on a million things. She tried to sort them out and settle them in an orderly fashion.

Cassell had a plan. That much was clear, and that was the thing which mattered most, and that was what everything revolved around.

Cassell himself was above suspicion. You would never suspect Cassell of any criminal plot, because he was so big you couldn't see anything but his importance. Cassell was so big that plots and plans would be, in a sense, difficult. He couldn't hire thugs to do his dirty work. True, Cassell had Brand and Stragg, but Brand had been about to cut and run, and of course Stragg would blackmail Cassell for the rest of his life. Cassell probably had something on Stragg, too, as he apparently had on Brand. But, when you came right down to it, Cassell would have to carry out his plans himself.

Daisy stopped and waited for three ornate floats to pass by.

That was where they came in, the five of them on the train. If Cassell could plan to have a group of innocent bystanders ready to be seized on as suspects, that would work out beautifully for him. If Cassell could pull wires so that a group of innocent people were thrust into a position where it looked as if they were plotting against him, that was even better. They were the stooges in Cassell's plan.

Those tickets were Cassell's own idea, and if Brand had been speaking the truth to Andrew, Cassell had somehow compelled Eggy to act for him in hiring Cherry. It was Cassell himself who had sent the message to the train about letting the ticket-holders on. On the train, it was Cassell himself who put on the act, first to scare them, and then to win them over and remove any suspicions they might feel about the ticket situation. Whitty had reacted as Cassell expected his five people, or any five people, to react. That change-over of moods was good, Daisy thought. Good, at least, for people like Whitty, who probably were equally moved when political orators dropped their voices from a bellow to a whisper. Cassell's psychology had been sound enough, even if he had overacted.

Daisy shifted and started off as the floats finally got by.

Eggy was beginning to fit into things, she thought. Eggy did not just want money. He required a large sum of money, and he required it quickly. Eggy must have gone to see Cassell at the Bottome house very early Saturday morning, because Cherry said she had been hired to distribute the pink slips and the envelopes containing the tickets some time in the morning. Very likely, as Sam suggested, Eggy had gone to Cassell with the hope of wheedling a large policy out of him. He might have gone for some other reason, but under the circumstances that seemed the most logical purpose of Eggy's visit.

But Cassell had a plan. From his dismissing Andrew, and with all the reporters harassing him, it was easy to guess that Cassell was in no mood to be wheedled by Egleston Tower. Probably he had brushed Eggy aside by giving him the task of hiring a girl to distribute the pink slips. He could have explained it simply enough by saying that he was checking up on advertising. Eggy never would have questioned him, anyway, and if Eggy thought he stood a chance of getting a policy from Cassell, very likely he would gladly have stood on his head in Frog Pond if Cassell suggested doing it. Why he should have been disguised as a doddering old man, Daisy couldn't imagine, unless Cassell thought it would confuse people if any slip-ups occurred. Cassell would have had some explanation for Eggy, and Eggy would have accepted it without question. Gert had spoken the truth in calling Eggy a sucker.

Having hired Cherry, a task which must have struck Eggy as being hilariously funny, Eggy would march right back to the Bottome house and continue his dogged wheedling. That must have been about the time that the reporters were thickest, about the time that Sam had penetrated the sitting room.

There, Daisy decided, Sam must have done or seen something, even though the significance of it was lost to him, that moved Cassell to call Standish and have him fired. That seemed, on the whole, like a gesture of panic on Cassell's part.

But it had also given Cassell a chance to get rid of Eggy, by ordering him to follow Sam. That removed the nuisance of Eggy, and if it turned out that Sam had really caught on to anything in the sitting room, Cassell would know.

Somehow, after following Sam to the station, Eggy had managed to get on the Golden Dart. Not even Brand understood how, and the chances of finding out the truth appeared remote. The thing that mattered was that Eggy had got on the train. Perhaps, realizing that he had been sidetracked, Eggy waited until after the poker game before making his presence known. Then, if Daisy knew Eggy Tower, he started wheedling Cassell again.

Then came the hard part, about which Carter would be sure to ask her first, Daisy thought, and for which her answer would be sadly inadequate. Why had Cassell killed Eggy? What possible motive could he have had?

She could only say that Eggy was killed because he had found out Cassell's plan, or he appeared to Cassell to be in the way of it. Eggy's murder must have been incidental to something else. It had to be. Certainly Cassell, after his elaborate scheme to get the five of them on the train, would never set out from Boston with the sole purpose of killing Egleston Tower!

Daisy knew what Carter would ask her next.

What plan?

Daisy sighed. She didn't know even now what the plan was. She knew only that it existed. Neither Brand nor Andrew knew, and she doubted if Stragg did. Like her, they only knew something was going on.

It had to have something to do with pictures. Why was Cassell stealing his own pictures? Why was he removing them?

Daisy nearly hit a van full of men dressed in the buff and blue of the Continental Army.

Cassell wasn't stealing pictures! How stupid she had been. Cassell was not stealing pictures. He was removing them! And there was only one reason for people to remove things, and that was disaster of some sort. You removed things like that when fire threatened, or something like that.

That was why there had been the delays. Why the gun had been removed for a time, and then put in the garbage pail. Why labels had been removed to delay identification. Why there had been a delay in finding the five of them.

Cassell was killing time for something that was

going to happen. And before it happened, he was removing his favorite pictures. Not the most valuable ones at the fair, but the ones he wanted—

"Hey, lady!"

Daisy was so absorbed that she didn't hear the trooper hailing her.

"Lady, you can't go no further!"

"I didn't hear you," Daisy said. "I was thinking about a story—have I got to stop here?"

"All traffic's stopped here before the pageant."

Daisy looked around. She had almost forgotten the crowds, and now there seemed to be even more people.

"Over nine hundred thousand," the trooper said in answer to her question, "and more still coming—sure, leave your car over there with those others. There's room for two more, and then I start turning 'em back."

Swinging the car into the indicated space, Daisy locked it and hurried on foot through the milling crowds to Cassell's building. It was like election night in Times Square, she thought, as she shoved and pushed along, only there were more people and more noises.

Outside the hourglass building, weary-looking troopers were clearing a passageway.

"Is the reception over?" Daisy asked a woman.

"Yes. But lots of 'em haven't come out—have you seen the—oh, there! They're taking her out now!"

Daisy craned her neck to see.

The troopers were carrying a stretcher out through the way they had cleared.

"Has someone fainted?" Daisy asked.

"Oh, no," the woman beside her said. "That's that lady that forced her way into that office where Conrad Cassell was. She's the woman who committed suicide."

Daisy opened her mouth, but she couldn't speak. She couldn't utter a word.

She could only stare speechlessly at the trooper who pushed past her, carrying a blue coat over his arm, and in his hand, a hat with feathers. That awful hat with feathers!

Daisy shook her head as if to clear it, and spoke to the woman next her.

"You didn't—you didn't happen to see her? The one who committed suicide?"

"I was just as near to her," the woman said proudly, "as I am to you. That was when she was arguing with some cops. Before she got to Cassell. She had on a blue and white print dress, and I think she was crazy then. She was trying to find an Aunt Daisy, only she said 'Ont' for Aunt—"

"Elfrida!" Daisy said, and closed her eyes. "Oh, Elfrida!"

10

The woman standing next to Daisy was too excited to notice either Daisy's pallor or her poignant little cry.

"Poor Mr. Cassell!" Putting a hand on Daisy's shoulder, the woman stood on tiptoe to watch the stretcher being borne away. "Poor man. First he has pictures stolen on his train, and then that murder, then more pictures stolen here, and now here's this woman killing herself in his lovely building! Poor man, I certainly think it's a shame—"

Someone gripped Daisy's arm.

"Daisy Tower!" Sam said. "Daisy, we're out of our minds worrying about you! I went and got Whitty and Cherry and Gert and Al, and we came here in his car—we hoped you'd come back here, too. We couldn't think where else you might go. Move back out of this crush—Daisy, where have you been? What have you been doing? I couldn't get Carter on the phone, by the way. They told me he was already here at the Fair."

Sam piloted her through the throng around the building, where the rest were waiting on the wide steps of another entrance.

It was good to see them all, Daisy thought. It was good to hear Al's ringing cry of "Mother!" It was good to have Cherry's arm to lean on, good even to smell Whitty's stogie and see Gert's little suitcase once more.

"But you all look so different!" Daisy said, pointing to Sam's brown suit.

"I picked up Wecky's costumes on my way back in the truck," Sam told her. "Out of sheer gratitude, he lent me this. His cast had recovered, and he was riding a cloud. Cherry changed before she left with Whit, and the Liberty Boys fixed him up in the blue serge. Al pulled more robes out of a box in the car, and he made Gert change, too. They look a little Ku Kluxish, but I think the white's an improvement over that yellow—Daisy, where have you *been?* Where did you go when you left the truck—"

"I've got a cape for you, Daisy," Cherry interrupted. "You've probably caught cold, going around in that cotton dirndl without any coat! Oh, Daisy, do you know what's happened now? Did you see that stretcher going out?"

"Yes," Daisy said, slipping into the long black velvet cape that Cherry held out. "Yes. Elfrida. I know. I saw that hat. Whatever happened? What could have

246

happened? That woman beside me said she committed suicide, but of course she never did! Did you see her? Do you know anything about it all?"

"She was here when we came," Sam said. "Cherry saw her, darting around and arguing about getting in to the reception. She kept saying she wanted to see Mr. Cassell about her aunt, and she told one trooper and one attendant after another. Finally she worked her way to the lobby inside, and we followed—"

"Did you get in?"

Gert nodded. "They almost forced us in," she said, "when they caught sight of Al. They almost dragged us in. They even gave us food. They wanted us to go in some other room and shake hands with people, but we said no. Honestly, Al's like the key to the city, Daisy; we were the last car they let over from the midway—"

"We stayed out in the lobby," Cherry broke in, "because we wanted to watch Elfrida, and we wanted to watch out for you. Sam thought you might have followed her here from the train— Daisy, how did she find out about Eggy? She must have. I heard her telling one man that she was Mrs. Egleston Tower, and she wanted to see Mr. Cassell immediately on a matter of the greatest importance. She—"

"Elfrida a suicide!" Daisy said. "I don't believe it. And she couldn't have known about Eggy. She didn't know at the train. She told—"

"Daisy," Sam said, "were you at the train? Have you been at the train all this time?"

"On it. But don't let's go into that now. I've too much to think about. Elfrida told the guards there that Eggy was on a silly fishing trip. I even remember the phrase. Silly fishing trip. Oh, there's no woman in this world less likely to kill herself than Elfrida! I don't see how she could have found out about Eggy between the train and here, and even if she did, I can't imagine her being more than just remorseful! I know Elfrida! She simply could not have killed herself! Tell me what more you know."

"Finally they let her into some downstairs ante room to see Cassell," Sam said. "I suppose they thought it would be the only way to shut her up. Right after she went in, there was a shot, and then Cassell came rushing out—"

Daisy's eyes narrowed.

"She and Cassell were alone in that ante room, were they? I see. Go on."

"I was right there by the door," Whitty said. "I heard what Cassell told the detective—gee, he looked terrible, Daisy. He looked green. He told this detective that she grabbed the gun from his desk, and—"

"It was Debbon," Sam said. "Debbon himself, Daisy. He asked if it was the gun he made Cassell take, and Cassell said yes. He said this woman grabbed the gun and shot herself. Debbon tried to calm him down, and said not to take it so hard, and that she was the excitable sort of woman who shot herself on the White House lawn, or jumped off the Empire State, and it was just Cassell's hard luck that it happened here."

"Elfrida," Daisy said, "never killed herself in this world! He shot her—"

"For God's sakes," Sam said anxiously, "if you're going to say things like that, whisper 'em!"

"But he must have!" Daisy said. "Don't you see? She told everyone she was Mrs. Egleston Tower, and she wanted to see him on a matter of great importance. He had to shoot her, don't you understand, Sam? He had to! He thought she had found out about Eggy. He didn't wait to go into the matter with her. He shot. It's another gesture of panic, like his having you followed—Sam, I wish you'd close your mind to everything else, and think over what you did or what you saw, in that Bottome woman's sitting room yesterday. If I can only find that out!"

"If you think, Daisy," Sam said, "that I can close my mind to all this, and concentrate on that damned chintzey sitting room in Boston, you're crazy! Look, how'd you get on that train? What did you find out? Did you find out anything about the pictures that were stolen there?"

"You mean the first ones, the ones that were taken this morning? Those were just to set the stage," Daisy said. "Like—well, if you wanted to burn down your house to get the insurance money, you might conceivably burn a few barns down first, to implant the firebug notion in people's minds. Then the burning of your own house wouldn't come as such a shock. Those pictures were said to be stolen from the train only to soften the blow of the next pictures being stolen. Is Cassell still here in the building?"

"He's inside," Sam said. "What—"

"Cherry, take off this bonnet, will you?" Daisy asked. "And the curls. And can you straighten my hair out? Fine."

She drew the velvet cape around her. It made her seem taller, and instead of being a tiny little woman in a quaint-looking cotton dress, she suddenly became Mrs. Boylston Tower.

She drew a long breath.

"Come, all of you," she said. "We're going to see Mr. Cassell."

"You are going to what?" Sam demanded.

"See Mr. Cassell," Daisy returned. "We are going to confront him, if you want to be melodramatic about it. Cherry, have you my pocketbook? Give it back to me. We are going to confront Mr. Cassell, and I am going to tell him who I am. This wholesale slaughter of the Tower family is going to stop!"

"He'll have us arrested," Cherry said, "before you can say a word. We were all right when we went in before, because we stayed out of his way, but you can't go up to him and—"

"If he arrests us," Daisy said, "I'll know he is innocent. If he arrests us, we'll crawl out somehow. If he doesn't—well, come along!" She took Al's arm. "Lead the way with Mother, Al."

The attendants at the door bowed in Al's direction and admitted the party without question.

With Al at her side, and the rest following, Daisy walked across the lobby.

She paused as Cassell, surrounded by guards and troopers and Fair officials, entered the lobby from a room on her right. He had a watch in his hand, and he was talking earnestly to a man Sam identified, in a quick whisper, as Debbon.

"I've got to meet the ambassador before the opening pageant—"

Daisy walked tranquilly over to him.

"Oh, Mr. Cassell," she said, "just a moment, if you please."

Her voice was low and firm, but there was a certain note in it that Sam had never heard before. Cherry had. She had seen even Boy Tower waver at that voice.

Cassell turned and looked at her. He didn't start, or show any sign of surprise, but those small beady eyes half closed, and the thumb of his plump white hand rubbed back and forth over the face of his watch. If he recognized her, he gave no indication of it.

"I'm extremely busy," Cassell said. "If you will excuse me—"

"I know," Daisy said. "But I'm Mrs. Boylston

Tower. With all the confusion on the train, that point was not made clear. I should like to speak with you privately—"

"Daisy Tower!" Carter appeared from behind the guards and Fair officials.

"Carter," Daisy said honestly, "I'm terribly, terribly glad to see you! Perhaps you can persuade Mr. Cassell to give me a few minutes of his time? I've something so important to talk to him about, and he says he's so busy."

There, she thought to herself, let Cassell crawl out of that! He couldn't refuse to talk with her, now. If he said no, Carter would have to plead in her behalf, simply out of politeness.

"It's about all these things that have been happening," Daisy went on. "I'm sure you can spare a few minutes, can't you, Mr. Cassell, so that we can talk—"

"Certainly!" Cassell's heartiness was a little forced. "Of course, Mrs. Tower. The ambassador may be delayed, but I'm sure he won't mind being delayed for such a charming person. Suppose you come up to my office, and—"

"All of us?" Daisy said. "The Prince, and all of us?"

"Certainly! Yes, of course. Carter, should you care to come?"

Carter looked at Daisy's face, and smiled.

"Wouldn't miss it," he said.

Cassell waved a plump hand toward the elevators.

"Will you wait here?" he asked Debbon. "Oh, Brand and Stragg should be here, by the way. They should have been here long ago. Tell them to wait, as I said, will you?"

"Yes," Debbon said. "Don't you want one of us to go with you now?"

"No, no, my dear fellow," Cassell said, "I'm quite all right. Quite. Tell me, when did the Fair director leave? He has gone, hasn't he?"

"Must have," Debbon said. "I haven't seen him for a long while."

"With all this going on," Cassell said, "I missed him. I'll be only a few minutes, if there's a call from the train."

Daisy watched Cassell carefully as he got into the elevator.

He was looking as he had looked the night before, when they first saw him on the train. His eyes were almost hidden in the folds of flesh, and his mouth made that strange jaw look convex.

Sam felt the eyes on him, and he knew that Cassell recognized him, now that he had shed the Harold Lloyd glasses. Cherry felt the beady eyes, too. Unconsciously, she moved nearer Sam.

"Now," Cassell said as the elevator stopped, "if you'll all just come into my office."

"I keep thinking," Sam breathed in Daisy's ear, "of the spider and the fly."

She seemed not to hear him.

The floor was deserted, and their footsteps echoed hollowly as Cassell led them rapidly down the corridor and into a large circular reception room, walled with pastel glass bricks.

Unlocking a door on the left, Cassell snapped on a light switch and stood to one side to let them pass in.

"Now, if you'll just sit down for a moment," he said, "I'll join you as soon as I have phoned—"

"No," Daisy said, her blandness matching his, "I think your phone call can wait, Mr. Cassell. I think, now, you'd best give us your whole-hearted and undivided attention."

Carter, lounging on the arm of a leather office chair, looked at her interestedly.

"I'm sorry," Cassell said, "but my call is more important—"

Daisy moved over to the doorway, and stood between him and the reception room.

"No," she said. "I think, now, that you—"

Cassell made the mistake of trying to push past her.

Instantly, Al was on the scene, his curved sword-tip pricking the middle button on Cassell's vest.

"No!" Al said angrily.

"Thank you, Al," Daisy said. "No, Mr. Cassell, you are not going to make any phone calls now. Put your watch back. Suppose you just sit down until we've got things settled. Otherwise, I shall ask Al to do things with his sword. After we've settled things, you can make all the phone calls you wish—"

Cassell, in a fury, turned to Carter.

"This is a plot!" he said. "You're a witness to this!"

"Yes," Carter was sitting up, now. "I'm a witness, but I don't understand it. Daisy, what are you driving at?"

"We," Daisy said, "are the five people who came to the Fair in his train. The motley group. And Mr. Cassell has killed my nephew Egleston Tower, and his wife Elfrida. And I want a confession from him."

Carter stood up.

"Are you serious, Daisy? You can't be serious!"

"Serious?" Cassell was roaring. "She's crazy! This is a plot! Andrew and these people—they're trying to blackmail me! Here, you, take that sword away! Take it away—"

"He doesn't speak English," Gert said, putting her suitcase on the desk. "There's no use shouting at him."

"There's no use shouting at us, either," Daisy said. "We know all about the tickets, Mr. Cassell, and your fake message to the train, and about Eggy's gun that you shot him with. It was my gun, you see, and that made it easier for us to connect everything. We know how you put it in the garbage pail. And we know all about Eggy's wife. You made a bad mistake there. She didn't even know that Eggy was here, or that he'd been killed. All she wanted from you was tickets to your reception. Oh, and we know about the pictures, too. And the curtain shades. We know so much, Mr. Cassell!"

"Carter!" Cassell said. "Carter, do something about this bunch of blackmailers! Phone—"

"There isn't any phone in here, is there?" Carter said. "I don't see any. Frankly, Cassell, I still don't understand all this, but I know Daisy, and I know Harvey Bolling's boy, and neither of 'em could be described as a bunch of blackmailers. I'm sure there's some explanation, if you'll just explain."

"There's really only one thing I want explained," Daisy said, "and that is what Sam saw that you had him fired for, Mr. Cassell. Oh, yes, we know all about that, too. I talked with Standish. Now, will you sit down and write your confession, Mr. Cassell, before we proceed to the next point? I want to get these murders settled first. I shan't press you for details. We know most of them, anyway. Just write that you are responsible for both murders, and sign your name."

"Blackmailers!" Cassell said. "Blackmailers! You can't force me to write any such lies! Not even if you order this Turk here to cut me into ribbons! It's blackmail! You can't force me to—"

Daisy hardly heard him as he continued to rant and shout.

Her eyes were fixed on Gert.

Gert was bending over that suitcase on the desk.

Gert was opening the suitcase.

"Up, Renfrew!" Gert said quietly.

256

Daisy felt her nails digging into the moist palms of her hands as a black snake uncoiled itself and glided out of the suitcase onto the polished desk top.

Gert snapped her fingers toward Cassell.

"Go on, Renfrew!" she said. "Over there!"

Cassell stopped shouting. His beady eyes began to open as he stared at Renfrew. They began to glaze as the snake glided over the desk top, onto the chair, and down on the soft pile carpet. His mouth began to work as the creature soundlessly slid toward him.

Cassell began to gibber.

"Go on, Renfrew!" Gert said. "Go on!"

Cassell began to retreat into the corner on legs that seemed to have suddenly lost all substance.

He stumbled, and fell.

Daisy turned her eyes away from the writhing thing on the carpet.

"Had enough?" Gert said. "Going to sign?"

"Take it away!" Cassell's voice was no more than a terror-stricken squeal. "Take it away—I'll sign! I did it! I'll sign anything—take that away!"

It was Carter who took a fountain pen from his pocket, and wrote a few sentences on some paper from the desk.

"Sign," he said briefly.

His small white hand was shaking uncontrollably, but Cassell signed.

Daisy cleared her throat.

"Perhaps, Gert—"

"I'll put him right back," Gert said. "Come on, Renfrew. Back. Come on."

The snake glided back.

Casually, as though she were picking up a handkerchief, Gert picked it up and returned it to the suitcase.

Daisy cleared her throat again. There was only one thing in the world that she feared, and that was a snake.

"Why—er—why didn't you tell us about that, Gert?" she asked.

"You never asked me," Gert returned, snapping the lock on the suitcase. "You just asked me why I carried it. I never tell people unless I have to. Some folks are scared. I hope I didn't scare you, but I thought maybe if I sprung Renfrew on him quick, before he had a chance to think, it might bring him around. I thought you'd guessed, anyway, Daisy," she added. "I thought you'd notice the holes in the side. Say, he *is* scared!"

Cassell had managed to drag himself off the floor and into a chair. His eyes were still glazed, and he was breathing heavily and staring at his watch again.

Cherry beckoned to Daisy.

"Come here," she said. "Over here."

She drew Daisy over to the far corner of the office.

"Listen," she said, "this is queer! I mean, this office. Daisy, listen! I've been thinking. This is just exactly like the office I was working in this morning, but it isn't the same one. It looks the same, and all, but it isn't."

"What do you mean?" Daisy said.

"Well, it's got the same colored walls and the same furniture and carpet—"

She paused as Sam walked over to them.

"Can I listen, or are you—"

"I'm telling Daisy about this office here," Cherry said. "It's queer. It looks like the same one I was in this morning, but it's not. Those glass brick windows are the same size, and the draperies are the same. It's got bookcases, but I don't see those huge cartons of books, and no one could have unpacked them, because there aren't any books on the shelves. And he made an awful fuss about having those cartons placed just so. And there were plug-in phones, but the plugs were in a different corner. And I don't see that little clock radio that I plugged in. He ordered me to do that almost before I took my hat off. I couldn't understand why, because to my knowledge he never turned it on. He said he always had a radio in his office, though. He told me that twice."

"He must always carry one with him," Sam said, "because I noticed a little radio, a little clock one, yesterday. Stragg told me—"

"Oh, Carter," Daisy said, turning around. "Carter, come outside a moment, will you? Sam, you and the rest keep Cassell here. Gert, use Renfrew if he moves. Come out here, Carter—"

Cassell watched them go, and then he looked on the desk, and shrugged.

He was still sitting there, slumped in the chair, when Carter and Daisy returned, a few minutes later.

"I suppose," Cassell spoke to Daisy, "you want to know why I killed Tower? You want to know it all?"

Carter, in rather a strained voice, answered for her. "Tell us," he said.

"I made those plans about the tickets," Cassell said, taking out his watch again. "I made those plans a long while ago. I wanted five people to divert suspicion. Tower didn't know what was in the envelopes. I told him that I wanted to make a private check on some advertising, and I made him disguise himself, so if anything went wrong, nothing could be traced."

Slowly, Cassell went on with his story, about the fake message to the train staff, so that the five people would be admitted on the train. He told how he had planned first to frighten the group, then to win them over and allay any suspicions they might have by asking them to aid him in getting to the root of the ticket situation.

None of it seemed new to Daisy.

"Why," Carter interrupted, "are you telling us all this, Cassell?"

Cassell's eyes half closed, and his lips formed that sinister smile.

"In four minutes," he said, "the opening pageant will begin. The World's Fair will begin. But you won't see it. No one will see it. It's going to end before

260

it begins. You can leave this room, and you can get to the elevator. But it's locked. Did you find that out?"

Daisy nodded.

"And the windows are glass brick," Cassell said. "And the phones have been removed. You can't do anything about it. You can take my keys, but even then you can't unlock that elevator. That radio you plugged in for me," he turned to Cherry, "that was not a radio at all. That was a clock bomb, with an explosion set-up where the radio would be. The clock— not the clock on the face—that started when you plugged it in. And I was careful to have people see you plug it in. That was to be your reward, young woman, for playing tricks with those envelopes!"

Cherry, Sam, Gert and Whitty looked from Cassell to Daisy, sitting there calmly, with her hands folded.

"I don't get this!" Whitty said. "You mean, you're blowing something up?"

"When the primer explodes the stick of dynamite in my little cigar box," Cassell said, "then what you thought were cartons of books, young woman, will explode. They are not books. Each one of those cartons contains two twenty-five-pound cartridges of TNT. We have been blasting roads out on the Greenville estate, but no one will find that out. Because the man who got them for me and brought them here is down on the floor below, in the same room with Brand and Stragg. I had not planned for you five to be here. Not until you appeared downstairs. But since you are here—" Cassell shrugged.

Whitty, who had been staring at Daisy's folded hands, turned and looked at Cassell.

"Well, you dirty skunk!" he said. "You dirty skunk! You mean to sit there and tell us, when your thing goes off, it's going to set TNT going? Why, this whole building'll blow sky high! It'll smash into everything—all the people! Into the ball thing, and the pageant!"

"Yes," Cassell said. "And we will go with it."

Gert, Sam noticed, was also staring at Daisy's hands. So was Cherry. Then he caught on. Daisy's hands were folded, but her thumbs were pointing to the ceiling. Thumbs up!

Sam relaxed.

"So the radio I saw," he said, "was your gadget, was it? The one in Bottome's sitting room? And that's why you called Standish with that yarn, and had me fired —what a horrible pun," he added, "I could make on that now!"

"You might as well be flippant," Cassell said. "You have very little time left—"

"Then settle something else," Daisy said. "About Eggy. Of course, he was after money, and willing to jump through hoops for it—but you thought he was snooping around, didn't you? Because if he caught on to your clock bomb, he'd cancel your insurance, and you'd lose the money you planned to collect. Is that

262

right? Then, last night, he appeared from his hiding place on the train—am I right?—and saw the gadget in your private office."

Cassell nodded. "I had to shoot him, then," he said. "He saw the thing, and he understood."

He put his watch back in his pocket.

"Now," he said. "Now—"

"Now," Daisy got up, "it only seems fair to tell you that Carter and I have unplugged the radio, you know. I guessed when Cherry mentioned the clock radio. I have one at home. Boy gave it to me. He was always being sent clock bombs by that Happy Mosello, back in prohibition days. I got used to clock bombs. And of course, I knew something disastrous was going to happen here, or you wouldn't have removed your favorite pictures."

"But that was locked!" Cassell had slumped back in his chair again. "That office was locked—"

"Yes, but I had all your master keys," Daisy explained gently. "I got them before I tied Brand and Stragg up, on the train. We let the Fair director out, too. It was very smart, having two offices alike. You thought of everything. But so did we."

"The Fair director?" Sam asked blankly.

"He was in the other office, the one like this. Locked in, with the clock bomb and the TNT, no phones, glass brick windows, and a locked steel door. Even Debbon thought he'd gone, but he hadn't. You see," Daisy said, "Cassell decided long ago that if he couldn't be the Fair director, there wouldn't be one. If he couldn't run the Fair, he'd ruin it. And he very nearly did."

"By less," Carter said, "than ten minutes, I think, to judge from the hands of that clock. And I don't think the last ten minutes could have been any more harrowing if we hadn't unplugged the thing. Daisy, have you got all you want from him? Then somebody open that door and let those troopers in, quick!"

Later, outside Cassell's building, Daisy surveyed the Fair.

During their absence inside, it seemed to have burst into flame.

Fountains splashed every color of the rainbow. The trees and foliage glowed. The façades of the buildings stood out in brilliant relief. Dominating everything was the great dazzling bulk of the perisphere, which seemed to float on its colored fountains.

Thousands and thousands of people were waiting to mount the escalators leading up to the perisphere; thousands and thousands more stood below, watching.

Sam pressed a penny into Daisy's hand.

"I wasn't thinking much," Daisy said. "I just remembered the Tower of Jewels, and how wonderful we thought that was. At the Pan-American exposition. But compared to this, it was just an illuminated hamburg stand. Oh, look!"

The first part of the great parade had reached the esplanade, and still with flags and pennants flying, the endless color scheme wound down the helicline out of the great ball.

Whitty blew his nose. "Say, this gets you!" he said. "See Washington, there, on his white horse? Say, what's that thing they keep singing?"

"The Fair anthem, or hymn, or something," Gert said. "Al learned it from a calliope. He's been humming it all afternoon. Something about the dawn of a new day—"

"Fireworks!" Cherry said. "Look, Daisy, from over by the lake!"

Daisy looked, and then she sighed.

"I wonder," she said, "if someone could find my gold-knobbed cane over in Tomorrow Town, before we go back to the midway? I must be feeling my age. I really want that cane."

"You're not going back to the midway!" Cherry said. "Not tonight! You're going to bed."

"Yes," Daisy said, "I'm going to the midway. We must find Al's friends, and I told the Liberty Boys I'd come to their concert. They're going to play *The Pink Lady* for me, and some Strauss waltzes. I think a nice calm waltz would do me good. And Cherry, could you find me a copy of *Lady Audley's Secret?*"

"Of what?" Cherry said.

"Well, *Little Women* will do. To read myself to sleep with—Sam, what are you chuckling about?"

"None," Sam said, "none but the brave deserve the fair."

265

Afterword

by Ellen Nehr

THE 1939 New York World's Fair, billed as "The World of Tomorrow," was conceived by Grover Whalen as a means of reviving the fortunes of a city slow in recovering from the Depression. Whalen, something of a super salesman, was president of Wannamaker's Department Store for many years, and, having served in several appointed positions, was New York City's "Official Greeter." He headed a non-profit organization that transformed over twelve-hundred acres of Flushing wasteland into the Fair grounds, and created thousands of jobs as a result of subsequent construction. An international exposition, it celebrated the nation's sesquicentennial and commemorated George Washington's 1789 inauguration, which, like the Fair's opening, took place in New York City on April 30.

In the summer of 1937, Bennett Cerf, the thirty-nine year old President of Random House, had the idea of publishing a mystery featuring the nascent New York World's Fair. Through Marie Rodell[†] he learned of a relative newcomer to the mystery field, twenty-eight year old Phoebe Atwood Taylor, whom he commissioned to write the book. A contract providing for an advance of two hun-

---

[†]Mrs. Rodell began her publishing career in the 1930s typing contracts for William Morrow. At the end of the decade, she joined Duell, Sloan & Pearce as an associate editor and was eventually to found and direct their Bloodhound Mysteries imprint.

In 1945, Mrs. Rodell helped found the Mystery Writers of America.

dred and fifty dollars was signed on October 26, 1937 and a week later the publisher and author met for the first time.

Since she had been producing two mystery novels a year for W.W. Norton under her own name, the author chose to use Freeman Dana† for the proposed novel. She was still in the midst of writing *The Annulet of Gilt* for Norton at the time of the signing, so a deadline of May 1, 1938 was agreed upon.

Bennett Cerf was enthusiastic about the prospects of the proposed mystery and its author. He wrote Kay Swift, the Fair's publicist, asking for whatever information was available. And, referring back to the sensation caused by Sally Rand at the Chicago World's Fair (1933), jokingly enquired about the possible appearance of a naked dancer.

Mr. Cerf sent his author numerous maps and newspaper clippings, hoping that they would aid her in visualizing the prospective Fair grounds. PAT†† found that the information held a "certain common aura of the Merry-go-round" and wrote requesting "...anything that struck your fancy, whether or not it was directly connected to

---

†This pseudonym was derived from a combination of family names, and had previously been borne by a deceased relative. Earlier that year, Ms. Taylor had signed with the Collins Crime Club, London, for the publication of her rewritten novel *Beginning with a Bash* under the pseudonym Alice Tilton, which was comprised of the first and last names of her aunt, an invalid who lived with her.

††Phoebe Atwood Taylor, who often wrote of herself in the third person, customarily employed these initials, and I've adopted them for use here.

the Fair. Something very fine might pop out of the mouths of miniature engines and garbage choppers. And if you hear any gossip about the Sally Rand angle, that would be marvelous." (Gypsy Rose Lee did appear at the Fair but, of course, does not figure in the novel.) There is every indication that PAT was immersed in the material she received, at one point claiming, "I spent the whole day with crayons on the ground maps...my room is plastered with Fair, three thousand books, doors and ceiling are all covered with pictures."

On December 16, Mr. Cerf wrote that he had met Grover Whalen at a dinner party. The Fair's organizer was not disposed to offer much assistance with the mystery project, no doubt believing that even fictional homicide might be bad public relations. Indeed, he attempted to persuade the publisher to withhold the book until after the Fair's opening. The two agreed to meet again the following week, and Mr. Cerf prepared for the appointment by compiling an extensive list of notable sites where murders had been laid without adversely affecting the trade or reputation of the places involved. Though nothing conclusive resulted from this second meeting between the organizer and the publisher, the latter used it as the basis of an amusing letter to PAT in which he noted that Mr. Whalen promised to conduct a personal tour of the Fair for the author. While there is no indication that this ever occurred, she did visit the "Flushing mud flats" in January 1938, guided by Dr. Frank Monaghan, the Fair's director of research.

Deadlines began to loom larger in the author's mind. Having completed *The Annulet of Gilt* the day after

Christmas, PAT was slated to finish an Asey Mayo mystery, and meet a revised submission date for *Murder at the New York World's Fair* by the first of June. A doodle-covered manuscript page survives bearing the note: "Phoebe has one hundred and thirty days in which to write two books. Phoebe has written one book in fifteen days and does not care to repeat the process." Among listings for her water, gas, electricity and phone bills (as well as a skull and crossbones next to the entry for "Income Tax"!) it includes a sketch for a book cover that was strikingly similar to that which eventually appeared on the novel's dust jacket.

In a letter dating from late January 1938, the author wryly comments on her style of composition.

> I know there's nothing now but for me to get down to the business of writing; only it seems—well there's no point in disillusioning you, but my scripts usually reach people on time, via air express. They've never been known to reach anyone ahead of time, ever. It's all on acc't of my habit of not beginning a script until two weeks before it is due. Then the suspense, you see, is genuine. Taylor books have Pace. Eight years of fresh killed fiction has convinced me (have convinced, maybe) that you can't murder slowly. But of course, as Norton always says, 'I *think* beforehand, and That Is Something.' And I truly think I've got some things brewing for you.

On April 30, 1938, exactly a year before the scheduled opening, there was a preview at the Fair Grounds. PAT had written Random House requesting a ticket so that she could experience the novel's setting complete with crowds. Elaborating on rumors that Lloyd's was laying three to one odds that the Fair would, in fact, fail to materialize, she noted "...the best basis for a plot that I've yet found...involving insurance fraud. You insure your part in the WF and then take steps to see that there will be no WF, but there IS. It's too complicated to go into, but it may work out. And that will show you the state of mind that can be obtained from the intense writing of escapist fiction. I've been taking corpses out of ash barrells for a week."[†]

Having heard from her agent that Mr. Cerf would be in Europe at the time of the April 30 preview, the author provided a detailed account of the book's progress.

> It occurs to me at this point that you are more handicapped in not knowing what to expect of the WF than I am in not quite knowing what you want. Right now, I feel that what exists of the WF, I have built with my bare hands, including the meadow's ash removal. And I think I've got a plot—the obstacle removal has taken me months, by the way. You've no idea how many obstacles an incomplete Fair can make. I hadn't. And they assure me that they won't make more than thirty or forty major changes in the layout and plans, so that I can work with comparative confidence. The layout changes have balked me several times. But, if I could talk with you, it would be so much simpler. Are you really going to be away that weekend? Because if you are, I'll try to send you an outline of the abolition of obstacles and the ensuing birth of the plot and what not. That thought terrifies me, I have never outlined anything in my life. After all, the bare outline of a mystery plot is simply, X gets killed; dither; Y gets killed: less dither. A catches B. Most of the time that base plot rarely sticks its head above the surface...Or maybe you would rather someone else wrote the thing? I can tell them how *not* to do it.

[†]This last reference is to *Banbury Bog* which was begun on May 20, 1938 and completed some twenty days later.

As it turned out, Mr. Cerf postponed his European journey, but nevertheless declined to attend the festivities. PAT went, however, accompanied by Jane Wilson, who rendered some sketches of the Fair for her.[†]

Random House received the manuscript on June 2, accompanied by a somewhat tentative, apologetic note.

I'm sorry it is late, amazed that you are getting it at all. If you are wedded to the Little-did-we-guess-two-weeks-from-Candlemas-we-would-be-corpses School, you will loathe this. It isn't an orthodox mystery; it couldn't be. But it has corpses, a detective, suspects and an occasional clew.[††] I don't feel that I can accent too strongly two important points. The worst problem I faced was that of keeping the murder *at* the Fair. The minute the police arrived, there would be no Fair color, because everyone would be whipped away. For that reason, the characters had to be manipulated into positions where they couldn't go to the police, or be caught. That way, everyone stayed at the Fair, roamed at will and at random. The other problem was how to make people, who are wanted for and involved in a murder, actually *go* to a fair. There was one solution, and I hope you don't think the chases are overworked. So, before you and your readers uncork the vitriol bottle, I hope you'll bear those mechanical problems in mind. I shall be terribly surprised if you like the

[†] PAT's personal copy of the novel, archived at Boston University's Mugar Memorial Library, contains a circular badge that was given to her to wear that day. (A facsimile appears as the shade pull on the cover of this edition.) The volume is inscribed "Freeman Dana, her book." All other personal copies contain similar notations, bearing the names Phoebe Atwood Taylor or Alice Tilton.

[††] In PAT's correspondence with the Bobbs-Merrill Company, now housed in the University of Indiana at Bloomington's Lilly Library, she attributes her insistence on the use this spelling for "clue" to having spent her early years under the tutelage of an English governess, and subsequent education at the Boston Latin School.

book—if you feel there's any hope, I can, of course, add, subtract, delete, *ad inf.*, would be delighted to follow anyone's constructive thoughts for revision. And if you say the helicline with it (Trylon, perisphere, helicline, remember?) I said it first back in chapter three.

It is extremely fortunate that PAT was amenable to extensive revision. Mr. Cerf and a number of Random House staff members (one of whom had read and admired all the Asey Mayo novels) were unanimous in pointing to the manuscript's essential weakness. In a letter, the publisher baldly states that the novel was singularly marked by an apparent lack of interest on the part of the author.

PAT's response to this criticism testifies eloquently to her professionalism: "If you will blue pencil this mss to pieces, I will pick up the pieces and go on from there...I fear that your conception of a mystery story differs from mine, but, in this situation, your conception is the one that matters."

The correspondence between author and publisher at this point in the novel's genesis provides valuable insight into PAT's working habits (along with doubts and reservations), as well as Mr. Cerf's active role in shaping the final form of the book. Perhaps most importantly, in the author's estimation of her own strengths—particularly the evocation of setting—contemporary readers can appreciate that she quite deliberately cultivated that aspect of her work that continues to entertain after half a century.

I felt the very notion of the Fair precluded the typical harrowing mystery element, the typical earnest clew seeking, and I tried to accent the Fair, subordinate the mystery to it, thinking that any potential audience might include as many people interested in the Fair as in the murder. Similarly, in the Asey books, I subordinate plot to Cape Cod.

I could, of course, revise till doomsday without success, so, in order to cooperate as fully as I can with you and your ideas, I know you will be willing to send me specific criticisms and recommendations, which I shall follow, believe me, as conscientiously and closely as possible.

The publisher responded to this willingness with alacrity. Mr. Cerf's chapter-by-chapter emendations ran to some four legal-sized pages. They were nothing if not spirited and direct, and ran the gamut from cajoling to caustic.

However, the passage of a few days found Mr. Cerf in something of a more amiable and conciliatory mood, and a follow-up letter concludes with assurances that a compromise could be reached. He also urged the author to act with dispatch, since two motion picture studios and one of the most popular magazines of the day had expressed interest in the book.

In a letter dated August 22, 1938, Mr. Cerf wrote to express his gratitude for the final revisions of *Murder at the New York World's Fair*, and indicated that it was scheduled for immediate publication. This was confirmed by a transmittal order from the J.J. Little & Ives Company, calling for the printing and binding of 900 copies. And on November 17, the original manuscript was returned.

It should be noted that despite the apparent acrimony

surrounding the book's original publication, PAT and her husband later socialized with the Cerfs, and were guests at their Mount Kisco home. Before this was to be, however, a last pratfall ensued when an invoice dated November 30 charged $15.56 in Author's Alterations. Her agent, Frances Pindyck, quoted PAT's reaction in a letter to Random House. "How do you suppose they arrive at the conclusion of Author's Alterations, being as how I never read any proof...I rather resent paying, or even being charged for corrections that I never made...If I'd dallied with commas and changed spacing...I would be the last to carp." Happily, the charges were cancelled and though there is no indication that the novel was sent to either the film companies or the *Saturday Evening Post*, three copies were forwarded to World's Fair headquarters.